THOSE TIMES AND THESE

THE WORKS OF
IRVIN S. COBB

THOSE TIMES
AND THESE

Short Story Index Reprint Series

 BOOKS FOR LIBRARIES PRESS
FREEPORT, NEW YORK

First Published 1917

Reprinted 1972

Library of Congress Cataloging in Publication Data

Cobb, Irvin Shrewsbury, 1876-1944.
  Those times and these.

  (Short story index reprint series)
  At head of title: The works of Irvin S. Cobb.
  CONTENTS: Ex-fightin' Billy.--And there was light.--
Mr. Felsburg gets even. [etc.]
  I. Title.
PZ3.C6334Te7 [PS3505.O14]   813'.5'2   72-5862
ISBN 0-8369-4201-9

TO THE MEMORY

OF

MANDY MARTIN,

whose soul was as white as her skin was black,
and who for forty-two years, until her death,
was a loyal friend and servant of my people.

CONTENTS

CONTENTS

THOSE TIMES AND THESE

CHAPTER I
EX-FIGHTIN' BILLY

TO me and to those of my generation, Judge Priest was always Judge Priest. So he was also to most of the people of our town and our county and our judicial district. A few men of his own age—mainly men who had served with him in the Big War—called him Billy, right to his face, and yet a few others, men of greater age than these, spoke of him and to him as William, giving to the name that benignant and most paternal air which an octogenarian may employ in referring to one who is ten or fifteen years his junior.

I was a fairly sizable young person before ever I found out that once upon a time among his intimates the Judge had worn yet another title. Information upon this subject was imparted to me one summery afternoon by Sergeant Jimmy Bagby as we two perched in company upon the porch of the old boat-store. I don't know what mission brought Sergeant Bagby three blocks down Franklin Street from

his retail grocery establishment, unless it was
that sometimes the boat-store porch was cool
while the rest of the town baked. That is to
say, it was cool by comparison. Little wanton
breezes that strayed across the river paid fluttering visits there before they struck inland to
perish miserably of heat prostration.

For the moment the Sergeant and I had the
little wooden balcony to ourselves, nearly
everybody else within sight and hearing having
gone down the levee personally to enjoy the
small excitement of seeing the stern-wheel
packet *Emily Foster* land after successfully completing one of her regular triweekly round trips
to Clarksburg and way landings.

At the blast of the *Emily Foster's* whistles as
she rounded to and put her nose upstream preparatory to sliding in alongside the wharf,
divers coloured persons of the leisure class had
roused from where they napped in the shady
lee of freight piles and lined up on the outer gun-
wales of the wharf-boat ready to catch and
make fast the head-line when it should be
tossed across the intervening patch of water
into their volunteer hands.

Two town hacks and two town drays had
coursed down the steep gravelled incline, with
the draymen standing erect upon the jouncing
springless beds of their drays as was their way.
In the matter of maintaining a balance over
rough going and around abrupt turns, no
chariot racers of old could have taught them

anything. Only Sergeant Bagby and I, of all in the immediate vicinity, had remained where we were. The Sergeant was not of what you could exactly call a restless nature, and I, for the moment, must have been overcome by one of those fits of languor which occasionally descend upon the adolescent manling. We two bided where we sat.

With a tinkle of her engine bells, a calling out of orders and objurgations in the professionally hoarse, professionally profane voice of her head mate and a racking, asthmatic coughing and sighing and pounding from her exhaust pipes, the *Emily Foster* had found her berth; and now her late passengers came streaming up the slant of the hill—a lanky timberman or two, a commercial traveller—most patently a commercial traveller—a dressy person who looked as though he might be an advance agent for some amusement enterprise, and a family of movers, burdened with babies and bundles and accompanied by the inevitable hound dog. The commercial traveller and the suspected advance agent patronised the hacks —fare twenty-five cents anywhere inside the corporate limits—but the rest entered into the city afoot and sweating. At the very tail of the procession appeared our circuit judge, he being closely convoyed by his black house-boy, Jeff Poindexter, who packed the master's bulging and ancient valise with one hand and bore a small collection of law books under his other arm.

Looking much like a high-land terrapin beneath the shelter of his venerable cotton umbrella, Judge Priest toiled up the hot slant. Observed from above, only his legs were visible for the moment. We knew him, though, by his legs—and also by Jeff and the umbrella. Alongside the eastern wall of the boat-store, nearmost of all buildings to the water-front, he halted in its welcome shadows to blow and to mop his streaming face with a vast square of handkerchief, and, while so engaged, glanced upward and beheld his friend, the Sergeant, beaming down upon him across the whittled banister rail.

"Hello, Jimmy!" he called in his high whine.

"Hello, yourself!" answered the Sergeant. "Been somewheres or jest travellin' round?"

"Been somewheres," vouchsafed the newly returned; "been up at Livingstonport all week, settin' as special judge in place of Judge Given. He's laid up in bed with a tech of summer complaint and I went up to git his docket cleaned up fur him. He's better now, but still puny."

"You got back ag'in in time to light right spang in the middle of a warm spell," said Sergeant Bagby.

"Well," stated Judge Priest, "it ain't been exactly whut you'd call chilly up the river, neither. The present thaw appears to be gineral throughout this section of the country." He waved a plump arm in farewell and slowly

departed from view beyond the side wall of
the boat-store.

"Looks like Judge Priest manages to take
on a little more flesh every year he lives," said
the Sergeant, who was himself no lightweight,
addressing the remark in my direction. "You
wouldn't scursely think it to see him waddlin'
'long, atotin' all that meat on his bones; but
once't upon a time he was mighty near ez slim
ez his own ramrod and was commonly known
ez little Fightin' Billy. You wouldn't, now,
would you?"

The question I disregarded. It was the dis-
closure he had bared which appealed to my
imagination and fired my curiosity. I said:

"Mr. Bagby, I never knew anybody ever
called Judge Priest that?"

"No, you natchelly wouldn't," said the Sergeant—"not onless you'd mebbe overheared
some of us old fellers talkin' amongst ourselves
sometimes, with no outsiders present. It
wouldn't hardly be proper, ever'thing considered, to be referrin' in public to the presidin'
judge of the first judicial district of the State
of Kintucky by sech a name ez that. Besides
which, he ain't little any more. And then,
there's still another reason."

"How did they ever come to call him that
in the first place?" I asked.

"Well, young man, it makes quite a tale,"
said the Sergeant. With an effort he hauled
out his big silver watch, looked at its face, and

then wedged it back into a hidden recess under one of the overlapping creases of his waistband.

"He acquired that there title at Shiloh, in the State of Tennessee, and by his own request he parted from it some three years and four months later on the banks of the Rio Grande River, in the Republic of Mexico, I bein' present in pusson on both occasions. But ef you've got time to listen I reckin I've got jest about the time to tell it to you."

"Yes, sir—if you please." With eagerness, I hitched my cane-bottomed chair along the porch floor to be nearer him. And then as he seemed not to have heard my assent, I undertook to prompt him. "Er—what were you and Judge Priest doing down in Mexico, Mr. Bagby?"

"Tryin' to git out of the United States of America fur one thing." A little grin, almost a shamefaced grin, I thought, broke his round moist face up into fat wrinkles. He puckered his eyes in thought, looking out across the languid tawny river toward the green towhead in midstream and the cottonwoods on the far bank, a mile and more away. "But I don't marvel much that you never heared the full circumstances before. Our bein' down in Mexico together that time is a fact we never advertised 'round for common consumption—neither one of us."

He withdrew his squinted gaze from the hot vista of shores and water and swung his body about to face me, thereafter punctuating his narrative with a blunted forefinger.

"My command was King's Hell Hounds. There ought to be a book written some of these days about whut all King's Hell Hounds done endurin' of the unpleasantness—it'd make mighty excitin' readin'. But Billy and a right smart chance of the other boys frum this place, they served throughout with Company B of the Old Regiment of mounted infantry. Most of the time frum sixty-one to sixty-five I wasn't throwed with 'em, but jest before the end came we were all consolidated—whut there was remainin' of us—under General Nathan Bedford Forrest down in Mississippi. Fur weeks and months before that, we knowed it was a hopeless fight we were wagin', but somehow we jest kept on. I reckin we'd sort of got into the fightin' habit. Fellers do, you know, sometimes, when the circumstances are favourable, ez in this case.

"Well, here one mornin' in April, came the word frum Virginia that Richmond had fallen, and right on top of that, that Marse Robert had had to surrender. They said, too, that Sherman had Johnston penned off somewheres down in the Carolinas, we didn't know exactly where, and that Johnston would have to give up before many days passed. In fact, he had already give up a week before we finally heared about it. So then accordin' to our best information and belief, that made us the last body

of organised Confederates on the east bank of
the Mississippi River. That's a thing I was
always mighty proud of. I'm proud of it
yit.

"All through them last few weeks the army
was dwindlin' away and dwindlin' away.
Every mornin' at roll-call there'd be a few
more absentees. Don't git me wrong—I
wouldn't call them boys deserters. They'd
stuck that long, doin' their duty like men, but
they knowed good and well—in fact we all
knowed—'twas only a question of time till even
Forrest would have to quit before overpowerin'
odds and we'd be called on to lay down the
arms we'd toted fur so long. Their families
needed 'em, so they jest quit without sayin'
anything about it to anybody and went on
back to their homes. This was specially true
of some that lived in that district.

"But with the boys frum up this way it was
different. In a way of speakin', we didn't have
no homes to go back to. Our State had been
in Northern hands almost frum the beginnin'
and some of us had prices on our heads right
that very minute on account of bein' branded
ez guerrillas. Which was a lie. But folks didn't
always stop to sift out the truth then. They
were prone to shoot you first and go into the
merits of the case afterward. Anyway, betwixt
us and home there was a toler'ble thick hedge of
Yankee soldiers—in fact several thick hedges.
You know they called one of our brigades the

Orphan Brigade. And there were good reasons
fur callin' it so—more ways than one.

"I ain't never goin' to furgit the night of the
fifth of May. Somehow the tidin's got round
amongst the boys that the next mornin' the
order to surrender was goin' to be issued. The
Yankee cavalry general, Wilson—and he was
a good peart fighter, too—had us completely
blocked off to the North and the East, but the
road to the Southwest was still open ef anybody
cared to foller it. So that night some of us
held a little kind of a meetin'—about sixty of
us—mainly Kintuckians, but with a sprinklin'
frum other States, too.

"Ez I remember, there wasn't a contrary
voice raised when 'twas suggested we should
try to make it acrost the big river and j'ine in
under Kirby Smith, who still had whut was left
of the Army of the Trans-Mississippi.

"Billy Priest made the principal speech.
'Boys,' he says, 'South Carolina may a-started
this here war, but Kintucky has undertook the
contract to close it out. Somewheres out yonder in Texas they tell me there's yit a consid'ble
stretch of unconquered Confederate territory.
Speakin' fur myself I don't believe I'm ever
goin' to be able to live comfortable an' reconciled under any other flag than the flag we've
fit to uphold. Let's us-all go see ef we can't
find the place where our flag still floats.'

"So we all said we'd go. Then the question
ariz of namin' a leader. There was one man

that had been a captain and a couple more that
had been lieutenants, but, practically unanimously, we elected little Billy Priest. Even ef
he was only jest a private in the ranks we all
knowed it wasn't fur lack of chances to go
higher. After Shiloh, he'd refused a commission and ag'in after Hartsville. So, in lessen
no time a-tall, that was settled, too.

"Bright and early next day we started, takin'
our guns and our hosses with us. They were
our hosses anyway; mainly we'd borrowed 'em
off Yankees, or anyways, off Yankee sympathis-
ers on our last raid Northward and so that made
'em our pussonal property, the way we figgered
it out. 'Tennyrate we didn't stop to argue the
matter with nobody whutsoever. We jest
packed up and we put out—and we had almighty
little to pack up, lemme tell you.

"Ez we rid off we sung a song that was beginnin' to be right fashionable that spring
purty near every place below Mason and Dixon's line; and all over the camp the rest of the
boys took it up and made them old woodlands
jest ring with it. It was a kind of a farewell to
us. The fust verse was likewise the chorus and
it run something like this:

Oh, I'm a good old rebel, that's jest whut I am;
And fur this land of freedom I do not give a dam',
I'm glad I fit ag'in her, I only wish't we'd won,
And I don't ax your pardon fur anything I've
      done.

"And so on and so forth. There were several more verses all expressin' much the same trend of thought, and all entirely in accordance with our own feelin's fur the time bein'.

"Well, boy, I reckin there ain't no use wastin' time describin' the early stages of that there pilgrimage. We went ridin' along livin' on the land and doin' the best we could. We were young fellers, all of us, and it was springtime in Dixie—you know whut that means—and in spite of everything, some of the springtime got into our hearts, too, and drove part of the bitterness out. The country was all scarified with the tracks of war, but nature was doin' her level best to cover up the traces of whut man had done. People along our route had mighty slim pickin's fur themselves, but the sight of an old grey jacket was still mighty dear to most of 'em and they divided whut little they had with us and wish't they had more to give us. We didn't need much at that—a few meals of vittles fur the men and a little fodder fur our hosses and we'd be satisfied. We'd reduced slow starvation to an exact science long before that. Every man in the outfit was hard ez nails and slim ez a blue racer.

"Whut Northern forces there was East of the river we dodged. In fact we didn't have occasion to pull our shootin'-irons but once't, and that was after we'd cros't over into Louisiana. There wasn't any organised military force to regulate things and in the back districts civil

government had mighty near vanished altogether. People had went back to fust principles—wild, reckless fust principles they were,
too. One day an old woman warned us there
was a gang of bushwhackers operatin' down the
road a piece in the direction we were headin'—
a mixed crowd of deserters frum both sides, she
said, who'd jined in with some of the local bad
characters and were preyin' on the country,
harryin' the defenceless, and terrorisin' women
and children and raisin' hob ginerally. She
advised us that we'd better give 'em a wide
berth.

"But Billy Priest he throwed out scouts and
located the gang, and jest before sunrise next
mornin' we dropped in on 'em, takin' 'em by
surprise in the camp they'd rigged up in a live-
oak thicket in the midst of a stretch of cypress
slashes.

"And when the excitement died down ag'in,
quite a number of them bushwhackers had
quit whackin' permanently and the rest of 'em
were tearin' off through the wet woods wonderin', between jumps, whut had hit 'em. Ez
fur our command, we accumulated a considerable passel of plunder and supplies and a
number of purty fair hosses, and went on our
way rejoicin'. We hadn't lost a man, and only
one man wounded.

"When we hit the Texas border, news was
waitin' fur us. They told us ef we aimed to
ketch up with the last remainders of the army

we'd have to hurry, because Smith and Shelby, with whut was left of his Missoury outfit, and Sterlin' Price and Hindman with some of his Arkansaw boys and a right smart sprinklin' of Texans had already pulled up stakes and were headed fur old Mexico, where the natives were in the enjoyable midst of one of their regular revolutions.

"With the French crowd and part of the Mexicans to help him, the Emperor Maximilian was tryin' to hang onto his onsteady and topplin' throne, whilst the Republikins or Liberals, as they called themselves, were tryin' with might and main to shove him off of it. Ef a feller jest natchelly honed fur an opportunity to indulge a fancy fur active hostilities, Mexico seemed to offer a very promisin' field of endeavour.

"It didn't take us long to make up our minds whut course we'd follow. Billy Priest put the motion. 'Gentlemen,' he says, 'it would seem the Southern Confederacy is bent and determined on gittin' clear out frum under the shadder of the Yankee government. It has been moved and seconded that we foller after her no matter where she goes. All in favour of that motion will respond by sayin' *Aye*—contrarywise, *No*. The *Ayes* seem to have it and the *Ayes* do have it and it is so ordered, unanimously. By fours! Forward, march!'

"That happened in the town of Corsicana in the early summer-time of the year. So we went along acrost the old Lone Star State, headin' mighty nigh due West, passin' through Waco and Austin and San Antonio, and bein' treated mighty kindly by the people wheresoever we passed. And ez we went, one of the boys that had poetic leanin's, he made up a new verse to our song. Let's see, son, ef I kin remember it now after all these years."

The Sergeant thought a bit and then lifting his voice in a quavery cadence favoured me with the following gem:

> I won't be reconstructed; I'm better now than
> them;
> And fur a carpet-bagger I don't give a dam;
> So I'm off fur the frontier, fast ez I kin go,
> I'll purpare me a weepon and head fur Mexico.

"It was the middle of July and warm enough to satisfy the demands of the most exactin' when we reached the Rio Grande, to find out Shelby's force had done crossed over after buryin' their battle-flag in the middle of the river, wropped up in a rock to hold it down. On one side was cactus and greasewood and a waste of sandy land, that was already back in the Union or mighty soon would be. On the other side was more cactus and more greasewood and more sandy loam, but in a different country. So, after spendin' a few pleasant hours at the town of Eagle Pass, we turn't our backs to one country and cros't over to the other, alookin' fur the Confederacy wherever she might be. I figgered it out I was tellin' the United States of America good-by furever. I seem to remember that quite a number of us kept peerin' back over our shoulders toward the Texas shore. They tell me the feller that wrote 'Home Sweet Home' didn't have any home to go to but he writ the song jest the same. Nobody didn't say nothin', though, about weakenin' or turnin' back.

"Very soon after we hit Mexican soil we run into one of the armies—a Liberal army, this one was, of about twelve hundred men, and its name suited it to a T. The officers were liberal about givin' orders and the men were equally liberal about makin' up their minds whether or not they'd obey. Also, ez we very quickly discovered, the entire kit and caboodle of 'em were very liberal with reguards to other folks' property and other folks' lives. We'd acquired a few careless ideas of our own concernin' the acquirin' of contraband plunder durin' the years immediately precedin', but some of the things we seen almost ez soon ez we'd been welcomed into the hospitable but smelly midst of that there Liberal army, proved to us that alongside these fellers we were merely whut you might call amatoors in the confiscatin' line.

"I wish't I had the words to describe the outfit so ez you could see it the way I kin see it this minute. This purticular army was made up of about twelve hundred head, includin'

common soldiers. I never saw generals runnin'
so many to the acre before in my life. The
Confederacy hadn't been exactly destitute in
that respect but—shuckins!—down here you
bumped into a brigadier every ten feet. There
was a consider'ble sprinklin' of colonels and
majors and sech, too; and here and there a
lonesome private. Ef you seen a dark brown
scarycrow wearin' fur a uniform about enough
rags to pad a crutch with, with a big sorry straw
hat on his head and his feet tied up in bull hides
with his bare toes peepin' coyly out, and ef he
was totin' a flint lock rifle, the chances were
he'd be a common soldier. But ef in addition
to the rest of his regalia he had a pair of epau-
lettes sewed onto his shoulders you mout safely
assume you were in the presence of a general
or something of that nature. I ain't exagger-
atin'—much. I'm only tryin' to make you git
the picture of it in your mind.

"Well, they received us very kindly and
furnished us with rations, sech ez they were—
mostly peppers and beans and a kind of batter-
cake that's much in favour in them parts, made
out of corn pounded up fine and mixed with
water and baked ag'inst a hot rock. Ef a man
didn't keer fur the peppers, he could fall back
on the beans, thus insurin' him a change of
diet, and the corn batter-cakes were certainly
right good-tastin'.

"Some few of our dark-complected friends
kin make a stagger at speakin' English, so

frum one of 'em Billy inquires where is the Confederacy? They explains that it has moved on further South but tells us that first General Shelby sold 'em the artillery he'd fetched with him that fur to keep it frum fallin' into the Yankees' hands. Sure enough there're the guns —four brass field-pieces. Two of 'em are twelve-pounders and the other two are fourteen-pounders. The Mexicans are very proud of their artillery and appear to set much store by it.

"Well, that evenin' their commandin' general comes over to where we've made camp, accompanied by his coffee-coloured staff, and through an interpreter he suggests the advisability of our j'inin' in with them, he promisin' good pay and offerin' to make us all high-up officers. He seems right anxious to have us enlist with his glorious forces right away. In a little while it leaks out why he's so generous with his promises and so wishful to see us enrolled beneath his noble banner. He's expectin' a call inside of the next forty-eight hours frum the Imperials that're reported to be movin' up frum the South, nearly two thousand strong, with the intention of givin' him battle.

"Billy Priest, speakin' fur all of us, says he'll give him an answer later. So the commandin' general conceals his disappointment the best he kin and retires on back to his own headquarters, leavin' us to discuss the proposition amongst ourselves. Some of the boys favour

throwin' in with the Liberals right away, bein'
hongry fur a fight, I reckin, or else sort of daz-
zled by the idea of becomin' colonels and majors overnight. But Billy suggests that mebbe
we'd better jest sort of hang 'round and observe the conduct and deportment of these
here possible feller warriors of our'n whilst
they're under hostile fire. 'Speakin' pussonally,' he says, 'I must admit I ain't greatly attracted to them ez they present themselves to
the purview of my gaze in their ca'mmer hours.
Before committin' ourselves, s'posen we stand
by and take a few notes on how they behave
themselves in the presence of an enemy. Then,
there'll be abundant time to decide whether
we want to stay a while with these fellers or go
long about our business of lookin' fur the
Southern Confederacy.'

"That sounded like good argument, so we
let Billy have his way about it, and we settled
down to wait. We didn't have long to wait.
The next day about dinner-time, here come the
Imperial army, advancin' in line of battle. The
Liberals moved out acrost the desert to meet
'em and we-all mounted and taken up a position
on a little rise close at hand, to observe the pur-
ceedin's.

"Havin' had consider'ble experience in sech
affairs, I must say I don't believe I ever witnessed such a dissa'pintin' battle ez that one
turn't out to be. The prevailin' notion on both
sides seemed to be that the opposin' forces

should march bravely toward one another ontil
they got almost within long range and then fur
both gangs to halt ez though by simultaneous
impulse, and fire at will, with nearly everybody
shootin' high and wide and furious. When
this had continued till it become mutually bore-
some, one side would charge with loud cheers,
ashootin' ez it advanced, but prudently slowin'
down and finally haltin' before it got close
enough to inflict much damage upon the foe or
to suffer much damage either. Havin' accomplished this, the advancin' forces would fall
back in good order and then it was time fur the
other side to charge. I must say this in justice
to all concerned—there was a general inclination to obey the rules ez laid down fur the prose-
cution of the kind of warfare they waged. Ez
a usual thing, I s'pose it would be customary
fur the battle to continue ez described until the
shades of night descended and then each army
would return to its own base, claimin' the victory. But on this occasion something in the
nature of a surprise occurred that wasn't down
on the books a-tall.

"Right down under the little rise where us
fellers sat waitin', stood them four guns that
the Liberals bought off of Shelby. Ef brass
cannons have feelin's—and I don't know no
reason why they shouldn't have—them cannons must have felt like something was radically
wrong. The crews were loadin' and firin' and
swabbin' and loadin' and firin' ag'in—all jest ez

busy ez beavers. But they plum overlooked one triflin' detail which the military experts have always reguarded ez bein' more or less essential to successful artillery operations. They forgot to aim in the general direction at the enemy. They done a plentiful lot of cheerin', them gun crews did, and they burnt up a heap of powder and they raised a powerful racket and hullabaloo, but so fur ez visible results went they mout jest ez well have been bombardin' the clear blue sky of heaven.

"Well, fur quite a spell we stayed up there on the brow of the hill, watchin' that there engagement. Only you couldn't properly call it an engagement—by rights it wasn't nothin' but a long distance flirtation. Now several of our boys had served one time or another with the guns. There was one little feller named Vince Hawley, out of Lyon's Battery, that had been one of the crack gunners of the Western Army. He held in ez long ez he could and then he sings out:

"'Boys, do you know whut's ailin' them pore mistreated little field-pieces down yonder? Well, I'll tell you. They're Confederate guns, born, bred, and baptised; and they're cravin' fur Confederate hands to pet 'em. It mout be this'll be the last chance a Southern soldier will ever git to fire a Southern gun. Who'll go 'long with me fur one farewell sashay with our own cannons?'

"In another minute eight or ten of our com-

mand were pilin' off their horses and tearin' down
that little hill behind Vince Hawley and bustin'
in amongst the Mexies and laying violent but
affectionate hands on one of the twelve-pounders. Right off, the natives perceived whut our
fellers wanted to do and they fell back and
gave 'em elbow-room. Honest, son, it seemed
like that field-piece recognised her own kind of
folks, even 'way off there on the aidge of a
Mexican desert, and strove to respond to their
wishes. The boys throwed a charge into her
and Hawley sighted her and then—kerboom—
off she went!

"Off the Imperial forces went, too. The
charge landed right in amongst their front
ranks ez they were advancin'—it happened to
be their turn to charge—takin' 'em absolutely
by surprise. There was a profound scatteration
and then spontaneous-like the enemy seemed to
come to a realisation of the fact that the other
side had broke all the rules and was actually
tryin' to do 'em a real damage. With one accord they turned tail and started in the general
direction of the Isthmus of Panama. Ef they
kept up the rate of travel at which they started,
they arrived there inside of a week, too—or
mebbe even sooner. I s'pose it depended largely
on whether their feet held out.

"Hawley and his gang run the gun forward
to the crest of a little swale ready to give the
retreatin' forces another treatment in case they
should rally and re-form, but a second dose

wasn't needed. Howsomever, before the squad came back, they scouted acrost the field to see whut execution their lone charge had done. Near to where the shell had busted they gathered up six skeered soldiers—fellers that had dropped down, skeered but unhurt, when the smash come and had been layin' there in a hollow in the ground, fearin' the worst and hopin' fur the best. So they brung 'em back in with 'em and turned 'em over to the Liberals ez prisoners of war.

"The rest of us were canterin' down on the flat by now. We arrived in time to observe that some of the victorious Liberals were engaged in lashin' the prisoners' elbows together with ropes, behind their backs, and that whut looked like a firin' squad was linin' up conveniently clos't by. Billy Priest went and located a feller that could interpret after a fashion and inquired whut was the idea. The interpreter feller explained that the idea was to line them six prisoners up and shoot 'em to death.

"'Boys,' says Billy, turnin' to us, 'I'm afeared we'll have to interfere with the contemplated festivalities. Our friends are too gently-inclined durin' the hostilities and too blame' bloodthirsty afterward to suit me. Let us bid an adieu to 'em and purceed upon our way. But first,' he says, 'let us break into the picture long enough to save those six poor devils standin' over there in a row, all tied up like beef-critters fur the butcher.'

"So we rid in betwixt the condemned and the firin' squad and by various devices such ez drawin' our carbines and our six-shooters, we made plain our purpose. At that a wave of disappointment run right through the whole army. You could see it travellin' frum face to face under the dirt that was on said faces. Even the prisoners seemed a trifle put-out and downcasted. Later we found out why. But nobody offered to raise a hand ag'inst us.

"'All right then,' says Billy Priest, 'so fur so good. And now I think we'd better be resumin' our journey, takin' our captives with us. I've got a presentiment,' he says, 'that they'd probably enjoy better health travellin' along with us than they would stayin' on with these here Liberals.'

"'How about them four field-pieces?' says one of the boys, speakin' up. 'There's plenty of hosses to haul 'em. Hadn't we better take them along with us, too? They'll git awful lonesome bein' left in such scurvy company— poor little things!'

"'No,' says Billy, 'I reckin that wouldn't be right. The prisoners are our'n by right of capture, but the guns ain't. These fellers bought 'em off Shelby's brigade and they're entitled to keep 'em. But before we depart,' he says, 'it mout not be a bad idea to tinker with 'em a little with a view to sort of puttin' 'em out of commission fur the time bein'. Our late hosts mout take a notion to turn 'em on us, ez we are goin' away frum 'em and there's a bare chance,' he says, 'that they might hit some of us—by accident.'

"So we tinkered with the guns and then we moved out in hollow formation with the six prisoners marchin' along in the middle and not a soul undertakin' to halt us ez we went. On the whole them Liberals seemed right pleased to get shet of us. But when we'd gone along fur a mile or so, one of the Mexicans flopped down on his knees and begin to jabber. And then the other five follered suit and jabbered with him. After 'while it dawned on us that they were beggin' us to kill 'em quick and not torture 'em, they thinkin' we'd only saved 'em frum bein' shot in order to do something much more painful to 'em at our leisure. So then four or five of the boys dropped down off their mounts and untied 'em and faced 'em about so the open country was in front of 'em and give 'em a friendly kick or two frum behind ez a notice to 'em to be on their way. They lit out into the scrub and were gone the same ez ef they'd been so many Molly Cottontails.

"Fur upward of a week then, we moved along, headin' mighty nigh due South. Considerin' that the country was supposed to be in the midst of civil war we saw powerful few evidences of it ez we rode through. Life fur the humble Mexican appeared to be waggin' along about ez usual, but was nothin' to brag about, at that. We seen him ploughin' amongst the prevalent desolation with a forked piece of wood, one fork bein' hitched to a yoke of oxen and the other fork bein' shod with a little strip of rusty iron. We seen him languidly gatherin' his wheat, him goin' ahead and pullin' it up out of the ground, roots and all and pilin' it in puny heaps, and then the women comin' along behind him and tyin' it in little bunches with strings. Another place we seen him and his women folks threshin' grain by beatin' it with sticks and de- pendin' on the wind to help 'em winnow the wheat from the chaff jest ez it is written 'twas done in the Bible days. We seen him in his hours of ease, fightin' his chicken-cock against some other feller's game-bird, and gamblin' and scratchin' his flea-bites and the more we seen of him the less we seemed to keer fur him. He mout of been all right in his way, but he wasn't our kind of folks; I reckin that was it.

"And he repaid the compliment by not ap- pearin' to keer very deeply fur us strangers neither, but the women seemed to take to us, mightily. They'd come out to us frum their little dried mud cabins bringin' us beans and them flat batter-cakes of their'n and even some- times milk and butter. Also they gave us roughage fur our hosses and wouldn't take pay fur none of it, indicatin' by signs that it was all a free gift. Whut between the grazin' they got and the dried fodder the women gave us, our hosses took on flesh and weren't sech ga'nted crowbaits ez they had been.

"Seven days of traversin' that miser'ble land and then, son, we ran smack into the Imperial scouts and found we'd arrived within less 'en a day's march of the city of Monterey. Purty soon out come a detachment of cavalry to meet us and inquire into our business and a most God-fursaken lookin' bunch they were, but with 'em they had half a dozen Confederates—Missoury boys, all of 'em exceptin' one, him bein' frum Louisiana; and these here Missoury fellers told us some news. It seemed that after Shelby and Price and Hindman got to Monterey their little army had split in two, most of its members headin' off toward the City of Mexico with no purticular object in view so fur ez anybody knowed but jest filled with a restless cravin' to stay in the saddle and keep movin', and the rest strikin' Westward toward the Pacific Coast.

"But about two hundred of 'em had stayed behind and enlisted at Monterey, havin' been given a bounty of six hundred dollars apiece and a promise of one hundred dollars a month in pay ef they'd fight fur Maximilian. The delegation that had rode out to meet us now were part and parcel of that two hundred. They seemed tickled to death to see us and they bragged about the money they were gittin', but ef you watched 'em kind of clos't you could tell, mighty easy, they weren't exactly overjoyed and carried away with enthusiasm over their present jobs. They told us in confidence that the French officers in their army were fine soldiers and done the best they could with the material they had, but that the rank and file were small potatoes and few in the hill. In fact, we gathered frum remarks let fall here and there that after servin' ez a Confederate fur a period of years and fightin' ag'inst husky fellers frum Indiana or Kansas or Michigan or somewheres up that way, bein' a soldier of fortune with the Imperials and fightin' ag'inst the Liberals was, comparatively speakin', a mighty tame pursuit—that you'd probably live longer so doin', but you wouldn't have anywheres near the excitement. On top of all that, though, they extended a cordial invitation to us to go on back to Monterey with 'em and enlist under the Maximilian government.

"Some of our outfit seemed to sort of lean toward the proposition and some to sort of lean ag'inst it, without exactly statin' their reasons why and wherefore. But amongst us all there wasn't a man but whut relied mighty implicit on Billy Priest's judgment, and besides which, you've got to remember, son, that discipline had come to be a sort of an ingrained habit with us. We'd got used to lookin' to our leaders to show us the way and give us our orders and then we'd try to obey 'em, spite of hell and high water. That's the way it had been with us for four long years and that's the way it still was with us. So under the circumstances, with sentiment divided ez it was, we-all waited to see how Billy Priest felt, because ez I jest told you,

we imposed a heap of confidence in his views on
purty near any subject you mout mention. The
final say-so bein' put up to him, he studied a
little and then he said to the Missoury boys that
hearin' frum them about the Confederacy havin'
split up into pieces had injected a new and a
different aspect into the case and in his belief
it was a thing that needed thinkin' over and
mebbe sleepin' on. Accordin'ly, ef it was all
the same to them, he'd like to wait till next
mornin' before comin' to a definite decision and
he believed that in this his associates would con-
cur with him. That was agreeable to the fellers
that had brung us the invitation, or ef it wasn't
they let on like it was anyhow, and so we left
the matter standin' where it was without further argument on their part.

"They told us good-by and expressed the
hope that they'd see us next day in Monterey
and then they rid on back to headquarters to
report progress on the part of the committee on
new members and to ask further time, I s'pose.
Ez fur us, we went into camp right where we
was.

"Most of us suspicioned that after we'd fed
the hosses and et our supper Billy would call a
sort of caucus and git the sense of the meetin',
but he didn't take no steps in that direction
and of course nobody else felt qualified to do so.
After a while the fires we'd lit to cook our
victuals on begin to die down low and the boys
started to turn in. There wasn't much talkin'

or singin', or skylarkin' round, but a whole heap of thinkin' was goin' on—you could feel it in the air. I was layin' there on the ground under my old ragged blankets with my saddle fur a pillow and the sky fur my bed canopy, but I didn't drop right off like I usually done. I was busy ponderin' over in my mind quite a number of things. I remember how gash'ly and on-earthly them old cactus plants looked, loomin' up all 'round me there in the darkness and how strange the stars looked, a-shinin' overhead. They didn't seem like the same stars we'd been used to sleepin' under before we come on down here into Mexico. Even the new moon had a different look, ez though it was another moon frum the one that had furnished light fur us to go possum-huntin' by when we were striplin' boys growin' up. This here one was a lonesome, strange, furreign-lookin' moon, ef you git my meanin'? Anyhow it seemed so to me.

"Somebody spoke my name right alongside of me, and I turn't over and raised up my head and there was Billy Priest hunkered down. He had a little scrap of dried greasewood in his hand and he was scratchin' with it in the dirt in a kind of an absent-minded way.

" 'You ain't asleep yet, Jimmy?' he says to me.

" 'No,' I says, 'I've been layin' here, study-in'.'

" 'That so?' he says. 'Whut about in par-ticular?'

"'Oh nothin' in particular,' I says, 'jest studyin'.'

"He don't say anything more fur a minute; jest keepin' on makin' little marks in the dirt with the end of his stick. Then he says to me:

"'Jimmy,' he says, 'I've been doin' right smart thinkin' myself.'

"'Have you?' I says.

"'Yes,' he says, 'I have. I've been thinkin' that whilst peppers make quite spicy eatin' and beans are claimed to be very nourishin' articles of food, still when taken to excess they're liable to pall on the palate, sooner or later.'

"'They certainly are,' I says.

"'Let's see,' he says. 'This is the last week in July, ain't it? Back in God's country, the first of the home-grown watermelons oughter be comin' in about now, oughten they? And in about another week from now they'll be pickin' those great big stripedy rattlesnake melons that grow in the river bottoms down below town, won't they?'

"'Yes,' I says, 'they will, ef th season ain't been rainy and set 'em back.'

"'Let us hope it ain't,' he says, and I could hear his stick scratchin' in the grit of that desert land, makin' a scrabblin' itchy kind of sound.

"'Jimmy Bagby,' he says, 'any man's liable to make a mistake sometimes, but that don't necessarily stamp him ez a fool onlessen he sticks to it too long after he's found out it is a mistake.'

"'Billy,' I says, 'I can't take issue with you there.'

"'F'r instance now,' he says, 'you take a remark which I let fall some weeks back touchin' on flags. Well I've been thinkin' that remark over, Jimmy, and I've about come to the conclusion that ef a man has to give up the flag he fout under and can't have it no longer, he mout in time come to be equally comfortable in the shadder of the flag he was born under. He might even come to love 'em both, mighty sincerely—lovin' one fur whut it meant to him once't and fur all the traditions and all the memories it stands fur, and lovin' the other fur whut it may mean to him now and whut it's liable to mean to his children and their children.'

"'But Billy,' I says, 'when all is said and done, we fit in defence of a constitutional principle.'

"'You bet we did,' he says; 'but it's mostly all been said and it's practically all been done. I figger it out this way, Jimmy. Reguardless of the merits of a given case, ef a man fights fur whut he thinks is right, so fur ez he pussonally is concerned, he fights fur whut is right. I ain't expectin' it to happen yit awhile, but I'm willin' to bet you something that in the days ahead both sides will come to feel jest that way about it too.'

"'Do you think so, Billy?' I says.

"'Jimmy,' he says, 'I don't only think so—

I jest natchelly knows so. I feel it in my bones.'

"'Then I persume you must be correct,' I says.

"He waits a minute and then he says: "'Jimmy,' he says, 'I don't believe I'd ever make a success ez one of these here passenger-pigeons. Now, a passenger-pigeon ain't got no regular native land of his own. He loves one country part of the time and another country part of the time, dividin' his seasons betwixt 'em. Now with me I'm afraid it's different.'

"'Billy,' I says, 'I've about re'ch the conclusion that I wasn't cut out to be a passenger-pigeon, neither.'

"He waits a minute, me holdin' back fur him to speak and wonderin' whut his next subject is goin' to be. Bill Priest always was a master one to ramble in his conversations. After a while he speaks, very pensive:

"'Jimmy,' he says, 'ef a man was to git up on a hoss, say to-morrow mornin' and ride along right stiddy he'd jest about git home by hog-killin' time, wouldn't he?'

"'Jest about,' I says, 'ef nothin' serious happened to delay him on the way.'

"'That's right,' he says, 'the spare ribs and the chitterlin's would jest about be ripe when he arrove back.'

"I didn't make no answer to that—my mouth was waterin' so I couldn't speak. Besides there didn't seem to be nothin' to say.

"'The fall revivals ought to be startin' up

about then, too,' he says, 'old folks gittin' religion all over ag'in and the mourners' bench overflowin', and off in the back pews and in the dark corners young folks flirtin' with one another and holdin' hands under cover of the hymn-books. But all the girls we left behind us have probably got new beaux by now, don't you reckin?'

"'Yes, Billy,' I says, 'I reckin they have and I don't know ez I could blame 'em much neither, whut with us streakin' 'way off down here like a passel of idiots.'

"He gits up and throws away his stick.

"'Well, Jimmy,' he says, 'I'm powerful glad to find out we agree on so many topics. Well, good night,' he says.

"'Good night,' I says, and then I rolled over and went right off to sleep. But before I dropped off I ketched a peep of Billy Priest, squattin' down alongside one of the other boys, and doubtless fixin' to read that other feller's thoughts like a book the same ez he'd jest been readin' mine.

"Well, son, the next mornin' at sun-up we were all up, too. We had our breakfast, sech ez it was, and broke camp and mounted and started off with Billy Priest ridin' at the head of the column and me stickin' clos't beside him. I didn't know fur sure whut was on the mind of anybody else in that there cavalcade of gentlemen rangers, but I was mighty certain about whut I aimed to do. I aimed to stick with

Billy Priest; that's whut. Strange to say, nobody ast any questions about whut we were
goin' to do with reguards to them Imperalists
waitin' there fur us in Monterey. You never
saw such a silent lot of troopers in your life.
There wasn't no singin' nor laughin' and
mighty little talkin'. But fur half an hour or
so there was some good, stiddy lopin'.

"Presently one of the boys pulled out of line
and spurred up alongside of our chief.

"'S'cuse me, commander,' he says, 'but it
begins to look to me like we were back trackin'
on our own trail.'

"Billy looks at him, grinnin' a little through
his whiskers. We all had whiskers on our
faces, or the startin's of 'em.

"'Bless my soul, I believe you're right!' says
Billy. 'Why, you've got the makin's of a
scout in you.'

"'But look here,' says the other feller, still
sort of puzzled-like, 'that means we're headin'
due North, don't it?'

"'It means I'm headin' North,' says Billy,
and at that he quit grinnin'. 'But you, nor
no one else in this troop don't have to foller along onlessen you're minded so to do.
Every man here is a free agent and his own
boss. And ef anybody is dissatisfied with the
route I'm takin' and favours some other, I'd
like fur him to come out now and say so. It
won't take me more'n thirty seconds to resign
my leadership.'

"'Oh, that's all right,' says the other feller, 'I was merely astin' the question, that's all. I ain't dissatisfied. I voted fur you ez commander fur the entire campaign—not fur jest part of it. I was fur you when we elected you, and I'm fur you yit.'

"And with that he wheeled and racked along back to his place. Purty soon Billy looked over his shoulder along the column and an idea struck him. Not fur behind him Tom Moss was joggin' along with his old battered banjo swung acrost his back. Havin' toted that there banjo of his'n all through the war he'd likewise brought it along with him into Mexico. He had a mighty pleasin' voice, too, and the way he could sing and play that song about him bein' a good old rebel and not carin' a dam' made you feel that he didn't care a dam', neither. Billy beckoned to him and Tom rid up alongside and Billy whispered something in his ear. Tom's face all lit up then and he onslung his banjo frum over his shoulder and throwed one laig over his saddle-bow and hit the strings a couple of licks and reared his head back and in another second he was singin' at the top of his voice. But this time he wasn't singin' the song about bein' a good old rebel. He was singin' the one that begins:

'The sun shines bright on my Old Kintucky Home;
  'Tis Summer, the darkies are gay,
The corn tops are ripe and the medders are in bloom,
  And the birds make music all the day.'

"In another minute everybody else was singin', too—singin' and gallopin'. Son, you never in your whole life seen so many hairy, ragged, rusty fellers on hoss-back a-tearin' along through the dust of a strange land, actin' like they were all in a powerful hurry to git somewheres and skeered the gates would be shut before they arrived. Boy, listen: the homesickness jest popped out through my pores like perspiration.

"It taken us all of seven days to git frum the border acros't that long stretch of waste to within a day's ride of the city of Monterey. It only taken us four and a half to git back ag'in to the border, the natives standin' by to watch us as we tore on past 'em. The sun was still several hours high on the evenin' of the fifth day when we come in sight of the Rio Grande River; and I don't ever seem to recall a stretch of muddy yaller water that looked so grateful to my eyes ez that one looked.

"We come canterin' down to the water's edge, all of us bein' plum' jaded and mighty travel-worn. And there, right over yond' on the fur bank we could see the peaky tops of some army tents standin' in rows and we heared the notes of a bugle, soundin' mighty sweet and clear in that still air. And it dawned on us that by a strange coincidence whut wouldn't be liable to happen once't in a dozen years had happened in our purticular case— that the United States Government, ez represented by a detachment of its military forces, had moved down to the line at a point almost opposite to the place where we aimed to cross back over.

"I ain't sure yit whut it was—it mout a-been the first sight of the foeman he'd fit ag'inst so long that riled him or it mout a-been merely a sort of sneakin' desire to make out like he purposed to hold off to the very last and then be won over by sweet blandishments—but jest ez we reached the river, a big feller hailin' frum down in Bland County rid up in front of Billy Priest and he says he wants to ast him a question.

"'Fire away,' says Billy.

"'Bill Priest,' says the Bland County feller, 'I take it to be your intention to go back into the once't free but now conquered state of Texas?'

"'Well, pardner,' says Billy in that whiny way of his'n, 'you certainly are a slow one when it comes to pickin' up current gossip ez it flits to and fro about the neighbourhood. Why do you s'pose we've all been ridin' hell-fur-leather in this direction endurin' of the past few days onlessen it was with that identical notion in mind?'

"'Never mind that now,' says the other feller. 'Circumstances alter cases. Don't you see that there camp over yonder is a camp of Yankee soldiers?'

"'Ef my suspicions are correct that's jest

whut it is,' says Billy very politely. 'Whut of it?'

"'Well,' says the other feller, 'did it ever occur to you that ef we cross here them Yankees will call on us to lay down the arms which we've toted so long? Did it ever occur to you that mebbe they'd even expect us to take their dam' oath of allegiance?'

"'Yes,' says Billy Priest, 'sence you bring up the subject, it had occurred to me that they mout do jest that. And likewise it has also occurred to me that when them formalities are concluded they mout extend the hospitalities of the occasion by invitin' us to set down with them to a meal of real human vittles. Why,' he says, 'I ain't tasted a cup of genuwyne coffee in so long that——!'

"The other feller breaks in on him before Billy can git done with whut he's sayin',

"'And you,' he says, sort of sneerful and insinuatin', 'you, here only some three or four months back was a ring-leader and a head-devil in formin' this here expedition. You was goin' round makin' your brags that you'd be the last one to surrender—you! And we've been callin' you Fightin' Billy! Fightin' Billy? Hell's fire!'

"Billy rammed his heels in his hoss's flanks and shoved over, only reinin' up when he was touchin' laigs with the Bland County feller. A shiny little blue light come into his eyes and the veins in his neck all swelled out.

"'My esteemed friend and feller-country-man,' says Billy, speakin' plenty slow and plenty polite, 'ef any gentleman present is inclined to make a pussonal matter of it, I'll undertake to endeavour to prove up my right to that there title right here and now. But ef not, I wish to state fur the benefit of all concerned that frum this minute I ain't figgerin' on wearin' the nick-name any longer. Frum where I set it looks to me like this is a mighty fitten and appropriate time to go out of the fightin' business and resume the placid and pleasant ways of peace. Frum now on, to friends ez well ez to strangers, I'm goin' to be jest plain William Pitman Priest, Esquire, attorney and counsellor-at-law. I ast you all to kindly bear it in mind. And further-more speakin' solely and exclusively fur the said William Pitman Priest, I will state it is my in-tention of gittin' acrost this here river in time to eat my supper on the soil of my own country. Ef anybody here feels like goin' along with me I'll be glad of his company. Ef not, I'll bid all you good comrades an affectionate farewell and jest jog along over all by my lonesome self.'

"But, of course, when he said that last he was jest funnin'—talkin' to hear hisself talk. He knowed good and well we would all go with him. And we did. And ez fur ez I know none of us ever had cause to regret takin' the step.

"By hurryin', we did git back home before hog-killin' time. And then after a spell, when we'd had our disabilities removed, some of us like Billy Priest started runnin' fur office and bein' elected with reasonable regularity and some of us, like me, went into business. We lived through bayonet rule and reconstruction and carpet-baggery, and we lived to see all them evils die out and a better feelin' and a better understandin' come in. We've been livin' ever since, sech of us ez are still survivin'. I've done consider'ble livin' myself. I've lived to see North and South united. I've even lived to see my own daughter married to the son of a Northern soldier, with the full consent of the families on both sides. And so that's how it happens I've got a grandson that's part Yankee and part Confederate in his breedin'. I reckin there ain't nobody that's ez plum' foolish ez I am about that there little, curly-headed sassy tike, without it's his grandfather on the other side, old Major Ashcroft. We differ radically on politics, the Major bein' a besotted and hopeless black Republikin; and try ez I will I ain't never been able to cure him of a delusion of his'n that the Ninth Michigan could a-helt its own ag'inst King's Hell Hounds ef ever they'd met up on the field of battle; but in other respects he's a fairly intelligent man; and he certainly does coincide with me that betwixt us we've got the smartest four-year-old youngster fur a grandchild that ever was born. There's hope fur a nation that kin produce sech children ez that one, ef I do say it myself."

He stood up and shook himself.

"In fact, son," concluded Sergeant Bagby, "you mout safely say that, takin' one thing with another, this country is turnin' out to be quite a success."

CHAPTER II

AND THERE WAS LIGHT

SO many things that at first seem amazingly complex turn out amazingly simple. The purely elemental has a trick of ambushing itself behind a screen of mystery; but when by deduction and elimination—in short, by the simple processes of subtraction and division—we have stripped away the mask, the fact stands so plainly revealed we marvel that we did not behold it from the beginning. Elemental, you will remember, was a favourite word with Mr. Sherlock Holmes, and one much employed by him in the elucidation of problems in criminology for the better enlightenment of his sincere but somewhat obvious-minded friend, the worthy Doctor Watson.

On the other hand, traits and tricks that appear to betray the characters, the inclinations and, most of all, the vocations of their owners may prove misleading clues, and very often do. You see a black man with a rolling gait, who spraddles his legs when he stands and sways his body on his hips when he walks; and, following

the formula of the deductionist cult of amateur
detectives, you say to yourself that here, beyond
peradventure, is a deep-water sailor, used to
decks that heave and scuppers that flood. Inquiry but serves to prove to you how wrong
you are. The person in question is a veteran
dining-car waiter.

Then along comes another—one with a hearty
red face, who rears well back and steps out with
martial precision. Evidently a retired officer of
the regular army, you say to yourself. Not at
all; merely the former bass drummer of a military brass band. The bass drummer, as will
readily be recalled, leans away from his instru-
ment instead of toward it.

For a typical example of this sort of thing, let
us take the man I have in mind for the central
figure of this tale. He was a square-built man,
round-faced, with a rather small, deep-set grey
eye, and a pair of big hands, clumsy-looking
but deft. He wore his hair short and his upper
lip long. Appraising him upon the occasion of
a chance meeting in the street, you would say
offhand that this, very probably, was a man who
had been reasonably successful in some trade
calling for initiative and expertness rather than
for technic. He wouldn't be a theatrical man-
ager—his attire was too formal; or a stock-
broker—his attire was not formal enough.

I imagine you in the act of telling yourself
that he might be a clever life-insurance solicitor,
or a purchasing agent for a trunk line, or a canny

judge of real-estate values—a man whose taste in dress would run rather to golf stockings than to spats, rather to soft hats than to hard ones, and whose pet hobby would likely be trout flies and not first editions. In a part of your hypothesis you would have been absolutely correct. This man could do things with a casting rod and with a mid-iron too.

Seeing him now, as we do see him, wearing a loose tweed suit and sitting bareheaded behind a desk in the innermost room of a smart suite of offices on a fashionable side street, surrounded by shelves full of medical books and by wall cases containing medical appliances, you, knowing nothing of him except what your eye told you, would probably hazard a guess that this individual was a friend of the doctor, who, having dropped in for social purposes and having found the doctor out, had removed his hat and taken a seat in the doctor's chair to await the doctor's return.

Therein you would have been altogether in error. This man was not the doctor's friend, but the doctor himself—a practitioner of high repute in his own particular line. He was known as a specialist in neurotic disorders; privately he called himself a specialist in human nature. He was of an orthodox school of medicine, but he had cast overboard most of the ethics of the school and he gave as little as possible of the medicine. Drugs he used sparingly, preferring to prescribe other things for most of his patients

[54]

—such things, for instance, as fresh air, fresh vegetables and fresh thoughts. His cures were numerous and his fees were large.

On the other side of a cross wall a woman sat waiting to see him. She was alone, being the first of his callers to arrive this day. A heavy, deep-cushioned town car, with a crest on its doors and a man in fine livery to drive it, had brought her to the doctor's address five minutes earlier; car and driver were at the curb outside. The woman was exquisitely groomed and exquisitely overdressed. She radiated luxury, wealth and the possession of an assured and enviable position. She radiated something else, too—unhappiness.

Here assuredly the lay mind might make no mistake in its summarising. There are too many like her for any one of us to err in our diagnosis when a typical example is presented. The city is especially prolific of such women. It breeds them. It coddles them and it pampers them, but in payment therefore it besets them with many devils. It gives them everything in reason and out of reason, and then it makes them long for something else—anything else, so long as it be unattainable. Possessed of the nagging demons of unrest and discontent and satiation, they feed on their nerves until their nerves in retaliation begin to feed on them. The result generally is smash. Sanitariums get them, and divorce courts and asylums—and frequently cemeteries.

The woman who waited in the reception room did not have to wait very long, yet she was hard put to it to control herself while she sat there. She bit her under lip until the red marks of her teeth showed in the flesh, and she gripped the arms of her chair so tightly and with such useless expenditure of nervous force that through her gloves the knuckles of her hands exposed themselves in sharp high ridges.

Presently a manservant entered and, bowing, indicated mutely that his master would see her now. She fairly ran past him through the communicating door which he held open for her passage. As she entered the inner room it was as though her coming into it set all its orderliness awry. Only the ruddy-faced specialist, intrenched behind the big table in the middle of the floor, seemed unchanged. She halted on the other side of the table and bent across it toward him, her finger tips drumming a little tattoo upon its smooth surface. He did not speak even the briefest of greetings; perhaps he was minded not to speak. He waited for her to begin.

"Doctor," she burst out, "you must do something for me; you must give me medicine —drugs—narcotics—anything that will soothe me. I did not sleep at all last night and hardly any the night before that. All night I sat up in bed or walked the floor trying to keep from screaming out—trying to keep from going mad. I have been dressed for hours—I made my

maid stay up with me—waiting for your office
to open so that I might come to you. Here I
am—see me! See the state I am in! Doctor,
you must do something for me—and do it now,
quickly, before I do something desperate!"

She panted out the last words. She put her
clenched hands to her bosom. Her haggard
eyes glared into his; their glare made the carefully applied cosmetics upon her face seem a
ghastly mask.

"I have already prescribed for you, madam,"
the doctor said. "I told you that what you
mainly needed was rest—complete and abso-
lute rest."

"Rest? Rest! How can I rest? What
chance is there for me to rest? I can't rest! If
I try to rest I begin to think—and then it is
worse than ever. I must keep on the go.
Something drives me on—something inside me,
here—to go and go, and to keep on going until
I drop. Oh, doctor, you don't know what I
suffer—what I have to endure. No one knows
what I have to endure. No one understands.
My husband doesn't understand me—my children do not, nor my friends.

"Friends? I have no friends. I can't get on
with any one—I quarrel with every one. I
know I am sick, that I am irritable and out-of-
sorts sometimes. And I know that I am self-
willed and want my own way. But I've always
been self-willed; it's a part of my nature. And
I've always had my own way. They should

appreciate that. But they don't. They cross me. At every turn somebody crosses me. The whole world seems in a conspiracy to deny me what I want.

"It can't be my fault always that I am forever quarrelling with people—with my own family; with my husband's family; with every one who crosses my path. I tell you they don't understand me, doctor. They don't make allowances for my condition. If they would only make allowances! And they don't give me any consideration. I can't stand it, doctor! I can't go on like this any longer. Please—please, doctor, do something for me!"

Mounting hysteria edged her voice with a sharpened, almost a vulgar shrillness. The austere and studied reserve of her class—a reserve that is part of it poise and the rest of it pose—dropped away from her like a discarded garment, and before her physician she revealed herself nakedly for what she was—a creature with the passions, the forwardness and the selfishness of a spoiled and sickly child; and, on top of these, superimposed and piled up, adult impulses, adult appetites, adult petulance. adult capacity for misery.

"I told you," he said, "to go away. I thought, until my man brought me your name a bit ago, that you had gone. Weeks ago I told you that travel might help you—not the sort of travel to which you have been used, but a different sort—travel in the quiet places, out of the beaten path, and rest. I told you the same thing again less than a week ago."

"But where?" she demanded. "Where am I to go? Tell me that! I have been everywhere —I have seen everything. What is there left for me to see in the world? What is there in the world that is worth seeing? You told me before there was nothing organically wrong with me, nothing fundamentally wrong with my body. Then it must be my mind, and travel couldn't cure a mind in the state that mine is in. How can I rest when I am so distracted, when small things upset me so, when——"

In the midst of this new outburst she broke off. Her eyes, wandering from his as she pumped herself up toward a frenzy, were focused now upon some object behind him. She pointed toward it.

"I never saw that before," she said. "It wasn't there when I was here last."

He swung about in his chair, its spiral creaking under his weight.

"No," he said; "you never saw that before. It came into my possession only a day or two ago. It is a——"

She broke in on him.

"What a wonderful face!" she said. "What beauty there is in it—what peace! I think that is what made me notice it—the peace that is in it. Oh, if I could only be like that! Doctor, the being to whom that face belonged must have had everything worth having. And to

think there can be such beings in this world—
beings so blessed, so happy—while I—I——"

Tears of self-pity came into her eyes. She
was slipping back again into her former mood.
With his gaze he caught and held hers, exerting
all his will to hold it. A brother psychologist
seeing him in that moment would have said
that to this man a possible way out of a di-
lemma had come—would have said that an inspiration suddenly had visited him.

"Perhaps you would like to see it at closer
range," he said, still steadfastly regarding her.
"There is a story regarding it—a story that
might interest you, madam."

He rose from his place, crossed the room and,
reaching up, took down a plaster cast of a face
that rested upright against the broad low
moulding that ran along his walls on two
sides.

As he brought it to her he saw that she had
taken a chair. Her figure was relaxed from
its recent rigidness. Her elbows were upon the
tabletop. He put the cast into her gloved
hands and reseated himself. She held it before
her at arm's length, and one gloved hand went
over its surface almost caressingly.

"It is wonderful!" she said. "I never saw
such an expression on any human face—why,
it is soothing to me just to look at it. Doctor,
where did you get it? Who was the original of
it—or don't you know? What living creature
sat for the artist who made it?"

"No living creature sat for it," he said slowly.

"Oh!" she said disappointedly. "Well, then, what artist had the imagination to conjure up such a conception?"

"No artist conjured it up." he told her.

"Then how——"

"That, madam," he said, "is a death mask."

"A death mask!" Her tone was incredulous. "A death mask, doctor?"

"Yes, madam—a death mask. See, the eyes are closed—are half closed, anyway."

"Do you mean to tell me that death can leave such an expression on any face? How could——"

She broke off, staring incredulously at the thing.

"That is what makes the story I mean to tell you," he said—"if you care to hear it?"

"Of course I want to hear it." Her manner was insistent, impatient, demanding almost. "Please go on."

He kept her in suspense a moment or two; and so they both sat, he squinting up at the ceiling as though marshalling a narrative in its proper sequence in his mind, she holding fast to the disked shape of white plaster. At length he began, speaking slowly.

"Here is the story," he said: "A few weeks ago an acquaintance of mine—a fellow physician—told me of a case he thought might interest me. Primarily it was a surgical case, and

I, as perhaps you know, do not practise surgery; but there was another aspect of it that did have a direct and personal appeal for me.

"It seems that some weeks before there had been put into his hands for treatment a man— a young man—who was stone-deaf and stone-blind, and whose senses of taste and of smell were greatly affected—perhaps I should say impaired. He could speak, more or less imperfectly, and his sense of touch was good; in fact, better than with ordinary mortals. These two faculties alone remained to him. He had been afflicted so from childhood; the attack, or the disease, which left him in this state had come upon him very early, before his mind had registered very many sensible impressions.

"Speech and feeling—these really were what remained intact. Yet his intelligence, considering these handicaps, was above the average, and his body was healthy, and his temperament, in the main, sanguine. Practically all his life he had been in an asylum—a charity institution. Until chance brought him to the attention of this acquaintance of mine it had seemed highly probable that he would spend the rest of his life in this institution.

"The physicians there regarded his case as hopeless. They were conscientious men—these physicians—and they were not lacking in sympathy, I think; but their hands and their thoughts were concerned with their duties, and perhaps—mind you, I say perhaps—perhaps an individual case more or less did not mean to them what it means to the physician in private practice. You understand? So this young man, who was well formed physically, who was normal in his mental aspects, seemed to be doomed to serve a life sentence inside walls of utter darkness and utter silence.

"Well, this man came under the attention of the surgeon I have mentioned. Possibly because it seemed so hopeless, the case interested the surgeon. He made up his mind that the affliction—afflictions rather—were not congenital, not incurable. He made up his mind that a tumorous growth on the brain was responsible for the present state of the victim. And he made up his mind that an operation—a delicate and a risky and a difficult operation—might bring about a cure. If the operation failed the subject would pass from the silence and the blackness he now endured into a silence and a blackness which many of us, similarly placed, would find preferable. He would die—quickly and painlessly. If the operation succeeded he probably would have back all his faculties—he would begin really to live. The surgeon was willing to take the chance, to assume the responsibility.

"The other man was willing to take his chance too. Both of them took it. The operation was performed—and it was a success. The man lived through it, and when he was lifted off the table my friend had every reason to believe—in fact, to know as surely as a man whose business is tampering with the human organism can know anything—that before very long this man, who had walked all his days in darkness, lacking taste and smell, and hearing no sound, would have back all that his afflictions had denied him.

"To my friend, the surgeon, it seemed likely that I, as a person concerned to a degree in psychologic manifestations and psychologic phenomena, would be glad of the opportunity to be present at the hour when this man, through his eyes, his ears, his tongue and his palate, first registered intelligible and actual impressions. And I was glad of the opportunity. Almost it would be like witnessing the rebirth of a human being; certainly it would be witnessing the mental awakening, through physical mediums, of a human soul.

"At first hand I would see what this world, to which you and I are accustomed and of which some of us have grown weary, meant to one who had been so completely, so utterly shut out from that world through all the more impressionable years of his life. Naturally I was enormously interested to hear what he might say, to see what he might do in the hour of his reawakening and re-creation.

"So I went with the surgeon on the day appointed by him for testing the success of his operation. Only five of us were present—the man himself, the surgeon who had cured him,

two others and myself. Until that hour and
for every hour since he had come out from
under the ether, the patient's eyes had been
bandaged to shut out light, and his ears had
been muffled to shut out sounds, and he had
been fed on liquid mixtures administered arti-
ficially."

"Why?" asked the woman, interrupting for
the first time.

For a moment the doctor hesitated. Then he
went on smoothly to explain:

"You see, they feared the sudden shock to
senses and to organs made sensitive by long dis-
use until he had completely rallied from the
operation. So they had hooded his eyes and his
ears."

"But food—why couldn't he have eaten
solid food before this?" she insisted. "That is
what I mean."

"Oh, that?" he said, and again he halted for
an instant. "That was done largely on my
account. I think the surgeon wanted the test
to be complete at one time and not developed in
parts. You understand, don't you?"

She nodded. And he continued, watching
her face intently as he proceeded:

"So, first of all, we led him into a partly
darkened room and sat him down at a table;
and we gave him food—very simple food—a
glass of cold water; a piece of bread, buttered;
a baked Irish potato, with butter and salt upon
it—that was all. We stood about him watching

him as he tasted of the things we put before him—for it was really the first time he had ever properly tasted anything.

"Madam, if I live to be a hundred years old, I shall never forget the look that came into his face then. Even though he lacked the words to express himself, as you and I with our greater vocabularies might conceivably have expressed ourselves had such an experience come to us, I knew that to him the bread was ambrosia and the water was nectar.

"He didn't wolf the food down as I had rather expected he might. He ate it slowly, extracting the flavour from every crumb of it. And the water he took in sips, allowing it to trickle down his throat, drop by drop almost. And then he spoke to us, touching the bread and the potato and the water glass. Mind you, I am reproducing the sense of what he said rather than his exact words. He said:

" 'What is this—and this—and this? What are these delicious things you have given me to eat? And what is this exquisite drink I have swallowed?'

"We told him and he seemed not to believe it at first. He said:

" 'Why, I have handled such things as these often. I have taken them up in my hands a thousand times and I have swallowed them. I should have known what they were by the touch of my fingers—but the taste of them deceived me. Can it be possible that these things are

common things—that even poor people can
feast upon such meals as this which I am eating? Can it even be possible that there is food
within the reach of ordinary mortals which has
a finer zest than this?'

"And when his friend, the surgeon, told him
'Yes'—told him 'Yes' many times and in many
ways—still he seemed loath to believe it. When
he had finished, to the last scrap of the potato
skin and the last morsel of the bread crust and
the last drop in the glass, he bowed his head and
outspread his hands before him as though returning thanks for a glorious benefaction.

"Perhaps I should have told you that this
took place late in the afternoon. We waited a
little while after that, and then just before sunset we took him outdoors into a little shabby
garden on the asylum grounds; and we freed his
eyes and we unmuffled his ears. And then we
drew back from him a distance and watched
him to see what he would do.

"For a little while he did nothing except
stand in his tracks, transfixed and transfigured.
He saw the sky and the sunlight and the earth
and the grass and the shadows upon the earth
and the trees and the flowers that were about
him—saw them literally in a celestial vision;
and he smelled the good wholesome smells of
the earth, and the scents of the struggling,
straggling flowers in the ill-kept flower beds, and
the scents of the green things growing there too.

"And just then, as though it had known and

had been inspired to choose this instant for
bringing to him yet another sensation, a thrush
—a common brown thrush—began singing in an
elm tree almost directly above him. Of course
it was merely a coincidence that a thrush should
begin singing then and there. Thrushes are
plentiful enough about the country in this climate at this season of the year. Central Park is
full of them, sometimes. Most of us scarcely notice them, or their singing either. But, you see,
with this man it was different. He literally was
undergoing re-creation, re-incarnation, resur-
rection. Call it what you please. It was one
of those three things. In a way of speaking it
was all three of them.

"At the first note oᵢ music from the bird he
gave a quick start, and then he threw back his
head and uplifted his face; and quite near at
hand he saw the little rusty-coloured chap, singing away there, with its speckled throat feathers
rising and falling, and he heard the sounds that
poured from the thrush's open beak. And as he
looked and listened he put his hands to his
breast as though something were hurting him
there. He didn't move until the bird had
fluttered away. Nor did we move either.

"Then he turned and came stumbling and
reeling toward us, literally drunk with joy. His
intoxication of ecstasy thickened his tongue and
choked him until he, at first, could not speak to
us. After a bit, though, the words came out-
pouring from his lips.

" 'Did you hear that?' he cried out. 'Did you hear it? Do you smell the earth and the flowers? And the sky—I have seen it! I can see it now. Oh, hasn't God been good to us to give us all this? Oh, hasn't He been good to me?'

"In an outburst of gratitude he seized the hand of my friend and kissed it again and again. I had meant to take notes of his behaviour as we went along, but I took none. I knew that afterward I could reproduce from memory all that transpired.

"Presently he was calmer, and the surgeon said to him:

" 'My son, there is something yet to be seen—something that you, having so many other things to see, have overlooked. Look yonder!' And he pointed to the West, where the sun was just going down.

"And, at that, the other man faced about and looked full into his first sunset. Instantly his whole mood changed. It became rapt, reverential—you might say worshipful. His lips moved, but no words came from them at first, and he made as though to shut out the sight with his hands, as though the beauty of the vision was too great for him to endure. I went to him and put my hand on his shoulder. He was quivering from head to foot in an ague of sheer happiness. He seemed hardly to know I was there. He did not look toward me. He kept his eyes fixed upon the West as if he were greedy to miss nothing of the spectacle.

"Until now the sunset had seemed to me less beautiful by far than many another summer sunset I had seen, for the sky was rather overcast and the colours not particularly vivid; but, standing there beside him, in physical contact with him, I caught from him something of what he felt, and I saw that glow in the west as something of indescribable grandeur and unutterable splendour, a miracle too glorious for words to describe or painters to reproduce upon squares of canvas.

"Presently ne spoke to me, still without turning his head in my direction.

" 'How often does this—this—come to pass?' he asked, panting the words out.

" 'Many times a year,' I told him. 'At this season nearly every evening.'

" 'And is it ever so beautiful as this?' he said.

" 'Often more beautiful,' I said. 'Often the colours are richer and deeper.'

" 'Why are there not more of us here to look upon it?' he asked. 'Surely at this hour all mankind must cease from its tasks—from whatever it is doing—to see this miracle—this free gift of the Creator!'

"I tried to tell him that mankind had grown accustomed to the daily repetition of the sunset, but he seemed unable to comprehend. As the last flattened ray of sunshine faded upon the grass, and the afterglow began to spread across the heavens, I thought he was

about to faint; and I put both my arms round
him to steady him. But he did not faint, though
he trembled all over and took his breath into
his lungs in great sobbing gulps. I showed him
the evening star where it shone in the sky, and
he watched it brighten, saying nothing at all.

"Suddenly he turned to me and said:

" 'At last I have lived, and I have found that
life is sweet. Life is sweeter than I ever dared
to hope it might be.'

"Then he said:

" 'I have a home. Will you show me where
it is? While I was blind I could feel my way to
it; but, now that I can see, I feel lost—all things
are so changed to me. Please lead me there—
I want to see with my own eyes what a home is
like.'

"So I took his hand in mine and we went
toward it, and the three others who were there
followed after us.

"Madam, his home—the only home he had, for
so far as we knew, he had no living kinspeople—
was a room in that big barn of an asylum. I led
him to the door of it. It was a barren enough
room—you know how these institutions are apt
to be furnished, and this room was no exception
to the rule. Bare walls, a bare floor, bare un-
curtained windows, a bed, a chair or two, a
bare table—a sort of hygienic and sanitary
brutality governed all its appointments.

"I imagine the lowest servant in your employ has a more attractively furnished room

than this was. Now, though, it was flooded with the afterglow, which poured in at the windows; that soft light alone redeemed its hideousness of outline and its poverty of furnishings.

"He halted at the threshold. We know what home means to most of us. How much must it have meant, then, to him! He could see the walls closing round to encompass him in their friendly companionship; he could see the roof coming down to protect him.

" 'Home!' he said to himself in a half whisper, under his breath. 'What a beautiful word home is! And what a beautiful place my home is!'

"Nobody gave the signal, none of us made the suggestion by word or gesture; but with one accord we four, governed by the same impulse, left him and went away. We felt in an inarticulate way that he was entitled to be alone; that no curious eye had any right to study his emotions in this supreme moment.

"In an hour we went back. He was lying where he had fallen—across the threshold of his room. On his face was a beatific peace, a content unutterable—and he was dead. Joy I think had burst his heart. That bit of plaster you hold in your hand is his death mask."

The doctor finished his tale. He bent forward in his chair to see the look upon his caller's face. She stood up; and she was a creature transformed and radiant!

"Doctor," she said—and even her voice was altered—"I am going home—home to my hus-

band and my children and my friends. I believe
I have found a cure for my—my trouble.
Rather, you have found it for me here to-day.
You have taught me a lesson. You have made
me see things I could not see before—hear things
I could not hear before. For I have been blind
and deaf, as blind and as deaf as this man was—
yes, blinder than he ever was. But now"—she
cried out the words in a burst of revelation—
"but now—why, doctor, I have everything to
live for—haven't I?"

"Yes, madam," he said gravely; "you have
everything to live for. If only we knew it, if
only we could realise it, all of us in this world
have everything to live for."

She nodded, smiling across the table at him.

"Doctor," she said, "I do not believe I shall
ever come back here to see you—as a patient
of yours."

"No," he affirmed; "I do not believe you
will ever come back—as a patient of mine."

"But, if I may, I should like to come sometimes, just to look at that face—that dead face
with its living message for me."

"Madam," he told her, "you may have it on
two conditions—namely, that you keep it in
your own room, and that you do not tell its
story—the story I have just told you—to any
other person. I have reasons of my own for
making those conditions."

"In my own room is exactly where I would
keep it," she said. "I promise to do as you ask.

I shall never part with it. But how can you part with it?"

"Oh, I think I know where I can get another copy," he said. "The original mould has not been destroyed. I am sure my—my friend—has it. This one will be delivered at your home before night. My servant shall take it to you."

"No," she said. "If you do not mind, I shall take it with me now—in my own hands."

She clasped the gift to her breast, holding it there as though it were a priceless thing—too priceless to be intrusted to the keeping of any other than its possessor.

For perhaps five minutes after the departure of his recent patient the great specialist sat at his desk smiling gently to himself. Then he touched with his forefinger a button under the desk. His manservant entered.

"You have heard of troubles being started by a lie, haven't you?" asked the doctor abruptly.

"Yes, sir—I think so, sir."

The man was not an Englishman, but he had been trained in the school of English servants. His voice betrayed no surprise.

"Well, did you ever hear of troubles being ended by a lie?"

"Really, sir, I can't say, sir—offhand."

"Well, it can be done," said the doctor; "in fact, it has been done."

The man stood a moment.

"Was that all, sir?"

"No; not quite," said the master. "Do you remember an Italian pedlar who was here the other day?"

"An Italian pedlar, sir?"

"Yes; don't you remember? A street vender who passed the door. I called him in and bought a plaster cast from him—for seventy-five cents, as I recall."

"Oh, yes, sir; I do remember now."

The man's eyes flitted to an empty space on the wall moulding above the bookcase behind his employer's chair, and back again to his employer's face.

"Well," said the doctor, "you keep a lookout for him, in case he passes again. I want to buy another of those casts from him. I think it may be worth the money—the last one was, anyhow."

CHAPTER III

MR. FELSBURG GETS EVEN

OF all the human legs ever seen in our town I am constrained to admit that Mr. Herman Felsburg's pair were the most humorous legs. When it came to legs—funny legs—the palm was his without a struggle. Casting up in my mind a wide assortment and a great range of legs, I recall no set in the whole of Red Gravel County that, for pure comedy of contour or rare eccentricity of gait, could compare with the two he owned. In his case his legs achieved the impossible by being at one and the same time bent outward and warped inward, so that he was knock-kneed at a stated point and elsewhere bow-legged. And yet, as legs go, they were short ones. For a finishing touch he was, to a noticeable extent, pigeon-toed.

I remember mighty well the first time Mr. Felsburg's legs first acquired for me an interest unrelated to their picturesqueness of aspect. As I think backward along the grooves of my memory to that occasion, it defies all the rules of perspective by looming on a larger scale and in brighter and more vivid colours than many a more important thing which occurred in a much more recent period. I reckon, though, that is because our Creator has been good enough to us sometimes to let us view our childhood with the big, round, magnifying eyes of a child.

I feel it to be so in my case. By virtue of a certain magic I see a small, inquisitive boy sitting on the top step of the wide front porch of an old white house; and as he sits he hugs his bare knees within the circle of his arms and listens with two wide-open ears to the talk that shuttles back and forth among three or four old men who are taking their comfort in easy-chairs behind a thick screen of dishrag and morning glory and balsam-apple vines.

I am that small boy who listens; and, as the picture forms and frames itself in my mind, one of the men is apt to be my uncle. He was not my uncle by blood ties or marriage, but through adoption only, as was the custom down our way in those days and, to a certain degree, is still the custom; and, besides. I was his namesake.

I know now, when by comparison I subject the scene to analysis, that they were not such very old men—then. They are old enough now —such of them as survive to this day. None of that group who yet lives will ever see seventy-five again. In those times grown people would have called them middle-aged men, or, at the most, elderly men; but when I re-create the vision out of the back of my head I invest them with an incredible antiquity and a vasty wisdom, because, as I said just now, I am looking at them with the eyes of a small boy again. Also, it seems to me, the season always is summer—late afternoon or early evening of a hot, lazy summer day.

It was right there, perched upon the top step of Judge Priest's front porch, that I heard, piece by piece, the unwritten history of our town—its tragedies and its farces, its homely romances and its homely epics. There I heard the story of Singin' Sandy Riggs, who, like Coligny, finally won by being repeatedly whipped; and his fist feud with Harve Allen, the bully; and the story of old Marm Perry, the Witch. I don't suppose she was a witch really; but she owned a black cat and she had a droopy lid, which hung down over one red eye, and she lived a friendless life.

And so when the babies in the settlement began to sicken and die of the spotted fever somebody advanced the very plausible suggestion that Marm Perry had laid a spell upon the children, and nearly everybody else believed it. A man whose child fell ill of the plague in the very hour when Marm Perry had spoken to the little thing took a silver dollar and melted it down and made a silver bullet of it—because, of course, witches were immune to

slugs of lead—and on the night after the day
when they buried his baby he slipped up to
Marm Perry's cabin and fired through the window at her as she sat, with her black cat in her
lap, mouthing her empty gums over her supper.
The bullet missed her—and he was a good shot,
too, that man was. Practically all the men who
lived in those days on the spot where our town
was to stand were good shots. They had to
be—or else go hungry frequently.

When the news of this spread they knew for
certain that only by fire could the evil charm
be broken and the conjure-woman be destroyed.
So one night soon after that a party of men
broke into Marm Perry's cabin and made prisoners of her and her cat. They muffled her
head in a bedquilt and they thrust the cat into
a bag, both of them yowling and kicking; and
they carried them to a place on the bluff above
Island Creek, a mile or so from the young settlement, and there they kindled a great fire of
brush; and when the flames had taken good
hold of the wood they threw Marm Perry and
her cat into the blaze and stood back to see
them burn. Mind you, this didn't happen at
Salem, Massachusetts, in or about the year
1692. It happened less than a century ago near
a small river landing on what was then the
southwestern frontier of these United States.

There were certain men, though—leaders of
opinion and action in the rough young community—who did not altogether hold with the

theory that the evil eye was killing off the babies. Somehow they learned what was afoot and they followed, hotspeed, on the trail of the volunteer executioners. As the tale has stood through nearly a hundred years of telling, they arrived barely in time. When they broke through the ring of witch burners and snatched Marm Perry off the pyre, her apron strings had burned in two. As for the cat, it burst through the bag and ran off through the woods, with its fur all ablaze, and was never seen again. I remember how I used to dream that story over and over again. Always in my dreams it reached its climax when that living firebrand went tearing off into the thickets. Somehow, to me, the unsalvaged cat took on more importance than its rescued owner.

There were times, too, when I chanced to be the only caller upon Judge Priest's front porch, and these are the times which in retrospect seem to me to have been the finest of all. I used to slip away from home alone, along toward suppertime, and pay the Judge a visit. Many and many a day, sitting there on that porch step, I watched the birds going to bed. His big front yard was a great place for the birds. In the deep grass, all summer long and all day long, the cock partridge would be directing the attention of a mythical Bob White to the fact that his peaches were ripe and over-ripe. If spared by boys and house cats until the hunting season began he would captain a covey. Now he was chiefly concerned with a family. Years later I found that his dictionary name was American quail; but to us then he was a partridge, and in our town we still know him by no other title.

Forgetting all about the dogs and the guns of the autumn before he would even invade Judge Priest's chicken lot to pick up titbits overlooked by the dull-eyed resident flock; and toward twilight, growing bolder still, he would whistle and whistle from the tall white gate post of the front fence, while his trim brown helpmate clucked lullabies to her speckled brood in the rank tangle back of the quince bushes.

When the redbirds called it a day and knocked off, the mocking birds took up the job and on clear moonlight nights sang all night in the honey locusts. Just before sunset yellow-hammers would be flickering about, tremendously occupied with things forgotten until then; and the chimney swifts that nested in Judge Priest's chimney would go whooshing up and down the sooty flue, making haunted-house noises in the old sitting room below.

Sprawled in his favourite porch chair, the Judge would talk and I would listen. Sometimes, the situation being reversed, I would talk and he listen. Under the spell of his sympathetic understanding I would be moved to do what that most sensitive and secretive of creatures—a small boy—rarely does do: I would bestow my confidences upon him. And if he felt like laughing—at least, he never laughed. And if he felt that the disclosures called for a lecture he rarely did that, either; but if he did the admonition was so cleverly sugar-coated by his way of framing it that I took it down without tasting it.

As I see the vision now, it was at the close of a mighty warm day, when the sun went down as a red-hot ball and all the west was copper-plated with promise of more heat to-morrow, when Mr. Herman Felsburg passed. I don't know what errand was taking him up Clay Street that evening—he lived clear over on the other side of town. But, anyway, he passed; and as he headed into the sunset glow I was inspired by a boy's instinctive appreciation of the ludicrous to speak of the peculiar conformation of Mr. Felsburg's legs. I don't recall now just what it was I said, but I do recall, as clearly as though it happened yesterday, the look that came into Judge Priest's chubby round face.

"Aha!" he said; and from the way he said it I knew he was displeased with me. He didn't scold me, though—only he peered at me over his glasses until I felt my repentant soul shrivelling smaller and smaller inside of me; and then after a bit he said: "Aha! Well, son, I reckin mebbe you're right. Old Man Herman has got a funny-lookin' pair of laigs, ain't he? They do look kinder like a set of hames that ain't been treated kindly, don't they? Whut was it you

MR. FELSBURG GETS EVEN

said they favoured—horse collars, wasn't it?"

I tucked a regretful head down between my hunched shoulders, making no reply. After another little pause he went on:

"Well, sonny, ef you should be spared to grow up to be a man, and there should be a war comin' along, and you should git drawed into it some-way, jest you remember this: Ef your laigs take you into ez many tight places and into ez many hard-fit fights as I've saw them little crookedy laigs takin' that little man, you won't have no call to feel ashamed of 'em—not even ef yours should be so twisted you'd have to walk backward in order to go furward."

At hearing this my astonishment was so great I forgot my remorse of a minute before. I took it for granted that off yonder, in those far-away days, most of the older men in our town had seen service on one side or the other in the Big War—mainly on the Southern side. But some-how it never occurred to me that Mr. Herman Felsburg might also have been a soldier. As far back as I recalled he had been in the clothing business. Boylike, I assumed he had always been in the clothing business. So——

"Was Mr. Felsburg in the war?" I asked.

"He most suttinly was," answered Judge Priest.

"As a regular sure-nuff soldier!" I asked, still in doubt.

"Ez a reg'lar sure-nuff soldier."

I considered for a moment.

"Why, he's Jewish, ain't he, Judge?" I asked next.

"So fur as my best information and belief go, he's practically exclusively all Jewish," said Judge Priest with a little chuckle.

"But I didn't think Jewish gentlemen ever did any fighting, Judge?"

I imagine that bewilderment was in my tone, for my juvenile education was undergoing enlargement by leaps and bounds.

"Didn't you?" he said. "Well, boy, you go to Sunday school, don't you?"

"Oh, yes, sir—every Sunday—nearly."

"Well, didn't you ever hear tell at Sunday school of a little feller named David that taken a rock-sling and killed a big giant named Goliath?"

"Yes, sir; but——"

"Well, that there little feller David was a Jew."

"I know, sir; but—but that was so long ago!"

"It was quite a spell back, and that's a fact," agreed Judge Priest. "Even so, I reckin human nature continues to keep right on bein' human nature. You'll be findin' that out, son, when you git a little further along in years. They learnt you about Samson, too, didn't they—at that there Sunday school?"

I am quite sure I must have shown enthusiasm along here. At that period Samson was, with me, a favourite character in history. By reason of his recorded performances he held rank in my estimation with Israel Putnam and General N. B. Forrest.

"Aha!" continued the Judge. "Old Man Samson was right smart of a fighter, takin' one thing with another, wasn't he? Remember hearin' about that time when he taken the jaw-bone of an ass and killed up I don't know how many of them old Philistines?"

"Oh, yes, sir. And then that other time when they cut off his hair short and put him in jail, and after it grew out again he pulled the temple right smack down and killed everybody!"

"It strikes me I did hear somebody speakin' of that circumstance too. I expect it must have created a right smart talk round the neighbourhood."

I can hear the old Judge saying this, and I can see—across the years—the quizzical little wrinkles bunching at the corners of his eyes.

He sat a minute looking down at me and smiling.

"Samson was much of a man—and he was a Jew."

"Was he?" I was shocked in a new place.

"That's jest exactly what he was. And there was a man oncet named Judas—not the Judas you've heared about, but a feller with the full name of Judas Maccabæus; and he was such a pert hand at fightin' they called him the Hammer of the Jews. Judgin' by whut I've been able to glean about him, his enemies felt jest as well satisfied ef they could hear, before the hostilities started, that Judas was laid up sick in bed somewheres. It taken considerable of a load off their minds, ez you might say.

"But—jest as you was sayin', son, about David—it's been a good while since them parties flourished. When we look back on it, it stretches all the way frum here to B. C.; and that's a good long stretch, and a lot of things have been happenin' meantime. But I sometimes git to thinkin' that mebbe little Herman Felsburg has got some of that old-time Jew fightin' blood in his veins. Anyhow, he belongs to the same breed. No, sirree, sonny; it don't always pay to judge a man by his laigs. You kin do that with reguards to a frog or a grasshopper, or even sometimes with a chicken; but not with a man. It ain't the shape of 'em that counts—it's where they'll take you in time of trouble."

He cocked his head down at me—I saying nothing at all. There didn't seem to be anything for me to say; so I mairtained silence and he spoke on:

"You jest bear that in mind next time you feel moved to talk about laigs. And ef it should happen to be Mister Felsburg's laigs that you're takin' fur your text, remember this whut I'm tellin' you now: They may be crooked; but, son, there ain't no gamer pair of laigs nowheres in this world. I've seen 'em carryin' him into battle when, all the time, my knees was knockin' together, the same ez one of these here end men in a minstrel show knocks his bones together. His laigs may 'a' trembled a little bit too—I ain't sayin' they didn't—but they kept right on promenadin' him up to where the trouble was; and that's the main p'int with a set of shanks. You jest remember that."

Being sufficiently humbled I said I would remember it.

"There's still another thing about Herman Felsburg's laigs that most people round here don't know, neither," added Judge Priest when I had made my pledge: "All up and down the back sides of his calves, and clear down on his shins, there's a whole passel of little red marks. There's so many of them little scars that they look jest like lacework on his skin."

"Did he get them in the war?" I inquired eagerly, scenting a story.

"No; he got them before the war came along," said Judge Priest. "Some of these times, sonny, when you're a little bit older, I'll tell you a tale about them scars on Mr. Felsburg's laigs. There ain't many besides me that knows it."

"Couldn't I hear it now?" I asked.

"I reckin you ain't a suitable age to understand—yit," said Judge Priest. "I reckin we'd better wait a few years. But I won't forgit—I'll tell you when the time's ripe. Anyhow, there's somethin' else afoot now—somethin' that ought to interest a hongry boy."

I became aware of his house servant—Jeff Poindexter—standing in the hall doorway, waiting until his master concluded whatever he might be saying in order to make an important announcement.

"All right, Jeff!" said Judge Priest. "I'll be there in a minute." Then, turning to me: "Son-boy, hadn't you better stay here fur supper with me? I expect there's vittles enough fur two. Come on—I'll make Jeff run over to your house and tell your mother I kept you to supper with me."

After that memorable supper with Judge Priest—all the meals I ever took as his guest were memorable events and still are—ensues a lapse, to be measured by years, before I heard the second chapter of what might be called the tale of Mr. Felsburg's legs. I heard it one evening in the Judge's sitting room.

A squeak had come into my voice, and there was a suspicion of down—a mere trace, as the chemists say—on my upper lip. I was in the second week of proud incumbency of my first regular job. I had gone to work on the *Daily Evening News*—the cubbiest of cub reporters, green as a young gourd, but proud as Potiphar over my new job and my new responsibilities. This time it was professional duty rather than the social instinct that took me to the old Judge's house.

I had been charged by my editor to get from him divers litigatious facts relating to a decision he had that day rendered in the circuit court where he presided. The information having been vouchsafed, the talk took a various trend. Somewhere in the course of it Mr. Felsburg's name came up and my memory ran back like a spark along a tarred string to that other day when he had promised to·relate to me an episode connected with certain small scars on those two bandy legs of our leading clothing merchant.

The present occasion seemed fitting for hearing this long-delayed narrative. I reminded my host of his olden promise; and between puffs at his corncob pipe he told me the thing which I retell here and now, except that, for purposes of convenience, I have translated the actual wording of it out of Judge Priest's vernacular into my own.

So doing, it devolves upon me, first off, to introduce into the main theme a character not heretofore mentioned—a man named Thomas Albritton, a farmer in our country, and at one period a prosperous one. He lived, while he lived—for he has been dead a good while now—six miles from town, on the Massac Creek Road. He lived there all his days. His father before him had cleared the timber off the land and built the two-room log house of squared logs, with the open "gallery" between. With additions, the house grew in time to be a rambling, roomy structure, but from first to last it kept its identity; and even after the last of the old tenants died off or moved off, and new tenants moved in, it was still known as the Albritton place. For all I know to the contrary, it yet goes by that name.

From pioneer days on until this Thomas Albritton became heir to the farm and head of the family, the Albrittons had been a forehanded breed—people with a name for thrift. In fact, I had it that night from the old Judge that, for a good many years after he grew up, this Thomas Albritton enjoyed his due share of affluence. He raised as good a grade of tobacco and as many bushels of corn to the acre as anybody in the Massac Bottoms raised; and, so far as ready money went, he was better off than most of his neighbours.

Perhaps, though, he was not so provident as his sire had been; or perhaps, in a financial way, he had in his latter years more than his share of bad luck. Anyhow, after a while he began to go downhill financially, which is another way of saying he got into debt. Piece by piece he sold off strips of the fertile creek lands his father had cleared. There came a day when he owned only the house, standing in its grove of honey locusts, and the twenty acres surrounding it; and the title to those remaining possessions was lapped and overlapped by mortgages.

It is the rule of this merry little planet of

ours that some must go up while others go down.
Otherwise there would be no room at the top
for those who climb. Mr. Herman Felsburg
was one who steadily went up. When first I
knew him he was rated among the wealthy men
of our town. By local standards of those days
he was rich—very rich. To me, then, it seemed
that always he must have been rich. But
here Judge Priest undeceived me.

When Mr. Felsburg, after four years of honourable service as a private soldier in the army
of the late Southern Confederacy, came back
with the straggling handful that was left of
Company B to the place where he had enlisted,
he owned of this world's goods just the rags he
stood in, plus a canny brain, a provident and
saving instinct, and a natural aptitude for bar-
ter and trade.

Somewhere, somehow, he scraped together a
meagre capital of a few dollars, and with this
he opened a tiny cheap-John shop down on
Market Square, where he sold gimcracks to
darkies and poor whites. He prospered—it
was inevitable that he should prosper. He took
unto himself a wife of his own people; and between periods of bearing him children she
helped him to save. He brought his younger
brother, Ike, over from the old country and
made Ike a full partner with him in his growing
business.

Long before those of my own generation were
born the little store down on Market Square

was a reminiscence. Two blocks uptown, on the busiest corner in town, stood Felsburg Brothers' Oak Hall Clothing Emporium, then, as now, the largest and the most enterprising merchandising establishment in our end of the state. If you could not find it at Felsburg Brothers' you simply could not find it anywhere—that was all. It was more than a store; it was an institution, like the courthouse and the county-fair grounds.

The multitudinous affairs of the industry he had founded did not engage the energies of the busy little man with the funny legs to the exclusion of other things. As the saying goes, he branched out. He didn't speculate—he was too conservative for that; but where there seemed a chance to invest an honest dollar with a reasonable degree of certainty of getting back, say, a dollar-ten in due time, he invested. Some people called it luck, which is what some people always call it when it turns out so; but, whether it was luck or just foresight, whatsoever he touched seemed bound to flourish and beget dividends.

Eventually, as befitting one who had risen to be a commanding figure in the commercial affairs of the community, Mr. Felsburg became an active factor in its financial affairs. As a stockholder, the Commonwealth Bank welcomed him to its hospitable midst. Soon it saw its way clear to making him a director and vice president. There was promise of profit in the use of his name. Printed on the letter-heads, it gave added solidity and added substantiality to the bank's roster. People liked him too. Behind his short round back they might gibe at the shape of his legs, and laugh at his ways of butchering up the English language and twisting up the metaphors with which he besprinkled his everyday walk and conversation; but, all the same, they liked him.

So, in his orbit Mr. Herman Felsburg went up and up to the very peaks of prominence; and while he did this, that other man I have mentioned—Thomas Albritton—went down and down until he descended to the very bottom of things.

In the fullness of time the lines of these two crossed, for it was at the Commonwealth Bank that Albritton negotiated the first and, later, the second of his loans upon his homestead. Indeed, it was Mr. Felsburg who both times insisted that Albritton be permitted to borrow, even though, when the matter of making the second mortgage came up, another director, who specialised in county property, pointed out that, to begin with, Albritton wasn't doing very well; and that, in the second place, the amount of his indebtedness already was as much and very possibly more than as much as the farm would bring at forced sale.

Even though the bank bought it in to protect itself—and in his gloomy mind's eye this director foresaw such a contingency—it might

mean a cash loss; but Mr. Felsburg stood pat;
and, against the judgment of his associates, he
had his way about it. Subsequently, when Mr.
Felsburg himself offered to relieve the bank
of all possibility of an ultimate deficit by buying Albritton's paper, the rest of the board
felt relieved. Practically by acclamation he
was permitted to do so.

Of this, however, the borrower knew nothing at all, Mr. Felsburg having made it a condition that his purchase should be a private
transaction. So far as the borrower's knowledge went, he owed principal and interest to
the bank. There was no reason why Albritton should suspect that Mr. Herman Felsburg
took any interest, selfish or otherwise, in his
affairs, or that Mr. Felsburg entertained covet-
ous designs upon his possessions. Mr. Felsburg wasn't a money lender. He was a clothing merchant. And Albritton wasn't a business man—his present condition, stripped as
he was of most of his inheritance, and with
the remaining portion heavily encumbered,
gave ample proof of that.

Besides, the two men scarcely knew each
other. Albritton was an occasional customer
at the Oak Hall. But, for the matter of that,
so was nearly everybody else in Red Gravel
County; and when he came in to make a purchase it was never the senior member of the
firm but always one of the clerks who served
him. At such times Mr. Felsburg, from the

back part of the store, would watch Mr. Albritton steadily. He never approached him,
never offered to speak to him; but he watched
him.

One day, not so very long after the date
when Mr. Felsburg privately took over the
mortgages on the Albritton place, Albritton
drove in with a load of tobacco for the Buckner
& Keys Warehouse; and, leaving his team and
loaded wagon outside, he went into the Oak
Hall to buy something. Adolph Dreifus, one
of the salesmen, waited on him as he often had
before.

The owners of the establishment were at the
moment engaged in conference in the rear of
the store. Mr. Ike Felsburg was urging, with
all the eloquence at his command, the advisability of adding a line of trunks and suit cases
to the stock—a venture which he personally
strongly favoured—when he became aware that
his brother was not heeding what he had to
say. Instead of heeding, Mr. Herman was
peering along a vista of counters and garment
racks to where Adolph Dreifus stood on one
side of a show case and Tom Albritton stood
on the other. There was a queer expression
on Mr. Felsburg's face. His eyes were squinted
and his tongue licked at his lower lip.

"Hermy," said the younger man, irritated
that his brother's attention should go wandering afar while a subject of such importance
was under discussion, "Hermy, would you

please be so good as to listen to me what I am saying to you?"

There was no answer. Mr. Herman continued to stare straight ahead. Mr. Ike raised his voice impatiently:

"Hermy!"

The older man turned on him with such suddenness that Mr. Ike almost slipped off the stool upon which he was perched.

"What's the idea—yelling in my ear like a graven image?" demanded Mr. Herman angrily. "Do you think maybe I am deef or something?"

"But, Hermy," complained Mr. Ike, "you ain't listening at all. Twice now I have to call you; in fact, three times."

"Is that so?" said Mr. Herman with elaborate sarcasm. "I suppose you think I got nothing whatever at all to do except I should listen to you? If I should spend all my time listening to you where would this here Oak Hall Clothing Emporium be? I should like to ask you that. Gabble, gabble, gabble all day long—that is you! Me, I don't talk so much; but I do some thinking."

"But this is important, what I am trying to tell you, Hermy. Why should you be watching yonder, with a look on your face like as if you would like to bite somebody? Adolph Dreifus ain't so dumb in the head but what he could sell a pair of suspenders or something without your glaring at him every move what he makes."

"Did I say I was looking at Adolph Dreifus?" asked Mr. Herman truculently.

"Well, then, if you ain't looking at Adolph, why should you look so hard at that Albritton fellow? He don't owe us any money, so far as I know. For what he gets he pays cash, else we positively wouldn't let him have the goods. I've seen you acting like this before, Hermy. Every time that Albritton comes in this place you drop whatever you are doing and hang round and hang round, watching him. I noticed it before; and I should like to ask——"

"Mister Ikey Felsburg," said Mr. Herman slowly, "if you could mind your own business I should possibly be able to mind mine. Remember this, if you please—I look at who I please. You are too nosey and you talk too damn much with your mouth! I am older than what you are; and I tell you this—a talking jaw gathers no moss. Also, I would like to know, do my eyes belong to me or do they maybe belong to you, and you have just loaned 'em to me for a temporary accommodation?"

"But, Hermy——"

"Ike, shut up!"

And Mr. Ike, warned by the tone in his brother's voice, shut up.

One afternoon, perhaps six months after this passage between the two partners, Mr. Herman crossed the street from the Oak Hall to the Commonwealth Bank to make a deposit.

Through his wicket window Herb Kivil, the cashier, spoke to him, lowering his voice:

"Oh, Mr. Felsburg; you remember that Albritton matter you were speaking to me about week before last?"

Mr. Felsburg nodded.

"Well, the last interest payment is more than a month overdue now; and, on top of that, Albritton still owes the payment that was due three months before that. There's not a chance in the world of his being able to pay up. He practically admitted as much when he was in here last, asking for more time. So I've followed your instructions in the matter."

"That's a good boy, Herby—a very good boy," said Mr. Felsburg, seemingly much gratified. "You wrote him, then, like I told you?"

"Yes, sir; I wrote him. Yesterday I served notice on him by mail that we would have to go ahead and foreclose right away. So this morning he called me up by telephone from out in the country and asked us to hold off, please, until he could come in here and talk the thing over again."

"Does he think maybe he can pay his just debts with talk?" inquired Mr. Felsburg.

"Well, if he does I'll mighty soon undeceive him," said Kivil. "And yet I can't help but feel sorry for the poor devil—he's had an awful run of luck, by all accounts. But here's the thing I mainly wanted to speak to you about: You see, he still thinks the bank holds these mortgages. He doesn't know you bought 'em from the bank; and what I wanted to ask you was this: Do you want me to tell him the truth when he comes in, or would you rather I waited and let him find it out for himself when the foreclosure goes through and the sheriff takes possession?"

"Don't do neither one," ordered Mr. Felsburg. "You should call him up right away and tell him to come in to see about it to-morrow at ten o'clock. And then, Herby, when he does come in, you should tell him he should step over to the Oak Hall and see me in my office. That's all what you should tell him. I got reasons of my own why I should prefer to break the news to him myself. Understand, Herby?"

"I understand, Mr. Felsburg," said Mr. Kivil. "The minute he steps in here—before he's had time to open up the subject—I'm to send him over to see you. Is that right?"

"That's exactly right, Herby." And, with pleased puckers at the corners of his eyes, Mr. Felsburg turned away and went stumping out.

Physically Mr. Felsburg didn't in the least suggest a cat, and yet, after he was gone, Cashier Kivil found himself likening Mr. Felsburg to a cat with long claws—a cat that would play a long time with a captive mouse before killing it. He turned to his assistant, Emanuel Moon.

"What's bred in the bone is bound to show sooner or later," said Herb Kivil sagely. "I never thought of it before—but I guess there must be a mighty mean streak in Mr. Felsburg somewheres. I know this much: I'd hate mightily to owe him any money. Did you see that look on his face? He looked like a regular little old Shylock. I'll bet you he takes his pound of flesh every pop—with an extra half pound or so thrown in for good measure."

Long before ten o'clock the following morning Mr. Felsburg sat waiting in his little cubicle of a private office on the mezzanine floor at the back of the Oak Hall. He kept taking out his watch and looking at it. About ten minutes past the hour one of the clerks climbed the stairs to tell him that Mr. Thomas Albritton, from out in the Massac Creek neighbourhood, was below, asking to see him.

"All right," said Mr. Felsburg; "you should send him up here to me right away. Tell him I said, please, he should step this way."

Presently, the clunk of heavy feet sounding on the steps, Mr. Felsburg reared himself back in his chair at his desk with an expectant, eager look on his face. In the doorway at the top of the stairs appeared the man for whom he waited—a middle-aged man with slumped shoulders, in worn, soiled garments, and in every line of his harassed face expressing the fact that here stood a failure, mutely craving the pardon of the world for being a failure. The yellow dust of country roads was thick, like powdered sulphur, in the wrinkles of his shoes and the creases of his shabby old coat. He had his hat in his hand.

"Good mornin', Mr. Felsburg," he said.

"Morning!"

Mr. Felsburg returned the greeting with a sharp and businesslike brevity. He did not invite the caller to seat himself. In the small room there was but one chair—the one that held Mr. Felsburg's short form. So, during the early part of the scene that followed, Albritton continued to stand, while Mr. Felsburg enjoyed the advantage of being seated and at his ease where, without stirring, he might, from beneath his lowered brows, look the other up and down.

"I've just come from over at the Commonwealth Bank," said Albritton, fumbling his hat. "I came in to see about getting an extension on my loans, and Mr. Kivil, over there, said I was to come on over here and talk to you first. He said you wanted to see me 'bout something—if I understood him right."

Mr. Felsburg nodded in affirmation of this, but made no other reply. Albritton, having halted for a moment, went on again:

"I suppose you want to talk to me about my affairs, you being a director of the bank?"

"And also, furthermore, vice president," supplemented Mr. Felsburg.

"Yes, suh. Just so. And that's what made me suppose——"

Mr. Felsburg raised a fat, short hand upon

which the biggest, whitest diamond in Red Gravel County glittered.

"You should not talk with me as an officer of that bank—if you will be so good, please," he stated. "You should talk with me now as an individual."

"An individual? I'm afraid I don't understand you, suh."

"Pretty soon you will, Mr. Albritton. This is an individual matter—just between you and me; because I, and not the bank, am the party what holds these here mortgages on your place."

"You hold 'em?"

"Sure! I bought both those mortgages off the bank quite some time ago. I own those mortgages—and not anybody else whatsoever."

"But I thought——"

"You don't need to think. You need only that you should listen at what I am telling you now. It is me—Herman Felsburg, Esquire, of the Oak Hall Clothing Emporium—to which you owe this money, principal and likewise interest. So we will talk together, man to man, if you please, Mr. Albritton. Do I make myself plain? I do."

The debtor dropped to his side the hand with which he had been rubbing a perplexed forehead. A little gleam, as of hope reawakening, came into his eyes.

"Well, suh," he said, "you sort of take me by surprise—I didn't have any idea that was the state of the case at all. Then, all along, the bank has just been representing you in the matter?"

"As my agent—yes," said the little merchant.

"Well, to tell you the truth, I'm not sorry to hear it," said Albritton. "A bank has got its rules, I reckin, and has to live up to 'em. But, dealing with you, suh, as an individual, is another thing altogether. Anyhow, I'm hoping so, Mr. Felsburg."

"How you make that out?"

Mr. Felsburg's tone was so sharply staccato that Albritton's face fell a little.

"Well, suh, I'm hoping that maybe you can see your way clear not to foreclose on me just yet a while. I'd hate mightily to lose my home—I would so! I was born there, Mr. Felsburg. And I've got a sickly wife and a whole houseful of children. I don't know where I'd turn to get another roof over their heads if I was driven off my place. I know I owe you the money and by law you're entitled to it; but I certainly would appreciate the favour if you'd give me a little more time."

"So? And was there any other little favour you'd like to ask from me, Mr. Albritton?" inquired Mr. Felsburg with impressive politeness.

Perhaps the other missed the note in the speaker's voice; or perhaps he was merely desperate. A drowning man does not pick and choose the straws at which he grasps.

"Yes, suh; since you bring up the subject yourself, there is something else, Mr. Felsburg. If you can see your way clear to giving me a little time, and, on top of that, if you could loan me, say, four hundred dollars more to help carry me over until fall, I believe I can pay you back everything and start clean and clear again."

"So-o-o!"

Mr. Felsburg turned himself in his chair, showing his back to his visitor, and, taking up a pen, bent over his desk and for a minute wrote briskly, as though to record notes of the proposition. Then he swung back again, facing Albritton.

"Let me see if I get you right, Mr. Albritton," he said, speaking slowly and prolonging the suspense. "Already you owe me money; and now, instead of paying up what you owe, you should like to borrow yet some more money, eh? What security should you expect to give, Mr. Albritton?"

"Only my word and my promise, Mr. Felsburg," pleaded Albritton. "You don't know me very well; but if you'll inquire round you'll find out I've got the name for being an honest man, even if I have had a power of hard luck these last few years. I ain't a drinking man, Mr. Felsburg, and I'm a hard worker. If there was somebody I knew better than I know you I'd go to him; but there ain't anybody. I'm right at the end of my rope—I ain't got anywhere to turn.

"I'm confident, if you'll give me a little help, Mr. Felsburg, I can make out to get a new start. But if I'm put off my place now I'll lose the crop I've put in—lose all my time and my labour too. It looks like tobacco is going to fetch a better price this fall than it's fetched for three or four years back, and the young plants I've put in are coming up mighty promising. But I need money to carry me over until I can get my tobacco cured and marketed. Don't you see how it is with me, Mr. Felsburg? Just a little temporary accommodation from you and I'm certain to——"

"Business is business, Mr. Albritton," said Mr. Felsburg, cutting in on him. "And all my life I have been a business man. Is it good business, I should like to ask you, that I should loan you yet more money when already you owe me money which you cannot pay? Huh, Mr. Albritton?"

"Maybe it ain't good business; but, just as one human being to another——"

"Oh! So now you put it that way? Well, suit yourself. We talk, then, as two human beings, eh? We make this a personal matter, eh? Good! That also is how I should prefer it should be. Listen to me for one little minute, Mr. Albritton. I am going to speak with you about a small matter which happened quite a long while ago. Do you perhaps remember something which happened in the

spring of the year eighteen hundred and sixty
—the year before the war broke out?"

"Why, yes," said Albritton after a moment
of puzzled thought. "That was the year my
father died and left me the place; the same
year that I got married too. I wasn't but just
twenty-two years old then. But I don't get
your drift, Mr. Felsburg. What's the year
eighteen-sixty got to do with you and me?"

"I'm coming to that pretty soon," said Mr.
Felsburg. He sat up straight now, his eyes
ashine and his hands clenched on the arms of
his chair. "Do you perhaps remember something else which also happened in that year,
Mr. Albritton?"

"I can't say as I do," confessed the puzzled
countryman.

"Then, if you'll be so good as to listen, Mr.
Albritton, I should be pleased to tell you.
Maybe I have got a better memory than what
your memory is. Also, maybe I have got
something on me to remember it by. Now
you listen to me!

"There was a hot day in the springtime of
that year, when you sat on the porch of your
house out there in the country, and a little
young Jew-boy pedlar came up your lane
from the road, with a pack on his back; and he
opened the gate of your horse lot, in the front
of your house, and he came through that gate.

"And you was sitting there on your porch,
just like I am telling you; and you yelled to

him that he should get out—that you did not
want to buy nothing from him. Well, maybe
he was new in this country and could not understand all what you meant. Or maybe it
was that he was very tired and hot, and that
he only wanted to ask you to let him sit down
and take his heavy pack off his back, and
drink some cool water out of your well, and
maybe rest a little while there. And maybe,
too, he had not sold anything at all that day
and hoped that if he showed you what he had
you would perhaps change your mind and buy
something from him—just a little something,
so that his whole day would not be wasted.

"So he came through that gate of your
horse lot and he kept on coming. And then
you cursed at him, and you told him again he
should get out. But he kept coming. And
then you called your dogs. And two dogs
came—big, mean dogs—out from under your
house.

"And when he saw the dogs come from
under the house, that young Jew boy he turned
round and he tried to run away and save himself. But the pack on his back was heavy,
and he was already so very tired, like I am
telling you, from walking in the sun all day.
And so he could not run fast. And the dogs
they soon caught him, and they bit him many
times in the legs; and then he was more worse
scared than before and the biting hurt him
very much, and he cried out.

"But you stood there on your porch; and you clapped your two hands together and you laughed to hear that poor little pedlar boy cry out. And your dogs chased him away down the lane, and they bit him still more in his legs. Maybe perhaps you thought a poor Jew would not have feelings the same as you? Maybe perhaps you thought he would not bleed when those sharp teeth bit him in his legs? So you clapped your hands and you laughed to see him run and to hear him yell out that way. Do you remember all that, Mr. Albritton?"

He stood up now, shaking all over; and his eyes glittered to match the diamond on his quivering hand. They glittered like two little hard bright stones.

Under the tan the face of the man at whom he glared turned a dull brick-dust red. Albritton put up a hand to one burning cheek; and as he made answer the words came from him haltingly, self-accusingly:

"I don't remember it, Mr. Felsburg; but if you say it's true—why, I reckin it must 'a' happened just the way you tell it. It was a low-down, cruel, mean thing to do; and if it was me I'm sorry for it—even now, after all these years. I wasn't much more than a boy, though; and——"

"You were a grown man, Mr. Albritton; anyhow, you were older than the little pedlar boy that your dogs bit. You say you are sorry now; but you forgot about it, didn't you? I

didn't forget about it, Mr. Albritton! All
these years I have not forgotten it. All these
years I have been waiting for this day to make
you sorry. All these years I have been waiting
for this day to get even with you. I was that
little Jew boy, Mr. Albritton. In my legs I
have now the red marks from your dogs' teeth.
And so now you come here and you stand here
before me"—he raised his chubby clenched
fists and shook them—"and you—you—you—
ask me that I should do you favours!"

"Mr. Felsburg," said Albritton—and his figure drooped as though he would prostrate himself before the triumphant little man—"I ain't
saying this because I hope to get any help
from you in a money way—I know there's no
chance of that now—I'm saying it because I
mean it from the bottom of my soul. I'm
sorry. If I thought you'd believe me I'd be
willing to go down on my knees and take my
Bible oath that I'm sorry."

"You should save yourself the trouble, Mr.
Albritton," said Mr. Felsburg, calmer now.
"In the part of your Bible which I believe in
it says 'An eye for an eye, and a tooth for a
tooth,' Mr. Albritton."

"All right!" said Albritton. "You've had
your say—you're even with me."

He turned from the gloating figure of the
other and started to go. From the chair in
which he had reseated himself, Felsburg, a picture of vengeance gratified and sated, watched

him, saying nothing until the bankrupt had descended the first step of the stairs and the second. Then he spoke.

"You wait!" he ordered in the tone of a master. "I am not yet done."

"What's the use?" said Albritton; but he faced about, humbled and crushed. "There ain't anything you could say or do that would make me feel any worse."

"Come back!" bade Felsburg; and, like a man whipped, the other came back to the doorway.

"You're even with me, I tell you," he said from the threshold. "What's the use of piling it on?"

Mr. Felsburg did not answer in words. He reached behind him to his desk, wadded up something in his fingers, and, once more rising, he advanced, with his figure distended, on Albritton. Albritton flinched, then straightened himself.

"Hit me if you want to," he said brokenly. "I won't hit back if you do. I deserve it."

"Yes, I will hit you," said Felsburg. "With this I will hit you."

Into Albritton's right hand he thrust a crumpled slip of paper. At the wadded paper Albritton stared numbly.

"I don't know what you are driving at," he said; "but, if this is a notice of foreclosure, I don't need any notice."

"Look at it—close," bade Felsburg.

And Albritton, obeying, looked; and his face turned from red to white and then to red again.

"Now you see what it is," said Felsburg. "It is my check for four hundred dollars. I loan it to you—without security; and to-day I fix up those mortgages for you. Mr. Albritton, I am even with you. All the days from now on that you live in your house I am getting even with you—more and more every day what passes. And now, please, go away."

He turned from the other, ignoring the fumbling hand that would have taken his own in its grasp; and, resting his elbows on his desk, he put his face in his cupped palms and spoke from between his fingers:

"I ask you again—please go away!"

When Judge Priest had finished telling me the story, in form much as I have retold it here, he sat back, drawing hard on his pipe, which had gone out. Bewildered, I pondered the climax of the tale.

"But if Mr. Felsburg really wanted to get even," I said at length, "what made him give that man the money?"

The Judge scratched a match on a linen-clad flank and applied the flame to the pipe-bowl; and then, between puffs, made answer slowly.

"Son," he said, "you jest think it over in your spare time. I reckin mebbe when you're a little older the answer'll come to you."

And sure enough, when I was a little older it did.

CHAPTER IV
THE GARB OF MEN

THEY used to say—and how long ago it seems since they used to say it!—that the world would never see another world war. They said that the planet, being more or less highly civilised with regard to its principal geographical divisions, and in the main peaceably inclined, would never again send forth armed millions to slit the throats of yet other armed millions. That was what they said back yonder in 1912 and 1913, and in the early part of 1914 even.

But something happened—something unforeseen and unexpected and unplausible happened. And, at that, the structure of amity between the nations which so carefully had been built up on treaty and pledge, so shrewdly tongued-and-grooved by the promises of Christian statesmen, so beautifully puttied up by the prayers of Christian men, so excellently dovetailed and mortised and rabbeted together, all at once broke down, span by span; just as it is claimed that a fiddler who stations himself in the middle of a bridge and plays upon his fiddle a certain note may, if only he keeps up his playing long enough, play down that bridge, however strong and well-piered it is.

We still regard the fiddle theory as a fable concocted upon a hypothesis of physics; but when that other thing happened—a thing utterly inconceivable—we so quickly adjusted ourselves to it that at once yesterday's impossibility became to-day's actuality and to-morrow's certain prospect.

This war having begun, they said it could not at the very most last more than a few months; that the countries immediately concerned could not, any of them, for very long withstand the drains upon them in men and money and munitions and misery; that the people at home would rise in revolt against the stupid malignity of it, if the men at the front did not.

Only a few war-seasoned elderly men, including one in a War Office at London and one in a General Staff at Berlin and one in a Cabinet Chamber at Paris, warned their respective people to prepare themselves for a struggle bloodier, and more violent and costlier, and possibly more prolonged, than any war within the memories of living men.

At first we couldn't believe that either; none of us could believe it. But those old men were right and the rest of us were wrong. The words of the war wiseacres came true.

Presently we beheld enacted the intolerable situation they had predicted; and in our own country at least the tallies of dead, as enumerated in the foreign dispatches, began to mean to us only headlines on the second page of the morning paper.

Then they said that when, by slaughter and maiming and incredible exertion, the manhood of Europe had been decimated to a given point the actual physical exhaustion of the combatants would force all the armies to a standstill. But the thing went on.

It went on through its first year and through its second year. We saw it going on into its third year, with no sign of abatement, no evidence of a weakening anywhere among the states and the peoples immediately affected. We saw our own country drawn into it. And so, figuring what might lie in front of us and them by what laid behind, we might, without violence to credibility, figure it as going on until all of Britain's able-bodied adult male population wore khaki or had been buried in it; until sundry millions of the men of France were corpses or on crutches; until Germania had scraped and harrowed and combed her domains for cannon fodder; until Russia's countless supply of prime human grist for the red hopper of this red mill no longer was countless but countable.

There is a town in the northern part of the Republic of France called Courney. Rather,

I should say that once upon a time there was
such a town. Considered as a town, bearing
the outward manifestations of a town and
nourishing within it the communal spirit of a
town, it ceased to exist quite a time back.
Nevertheless, it is with that town, or with the
recent site of it, that this story purports to
deal.

There is no particular need of our trying to
recreate the picture of it as it was before the
war began. Before the war it was one of a
vast number of suchlike drowsy, cosy little
towns lying, each one of them, in the midst of
tilled fat acres on the breasts of a pleasant
land; a town with the grey highroad running
through it to form its main street, and with
farms and orchards and vineyards and garden
patches round about it; so that in the springtime, when the orchard trees bloomed and the
grapevines put forth their young leaves and
the wind blew, it became a little island, set in
the centre of a little, billowy green-and-white
sea; a town of snug small houses of red brick
and grey brick, with a priest and a mayor, a
schoolhouse and a beet-sugar factory, a town
well for the gossips and a town shrine for the
devout.

Nor is there any especial necessity for us to
try to describe it as it was after the war had
rolled forward and back and forward again
over it; for then it was transformed as most
of those small towns that lay in the tracks of

the hostile armies were transformed. It became a ruin, a most utter and complete and squalid ruin, filled with sights that were affronts to the eye and smells that were abominations to the nose.

In this place there abode, at the time of which I aim to write, a few living creatures. They were human beings, but they had ceased to exist after the ordinary fashion of human beings in this twentieth century of ours. So often, in the first months and the first years of the war, had their simple but ample standards been forcibly upset that by now almost they had forgotten such standards had ever been.

To them yesterday was a dimming memory, and to-morrow a dismal prospect without hope in it of anything better. To-day was all and everything to them; each day was destiny itself. Just to get through it with breath of life in one's body and rags over one's hide and a shelter above one's head—that was the first and the last of their aim. They lived not because life was worth while any more, but because to keep on living is an instinct, and because most human beings are so blessed—or, maybe, so cursed—with a certain adaptability of temperament, a certain inherent knack of adjustability that they may endure anything—even the unendurable—if only they have ceased to think about the past and to fret about the future.

And these people in this town had ceased to think. They were out of habit with thinking. A long time before, their sensibilities had been rocked to sleep by the everlasting lullaby of the cannon; their imaginations were wrapped in a smoky coma. They lived on without conscious effort, without conscious ambition, almost without conscious desire: just as blind worms live under a bank, or slugs in a marsh, or protoplasms in a pond.

Once, twice, three times Courney had been a stepping-stone in the swept and garnished pathways of battle. Back in September of 1914 the Germans, sweeping southward as an irresistible force, took possession of this town, after shelling it quite flat with their big guns to drive out the defending garrison of French and British. Then, a little later, in front of Paris the irresistible force met the immovable body and answered the old, old question of the scientists; and, as the Germans fell back to dig themselves in along the Somme and the Aisne, there was again desperate hard fighting here, and many, very many, lives were spent in the effort of one side to take and retain, and of the other to gain and hold fast, the little peaky heaps of wreckage protruding above the stumps of the wasted orchard trees.

Now, though, for a long time things had been quiet in Courney. Though placed in debatable territory, as the campaign experts regard debatable territory, it had lapsed into an eddy

and a backwater of war, becoming, so to speak,
a void and a vacuum amid the twisting cur-
rents of the war. In the core of a tornado
there may be calm while about it the vortex
swirls and twists. If this frequently is true of
windstorms it occasionally is true of wars.

Often to the right of them and to the left of
them, sometimes far in front of them, and
once in a while far back in the rear of them,
those who still abode at Courney heard the
distant voices of the big guns; but their place
of habitation, by reasons of shifts in the war
game, was no longer on a route of communica-
tion between separate groups of the same fighting force. It was not even on a line of travel.
No news of the world beyond their limited
horizon seeped in to them. They did not know
how went the war—who won or who lost—and
almost they had quit desiring to know. What
does one colony of blind worms in a bank care
how fares it with colonies of blind worms in
other banks?

You think this state of apathy could not
come to pass? Well, I know that it can, because with my own eyes I saw it coming to pass
in the times while yet the war was new; while
it yet was a shock and an affront to our be-
liefs; and you must remember that now I
write of a much later time, when the world
war had become the world's custom.

Also, could you have looked in upon the surviving remnant of the inhabitants of Courney,

you would have had a clearer and fuller corroboration of the fact I state, because then you would have seen that here in this place lived only those who were too old or too feeble to care, or else were too young to understand.

All tallied, there were not more then than twenty remaining of two or three hundred who once had been counted as the people of this inconsequential village; and of these but two were individuals in what ordinarily would be called the prime of life.

One of these two was a French petty officer, whose eyes had been shot out, and who, having been left behind in the first retreat toward Paris, had been forgotten, and had stayed behind ever since. The other had likewise been a soldier. He was a Breton peasant. His disability seemed slight enough when he sustained it. A bullet bored across the small of his back, missing the spine. But the bullet bore with it minute fragments of his uniform coat; and so laden with filth had his outer garments become, after weeks and months of service in the field, that, with the fragments of cloth, germs of tetanus had been carried into his flesh also, and lockjaw had followed.

Being as strong as a bullock, he had weathered the hideous agonies of his disease; but it left him beset with an affliction like a queer sort of palsy, which affected his limbs, his tongue, and the nerves and muscles of his face.

Continually he twitched all over. He moved
by a series of spasmodic jerks, and when he
sought to speak the sounds he uttered came out
from his contorted throat in slobbery, unintelligible gasps and grunts. He was sane enough,
but he had the look about him of being an idiot.

Besides these two there were three or four
very aged, very infirm men on the edge of their
dotage; likewise some women, including one
masterful, high-tempered old woman and a
younger woman who wept continuously, with
a monotonous mewing sound, for a husband
who was dead in battle and for a fourteen-
year-old son who had vanished altogether out
of her life, and who, for all she knew, was dead
too. The rest were children—young children,
and a baby or so. There were no sizable youths
whatsoever, and no girls verging on maiden-
hood, remaining in this place.

So this small group was what was left of
Courney. Their houses being gone and family
ties for the most part wiped out, they con-
sorted together in a rude communal system
which a common misery had forced upon them.
Theirs was the primitive socialism that the cave
dweller may have known in his tribe. As I say,
their houses were gone; so they denned in
holes where the cellars under the houses had
been. Time had been when they fled to the
shelter of these holes as the fighting, swinging
northward or southward, included Courney
in its orbit.

Afterward they had contrived patchwork
roofage to keep out the worst of the weather;
and now they called these underground shel-
ters home, which was an insult to the word
home. Once they had had horse meat to eat—
the flesh of killed cavalry mounts and wagon
teams. Now perforce they were vegetarians,
living upon cabbages and beets and potatoes
which grew half wild in the old garden patches,
and on a coarse bran bread made of a flour
ground by hand out of the grain that sprouted
in fields where real harvests formerly had
grown.

The more robust and capable among the
adults cultivated these poor crops in a peck-
ing and puny sort of way. The children went
clothed in ancient rags, which partly covered
their undeveloped and stunted bodies, and
played in the rubbish; and sometimes in their
play they delved too deep and uncovered grisly
and horrible objects. On sunny days the blind
soldier and the palsied one sat in the sunshine,
and when it rained they took refuge with the
others in whichever of the leaky burrows was
handiest for them to reach. If they walked
the Breton towed his mate in a crippling, zig-
zag course, for one lacked the eyes to see where
he went and the other lacked the ability to
steer his afflicted legs on a direct line.

The wreckage of rafters and beams and house
furnishings provided abundant supplies of
wood and for fires. By a kind of general as-

sent, headship and authority were vested
jointly in the old tempestuous woman and the
blind man, for the reasons that she had the
strongest body and the most resolute will, and
he the keenest mind of them all.

So these people lived along, without a priest
to give them comfort by his preaching; without a physician to mend their ailments; with
no set code of laws to be administered and
none to administer them. Existence for them
was reduced to its raw elementals. Since frequently they heard the big guns sounding distantly and faintly, they knew that the war still
went on. And, if they gave the matter a
thought, to them it seemed that the war always would go on. Time and the passage of
time meant little. A day was merely a period
of lightness marked at one end by a sunrise
and at the other by a sunset; and when that
was over and darkness had come, they bedded
themselves down under fouled and ragged
coverlids and slept the dumb, dreamless sleep
of the lower animals. Except for the weeping
woman who went about with her red eyes continually streaming and her whining wail forever
sounding, no one among them seemingly gave
thought to those of their own kinspeople and
friends who were dead or scattered or missing.

Well, late one afternoon in the early fall of
the year, the workers had quit their tasks and
were gathering in toward a common centre,
before the oncoming of dusk, when they heard

cries and beheld the crotchety old woman who shared leadership with the blinded man, running toward them. She had been gathering beets in one of the patches to the southward of their ruins; and now, as she came at top speed along the path that marked where their main street had once been, threading her way swiftly in and out among the grey mounds of rubbish, she held a burden of the red roots in her long bony arms.

She lumbered up, out of breath, to tell them she had seen soldiers approaching from the south. Since it was from that direction they came, these soldiers doubtlessly would be French soldiers; and, that being so, the dwellers in Courney need feel no fear of mistreatment at their hands. Nevertheless, always before, the coming of soldiers had meant fighting; so, without waiting to spy out their number or to gauge from their movements a hint of their possible intentions, she had hastened to spread the alarm.

"I saw them quite plainly!" she cried out between pants for breath. "They have marched out of the woods yonder—the woods that bound the fields below where the highroad to Laon ran in the old days. And now they are spreading out across the field, to the right and the left. Infantry they are, I think—and they have a machine gun with them."

"How many, grandmother? How many of them are there?"

It was the eyeless man who asked the question. He had straightened up from where he sat, and stood erect, with his arms groping before him and his nostrils dilated.

"No great number," answered the old woman; "perhaps two companies—perhaps a battalion. And as they came nearer to me they looked—they looked so queer!"

"How? How? What do you mean by queer?" It was the blind man seeking to know.

She dropped her burden of beetroots and threw out her hands in a gesture of helplessness.

"Queer!" she repeated stupidly. "Their clothes now—their clothes seemed not to fit them. They are such queer-looking soldiers—for Frenchmen."

"Oh, if only the good God would give me back my eyes for one little hour!" cried the blind man impotently. Then, in a different voice, "What is that?" he said, and swung about, facing north. His ears, keener than theirs, as a blind man's ears are apt to be, had caught, above the babble of their excited voices, another sound.

Scuttling, shuffling, half falling, the palsied man, moving at the best speed of which he was capable, rounded a heap of shattered grey masonry that had once been the village church, and made toward the clustered group of them. His jaws worked spasmodically. With one fluttering hand he pointed, over his left shoulder, behind him. He strove to speak words, but from his throat issued only clicking, slobbery grunts and gasps.

"What is it now?" demanded the old woman. She clutched him, forcing him to a quaking standstill. He kept on gurgling and kept on pointing.

"Soldiers? Are there more soldiers coming?"

He nodded eagerly.

"From the north?"

He made signs of assent.

"Frenchmen?"

He shook his head until it seemed he would shake it off his shoulders.

"Germans, then? From that way the Germans are coming, eh?"

Again he nodded, making queer movements with his hands, the meaning of which they could not interpret. Indeed, none there waited to try. With one accord they started for the deepest and securest of their burrows—the one beneath the battered-down sugar-beet factory. Its fallen walls and its shattered roof made a lid, tons heavy and yards thick, above the cellar of it. In times of fighting it had been their safest refuge. So once more they ran to hide themselves there. The ragged children scurried on ahead like a flight of autumn leaves. The very old men and the women followed after the children; and behind all the rest, like a rearguard, went the cripple and the old woman, steering the blind man between them.

At the gullet of a little tunnel-like opening leading down to the deep basement below, these three halted a brief moment; and the palsied man and the woman, looking backward, were in time to see a skirmisher in the uniform of a French foot soldier cross a narrow vista in the ruins, perhaps a hundred yards away, and vanish behind a culm of broken masonry. Seen at that distance, he seemed short, squatty—almost gnomish. Back in the rear of him somewhere a bugle sounded a halting, uncertain blast, which trailed off suddenly to nothing, as though the bugler might be out of breath; and then—pow, pow, pow!—the first shots sounded. High overhead a misdirected bullet whistled with a droning, querulous note. The three tarried no longer, but slid down into the mouth of the tunnel.

Inside the cellar the women and children already were stretched close up to the thick stone sides, looking like flattened piles of rags against the flagged floor. They had taken due care, all of them, to drop down out of line with two small openings which once had been windows in the south wall of the factory cellar, and which now, with their sashes gone, were like square portholes, set at the level of the earth. Through these openings came most of the air and all of the daylight which reached their subterranean retreat.

The old woman cowered down in an angle of the wall, rocking back and forth and hugging her two bony knees with her two bony arms; but the maimed soldiers, as befitting men who had once been soldiers, took stations just beneath the window holes, the one to listen and the other to watch for what might befall in the narrow compass of space lying immediately in front of them. For a moment after they found their places there was silence there in the cellar, save for the rustling of bodies and the wheeze of forced breathing. Then a woman's voice was uplifted wailingly: "Oh, this war! Why should it come back here again? Why couldn't it leave us poor ones alone?"

"Hush, you!" snapped the blinded man in a voice of authority. "There are men out there fighting for France. Hush and listen!"

A ragged volley, sounding as though it had been fired almost over their heads, cut off her lamentation, and she hid her face in her hands, bending her body forward to cover and shield a baby that was between her knees upon the floor.

From a distance, toward the north, the firing was answered. Somewhere close at hand a rapid-fire gun began a staccato outburst as the gun crew pumped its belts of cartridges into its barrel; but at once this chattering note became interrupted, and then it slackened, and then it stopped altogether.

"Idiots! Fools! Imbeciles!" snarled the blind man. "They have jammed the magazine! And listen, comrade, listen to the rifle fire from over here—half a company firing, then the other half. Veterans would never fire so. Raw recruits with green officers—that's what they must be. . . . And listen! The Germans are no better."

Outside, near by, a high-pitched strained voice gave an order, and past the window openings soldiers began to pass, some shrilly cheering, some singing the song of France, the Marseillaise Hymn. Their trunks were not visible. From the cellar could be seen only their legs from the knees down, with stained leather leggings on each pair of shanks, and their feet, in heavy military boots, sliding and slithering over the cinders and the shards of broken tiling alongside the wrecked factory wall.

Peering upward, trying vainly at his angled range of vision to see the bodies of those who passed, the palsied man reached out and grasped the arm of his mate in a hard grip, uttering meaningless sounds. It was as though he sought to tell of some astounding discovery he had just made.

"Yes, yes, brother; I understand," said the blind man. "I cannot see, but I can hear. There is no swing to their step, eh? Their feet scuffle inside their boots, eh? Yes, yes, I know—they are very weary. They have come far to-day to fight these Huns. And how feebly

they sing the song as they go past us here!
They must be very tired—that is it, eh? But,
tired or not, they are Frenchmen, and they can
fight. Oh, if only the good God for one little
hour, for one little minute, would give me back
my eyes, to see the men of France fighting for
France!"

The last straggling pair of legs went sham-
bling awkwardly past the portholes. To the
Breton, watching, it appeared that the owner
of those legs scarcely could lift the weight of
the thick-soled boots.

Beyond the cellar, to the left, whither the
marchers had defiled, the firing became general. It rose in volume, sank to a broken and
individual sequence of crashes, rose again in
a chorus, grew thin and thready again. There
was nothing workmanlike, nothing soldierlike
about it; nothing steadfastly sustained. It
was intermittent, irregular, uncertain. Listening, the blind man waggled his head in a puzzled, irritated fashion, and shook off the grasp
of his comrade, who still appeared bent on trying to make something clear to him.

With a movement like that of a startled
horse the old leader-woman threw up her head.
With her fingers she clawed the matted grey
hair out of her ears.

"Hark! Hark!" she cried, imposing silence
upon all of them by her hoarse intensity.
"Hark, all of you! What is that?"

The others heard it too, then. It was a

whining, gagging, thin cry from outside, close up against the southerly wall of their underground refuge—the distressful cry of an unhappy child, very frightened and very sick. There was no mistaking it—the sobbing intake of the breath; the choked note of nausea which followed.

"It is a little one!" bleated one woman.

"What child is missing?" screeched another in a panic. "What babe has been overlooked?"

Each mother took quick and frenzied inventory of her own young, groping out with her hands to make sure by the touch of their flesh to her flesh that her offspring were safely bestowed. But when, this done, they turned to tell their leader that apparently all of Courney had been accounted for, she was gone. She had darted into the dark passage that led up and outward into the open. They sat up on their haunches, gaping.

A minute passed and she was back, half bearing, half pulling in her arms not a forgotten baby, but a soldier; a dwarfish and misshapen soldier, it seemed to them, squatting there in the fading light; a soldier whose uniform was far too large for him; a soldier whose head was buried under his cap, and whose face was hidden within the gaping collar of his coat, and whose booted toes scraped along the rough flagging as his rescuer backed in among them, dragging him along with her.

In the middle of the floor she released him,

and he fell upon his side in a clump of soiled cloth and loose accoutrement; and for just an instant they thought both his hands had been shot away, for nothing showed below the ends of the flapping sleeves as he pressed his midriff in his folded arms, uttering weak, tearful cries. Then, though, they saw that his hands were merely lost within the length of his sleeves, and they plunged at the conclusion that his hurt was in his middle.

"Ah, the poor one!" exclaimed one or two. "Wounded in the belly."

"Wounded?" howled the old woman. "Wounded? You fools! Don't you see he has no wound? Don't you see what it is? Then, look, you fools—look!"

She dropped down alongside him and wrestled him, he struggling feebly, over on his back. With a ferocious violence she snatched the cap off his head, tore his gripped arms apart, ripped open the coat he wore and the coarse shirt that was beneath it.

"Look, fools, and see for yourselves!"

Forgetting the danger to themselves of stray bullets, they scrambled to their feet and crowded up close behind her, peering over her shoulders as she reared back upon her bent knees in order that they might the better see.

They did see. They saw, looking up at them from beneath the mop of tousled black hair, the scared white face and the terror-widened eyes of a boy—a little, sickly, undernourished boy. He

could not have been more than fourteen—perhaps not more than thirteen. They saw in the
gap of his parted garments the narrow structure of his shape, with the ribs pressing tight
against the tender, hairless skin, and below the
arch of the ribs the sunken curve of his abdo-
men, heaving convulsively to the constant
retching as he twisted and wriggled his meagre
body back and forth.

"Oh, Mother above!" one yowled. "They
have sent a child to fight!"

As though these words had been to him a
command, the writhing heap half rose from the
flags.

"I am no child!" he cried, between choking
attacks of nausea. "I am as old as the rest—
older than some. Let me go! Let me go
back! I am a soldier of France!"

For all his brave words, his trembling legs
gave way under him, and he fell again and
rolled over on his stomach, hiding his face in
his hands, a whimpering, vomiting child, helpless with pain and with fear.

"He speaks true! He speaks true!" yelled
the old woman. Now she was on her feet, her
lean face red and swollen with a vast rage. "I
saw them—I saw them—I saw those others as
I was dragging this one in. He speaks true, I
tell you. There was a captain—he could not
have been more than fifteen. And his sword
—it was as long as he was, nearly. There are
soldiers out there like this one, whose arms are

not strong enough to lift the guns to their shoulders. They are children who fight outside—children in the garb of men!"

The widow, who continually wept, sprang forward. She had quit weeping and a great and terrible fury looked out of her red-lidded eyes. She screeched in a voice that rose above the wails of the rest:

"And it was for this, months ago, that they took away from me my little Pierre! Mother of God, they fight this war with babies!"

She threw herself down on all fours and, wriggling across the floor upon her hands and knees, gathered up the muddied, booted feet of the boy soldier and hugged them to her bosom.

In the middle of the circle the old woman stood, gouging at her hair with her hands.

"It is true!" she proclaimed. "They are sending forth our babies to fight against strong men."

The palsied man twisted himself up to her. He shook his head to and fro, as if in dissent of what she declared. He pointed toward the north; then at the sobbing boy at his feet; then north again; then at the boy; and, so doing, he many times and very swiftly nodded his head. Then he repeated the same gesticulations with his arms that he had made at the time of giving the first alarm of the approach of the enemy. Finally he stooped his back and shrank up his body and hunched in his shoulders

in an effort to counterfeit smallness and slight-
ness, all the while gurgling in a desperate attempt to make himself understood. All at once,
simultaneously his audience grasped the purport
of his pantomime.

"The Germans that you saw, they were children too—children like this one?" demanded
the old woman, her voice all thickened and
raspy with her passion. "Is that what you
mean?"

He jerked his head up and down in violent
assent, his jaws clicking and his face muscles
jumping. The old woman shoved him away
from in front of her.

"Come on with me!" she bade the other
women, in a tone that clarioned out high and
shrill above the sobbing of the boy on the floor,
above the gurgling of the cripple and the sound
of the firing without. "Come on!"

They knew what she meant; and behind her
they massed themselves, their bodies bent forward from their waists, their heads lowered
and their hands clenched like swimmers about
to breast a swift torrent.

"Bide where you are—you women!" the
blinded man commanded. He felt his way out
to the middle of the room, barring their path
with his body and his outspread arms. "You
can do nothing. The war goes on—this fight
here goes on—until we win!"

"No, no, no, no!" shouted back the old bel-
dam, and at each word beat her two fists

against her flaccid breasts. "When babies
fight this war this war ends! And we—the
women here—the women everywhere—we will
stop it! Do you hear me? We will stop it!
Come on!"

She pushed him aside; and, led by her, the
tatterdemalion crew of them ran swiftly from
the cellar and into the looming darkness of the
tunnel, crying out as they ran.

Strictly speaking, the beginning of this story
comes at the end of it. One morning in the
paper, I read, under small headlines on an inner page, sandwiched in between the account
of a football game at Nashville and the story
of a dog show at Newport, a short dispatch that
had been sent by cable to this country, to be
printed in our papers and to be read by our
people, and then to be forgotten by them. And
that dispatch ran like this:

BOYS TO FIGHT WAR SOON
GERMANY USING SOME SEVENTEEN YEARS OLD. HAIG WANTS YOUNG MEN

LONDON—The war threatens soon to become a
struggle between mere boys. The pace is said to
be entirely too fast for the older men long to endure. It is declared here that by the middle of
1917, the Entente Allies will be facing boys of sev-
enteen in the German Army.

General Sir Douglas Haig, commanding the British Expeditionary Forces, is said to have objected
to the sending out of men of middle age. He wants

young men of from eighteen to twenty-five. After
the latter year, it is said, the fighting value of the
human unit shows a rapid and steady decline. . . .
The older men have their place; but, generally
speaking, it is said now to be in "the army behind
the army"—the men back of the line, in the supply and transport divisions, where the strain is not
so great. These older men are too susceptible to
trench diseases to be of great use on the firing line.
England already is registering boys born in 1899,
preparatory to calling them up when they attain
their eighteenth year.

So I sat down and I wrote this story.

CHAPTER V
THE CURE FOR
LONESOMENESS

THEY were on their way back from Father Minor's funeral. Going to the graveyard the horses had ambled slowly; coming home they trotted along briskly so that from under their feet the gravel grit sprang up, to blow out behind in little squills and pennons of yellow dust. The black plumes in the headstalls of the white span that drew the empty hearse nodded briskly. It was only their colour which kept those plumes from being downright cheerful. Also, en route to the cemetery, the pallbearers, both honorary and active, had marched in double file at the head of the procession. Now, returning, they rode in carriages especially provided for them.

The first carriage—that is to say, the first one following the hearse—held four passengers: firstly, the widowed sister of the dead man, from up state somewhere; secondly and third-

ly, two strange priests who had come over
from Hopkinsburg to conduct the services;
finally and fourthly, the late Father Minor's
housekeeper, a lean and elderly spinster whose
devoutness made her dour; indeed, a person
whom piety beset almost as a physical affliction.
Seeing her any time at all, the observer went
away filled with the belief that in her particular
case the more certain this woman might be of
blessedness hereafter, the more miserable she
would feel in the meantime. Now, as her grief-
drawn face and reddened eyes looked forth
from the carriage window upon the familiar
panorama of Buckner Street, all about her be-
spoke the profound conviction that this world,
already lost in sin, was doubly lost since Father
Minor had gone to take his reward.

In the second carriage rode four of the honorary pallbearers, and each of them was a
veteran, as the dead priest had been: Circuit
Judge Priest, Sergeant Jimmy Bagby, Doctor
Lake, and Mr. Peter J. Galloway, our leading blacksmith and horseshoer. Of these four
Mr. Galloway was the only one who wor-
shipped according to the faith the dead man had
preached. But all of them were members in
good standing of the Gideon K. Irons Camp.

As though to match the changed gait of the
undertaker's horses, the spirits of these old
men were uplifted into a sort of tempered
cheerfulness. So often it is that way after the
mourners come away from the grave. All that

kindly hands might do for him who was departed out of this life had been done. The
spade had shaped up and smoothed down the
clods which covered him; the flowers had been
piled upon the sexton's mounded handiwork
until the raw brown earth was almost hidden.
Probably already the hot morning sun was
wilting the blossoms. By to-morrow morning
the petals would be falling—a drifting testimony to the mortality of all living things.

On the way out these four had said mighty
little to one another, but in their present mood
they spoke freely of their departed comrade—
his sayings, his looks, little ways that he had,
stories of his early life before he took holy
orders, when he rode hard and fought hard,
and very possibly swore hard, as a trooper in
Morgan's cavalry.

"It was a fine grand big turnout they gave
him this day," said Mr. Galloway with a tinc-
ture of melancholy pride in his voice. "Almost as many Protestants as Catholics there."

"Herman Felsburg sent the biggest floral design
there was," said Doctor Lake. "I saw his name on
the card."

"That's the way Father Tom would have
liked it to be, I reckin," said Judge Priest from
his corner of the carriage. "After all, boys,
the best test of a man ain't so much the amount
of cash he's left in the bank, but how many'll
turn out to pay him their respects when they
put him away."

"Still, at that," said the sergeant, "I taken notice of several absentees—from the Camp, I mean. I didn't see Jake Smedley nowheres around at the church, or at the graveyard neither."

"Jake's got right porely," explained Judge Priest. "He's been lookin' kind of ga'nted anyhow, lately. I'm feared Jake is beginnin' to break."

"Oh, I reckin tain't ez bad ez all that," said the sergeant. "You'll see Jake comin' round all right ez soon ez the weather turns off cool ag'in. Us old boys may be gittin' along in years, but we're a purty husky crew yit. It's a powerful hard job to kill one of us off. I'm sixty-seven myself, but most of the time I feel ez peart and skittish ez a colt." He spoke for the moment vaingloriously; then his tone altered: "I'm luckier, though, than some—in the matter of general health. Take Abner Tilghman now, for instance. Sence he had that second stroke Abner jest kin make out to crawl about. He wasn't there to-day with us neither."

"Boys," said Doctor Lake, "I hope it's no reflection on my professional abilities, but it seems to me I've been losing a lot of my patients here recently. I'm afraid Ab Tilghman is going to be the next one to make a gap in the ranks. Just between us, he's in mighty bad shape. Did it ever occur to any of you to count up and see how many members of the

Camp we've buried this past year, starting in last January with old Professor Reese and winding up to-day with Father Minor?"

None of them answered him in words. Only Judge Priest gave a little stubborn shake of his head, as though to ward away an unpleasant thought. Tact inspired Sergeant Bagby to direct the conversation into a different channel.

"I reckin Mrs. Herman Felsburg won't know whut to do now with that extry fish she always fries of a Friday," said the sergeant.

"That's right too, Jimmy," said Mr. Galloway. "Well, God bless her anyway for a fine lady!"

Had you, reader, enjoyed the advantage of living in our town and of knowing its customs, you would have understood at once what this last reference meant. You see, the Felsburgs, in their fine home, lived diagonally across the street from the little priest house behind the Catholic church. Mrs. Felsburg was distinguished for being a rigid adherent to the ritualistic laws of her people. Away from home her husband and her sons might choose whatever fare suited their several palates, but beneath her roof and at the table where she presided they found none of the forbidden foods.

On Fridays she cooked with her own hands the fish for the cold *Shabbath* supper and, having cooked them, she set them aside to cool. But always the finest, crispest fish of all, while still hot, was spread upon one of Mrs. Felsburg's best company plates and covered over with one of Mrs. Felsburg's fine white napkins, and then a servant would run across the street with it, from Mrs. Felsburg's side gate to the front door of the priest house, and hand it in to the dour-faced housekeeper with Mrs. Felsburg's compliments. And so that night, at his main meal of the day, Father Minor would dine on prime river perch or fresh lake crappie, fried in olive oil by an orthodox Jewess. Year in and year out this thing had happened once a week regularly. Probably it would not happen again. Father Minor's successor, whoever he might be, might not understand. Mr. Galloway nodded abstractedly, and for a little bit nothing was said.

The carriage bearing them twisted out of the procession, leaving a gap in it, and stopped in front of Doctor Lake's red-brick residence. The old doctor climbed down stiffly and, leaning heavily on his cane, went up the walk to his house. Next Mr. Galloway was dropped at his shabby little house, snug in its ambuscade behind a bushwhacker's paradise of lilac bushes; and pretty soon after that it was Sergeant Bagby's turn to get out. As the carriage slowed up for the third stop Judge Priest laid a demurring hand upon his companion's arm.

"Come on out to my place, this evenin', Jimmy," he said, "and have a bite of supper with me. There won't be nobody there but jest you and me, and after supper we kin set a spell and talk over old times."

The sergeant shook his whity-grey head in regretful dissent.

"I wish't I could, Judge," he said, "but it can't be done—not to-night."

"Better come on!" The judge's tone was pleading. "I sort of figger that there old nigger cook of mine has killed a young chicken. And she kin mix up a batch of waffle batter in less'n no time a-tall."

"Not to-night, Billy; some night soon I'll come, shore. But to-night my wife is figurin' on company, and ef I don't show up there'll be hell to pay and no pitch hot."

"Listen, Jimmy; listen to me." The judge spoke fast, for the sergeant was out of the carriage by now. "I've got a quart of special licker that Lieutenant Governor Bosworth sent me frum Lexington. Thirty-two years old, Jimmy—handmade and run through a gum log. Copper nor iron ain't never teched it. And when you pour a dram of it out into a glass it beads up same ez ef it had soapsuds down in the bottom of it—it does fur a fact. There ain't been but two drinks drunk out of that quart."

"Judge, please quit teasin' me!" Like unto a peppercorn, ground between the millstones of duty and desire, the sergeant backed reluctantly away from between the carriage wheels.

"You know yourse'f how wimmin folks are. It's the new Campbellite preacher that's comin' to-night, and there won't be a drop to drink on the table exceptin' maybe lemonade or ice tea. But I've jest natchelly got to be on hand and, whut's more, I've got to be on my best behaviour too. Dern that new preacher! Why couldn't he a-picked out some other night than this one?"

"Jimmy, listen——"

But the sergeant had turned and was fleeing to sanctuary, beyond reach of the tempter's tongue.

So for the last eighth-mile of the ride, until the black driver halted his team at the Priest place out on Clay Street, the judge rode alone. Laboriously he crawled out from beneath the overhang of the carriage top, handed up two bits as a parting gift to the darky on the seat, and waddled across the sidewalk.

The latch on the gate was broken. It had been broken for weeks. The old man slammed the gate to with a passionate jerk. The infirm latch clicked weakly, then slipped out of the iron nick and the gate sagged open—an invitation to anybody's wandering livestock to come right on in and feast upon the shrubs, which from lack of pruning had become thick, irregular little jungles. Clumps of rank grass, like green scalp locks, were sprouting in the walk, and when the master had mounted the creaking steps he saw where two porch planks had warped apart, leaving a gap between them. In and out of the space ran big black ants. The house needed painting, too, he noticed; in places where the rain water had dribbled out of a rust-hole in the tin gutter overhead, the grain of the clapboarding showed through its white coating. Mentally the judge promised himself that he would take a couple of days off sometime soon and call in workmen and have the whole shebang tidied and fixed up. Once a place began to run down it seemed to break out with neglect all over, as with a rash.

Halfway through his supper that evening the judge, who had been strangely silent in the early part of the meal, addressed his house boy, Jeff Poindexter, in the accents of a marked disapproval.

"Look here, Jeff," he demanded, "have I got to tell you ag'in about mendin' the ketch on that front gate?"

"Yas, suh—I means no, suh," Jeff corrected himself quickly. "Ise aimin' to do it fust thing in de mawnin', suh," added Jeff glibly, repeating a false pledge for perhaps the dozenth time within a month. "I got so many things to do round yere, Jedge, dat sometimes hit seems lak I can't think whut nary one of 'em is."

"Huh!" snorted his employer crossly. Then he went on warningly: "Some of these days there's goin' to be a sudden change in this house ef things ain't attended to better—whole place goin' to rack and ruin like it is."

Wriggling uneasily Jeff found a pretext for withdrawing himself, the situation having become embarrassing. It wasn't often that the judge gave way to temper. Not that Jeff feared the covert threat of discharge. If anybody quit it wouldn't be Jeff, as Jeff well knew. Usually Jeff had an excuse ready for any accusation of shortcomings on his part; thinking them up was his regular specialty. But this particular moment did not seem a propitious one for offering excuses. Jeff noiselessly evaporated out of sight and hearing.

In silence the master hurried through the meal, eating it with what for him was unusual speed. He was beset with an urge to be out of the big high-ceiled dining room. Looking about it he told himself it wasn't a dining room at all —just a bare barracks, full of emptiness and mighty little else.

After supper he sat on the porch, while the long twilight gloomed into dusk and the dusk into night. He was half-minded to walk downtown in the hope of finding congenial company at Soule's drug store, the favoured loafing place of his dwindling set of cronies. But he changed his mind. Since Mr. Soule, growing infirm, had taken a younger man for a partner, the drug store was changed. Its old-time air of hospitality and comfort had somehow altered.

The judge smoked on, rocking back and forth in his chair. The bull bats, which had been dodging about in the air as long as the daylight lasted, were gone now, and their shy cousin, the whippoorwill, began calling from down in the old Enders orchard at the far end of the street. Two or three times there came to Judge Priest's ears the sound of footsteps clunking along the plank sidewalk on his side of the road, and at that he sat erect, hoping each time the gate hinges would whine a warning of callers dropping in to bear him company. But the unseen pedestrians passed on without turning in. The whippoorwill moved up close to Judge Priest's side fence. A little night wind that had something on its mind began with a mournful whispering sound to swish through the top of the big cedar alongside the porch.

The judge stood it until nearly half-past nine o'clock. Even under the most favourable circumstances a whippoorwill and a remorseful night wind, telling its troubles to an evergreen tree, do not make what one would call exhilarating company. He closed and locked the front door, turned out the single gas light which burned in the hall and went up the stairs. In its main design the house was Colonial—Southern Colonial. But his bedroom was in an ell, above a side porch overlooking the croquet ground, and this ell was adorned with plank curlicues under its gables, and a square, ugly, useless little balcony, like a misplaced wooden moustache, adhered to its most prominent elevation on the side facing the front. The judge

frequently said that, as nearly as he could figure it out, the extension belonged to the Ruth-
erford B. Hayes period of American archi-
tecture.

Except for him the house was empty. Aunt
Dilsey didn't stay on the place at night and
Jeff's sleeping quarters were over the stable at
the back. As Judge Priest felt his way through
the upper hall and made a light in his bedchamber, the house was giving off those little
creaking, complaining sounds from its joints
that an old tired house always gives off when
it is lonely for a fuller measure of human occupancy.

His own room, revealed now in its homely
contour and its still homelier furnishings, was
neat enough, with Jeff's ideas of neatness, but
all about it indubitably betrayed the fact that
only male hands cared for it. The tall black-
walnut bureau lacked a cover for its top; the
mantel was littered with cigar boxes and old
law reports; the dead asparagus ferns, banked
in the grate, were faded to a musty yellow; and
some of the fronds had fallen out across the
hearth so that remotely the fireplace suggested
the mouth of a big cow choking on an overly
large bite of dried hay. In places the matting
on the floor was frayed almost through.

Just from the careless skew of the coverlid
and the set of the pillows against the white
bolster, you would have known at a glance
that a man had made up the bed that morning.

Barring one picture the walls were bare. This lone picture hung in a space between the two front windows, right where the occupant of the room, if so minded, might look at it the last thing at night and the first thing in the morning. Beyond any doubt a lover of the truly refined in art would have looked at it with a shudder, for it was one of those crayon portraits—a crayon portrait done in the most crayonsome and grewsome style of a self-taught artist working by the day rather than by the piece. Plainly it had been enlarged, as the trade term goes, from a photograph; the enlarger thereof had been lavish with his black leads; that, too, was self-evident. The original photographer had done his worst with the subject; the retoucher had gone him one better.

It was a likeness—you might call it a likeness—of a woman dressed in the abominable style of the late seventies—with heavy bangs down in her eyes, and a tight-fitting basque with enormous sleeves, and long pendent eardrops in her ears. The artist, whoever he was, had striven masterfully to rob the likeness of all expression. There alone his craftsmanship had failed him. For even he had not altogether taken away from the face a certain suggestion of old-fashioned wistfulness and sweetness. In all other regards, though, he had had his reckless way with it. The eyes were black and staring, the lines of the figure stiff and artificial, and the background for the head was a pastel nightmare.

For so long had Judge Priest been wifeless and childless that many of the younger genera- tion in our town knew nothing of the tragedy in this old man's life—which was that the same diphtheria epidemic that took both his babies in one week's time had widowed him too. We knew he loved other people's children; some of us never suspected that once upon a time he had had children of his own to love. Except in his memory no images of the dead babies endured, and this crayon portrait was the sole sentimental reminder left to him of his married life. And so, to him, it was a perfect and a matchless thing. He wouldn't have traded it for all the canvases of all the old masters in all the art galleries in this round big world.

This night, before he undressed, he went over and stood in front of it and looked at it for a while. There was dust in the grooves of the heavy tarnished gilt frame. From the top bureau drawer he took a big silk handkerchief and carefully he wiped the dust away. Then, before he put the handkerchief back in its place, he straightened the thing upon the nail which held it, and gave the glass front an awk- ward little caress with his pudgy old hand.

"It's been a long, long time, honey, since you went away and left me," he said slowly, in the voice of one addressing a hearer very near at hand; "but I still miss you and the babies powerfully. And sometimes it's sorter lonesome here without you."

A little later, when the light had been turned out, a noise like a long, deep sigh sounded out in the darkness. That, though, might have been the wheeze of the afflicted bedsprings as the old judge let his weight down in the bed.

An hour passed and there was another small sound there—a muffled nibbling sound. Behind the wainscoting, between bedroom and bathroom, a young, adventuresome rat gnawed at a box of matches which he had found on the floor in the hall and had dragged to his nest in the wall. From within the box a strangely tantalising aroma escaped; the rat, being deluded thereby into the belief that phosphorus might be an edible dainty, was minded to sample the contents. Presently his teeth met throɪgh the cover of the box. There was a sharp flaring pop, followed by a swift succession of other pops, and the rat gave a jump and departed elsewhere in great haste, with a hot bad smell in his snout and his adolescent whiskers quite entirely singed away.

The Confederates, in ragged uniforms of butternut jeans, were squatted in a clump of pawpaw bushes on the edge of a stretch of ploughed ground. From the woods on the far side of the field Yankee skirmishers were shooting toward them. A shell from the batteries must have fallen nearby and set fire to the dried

leaves and the fallen brush, for the smoke kept
blowing in a fellow's face, choking him and
making him cough. Captain Tip Meldrum,
the commander of Company B, was just behind the men, giving the order to fire back.
High Private Billy Priest aimed his musket at
the thickets where the Yankees were hidden
and pulled the trigger, but the cap on the nip-
ple of his piece was defective or something, and
the charge wouldn't explode. "Fire! Fire!
Fire!" yelled Captain Tip Meldrum over and
over again, and then he yanked out his own
horse-pistol and emptied it into the hostile timber. But Private Priest's gun still balked. He
flung it down—and found himself sitting up
in bed, gasping.

The dream hadn't been altogether a dream
at that. For there was indeed smoke in the
judge's eyes and his nostrils—plenty of it. A
revolver was cracking out its shots somewhere
near at hand; somebody outside his window
was shrieking "Fire!" at the top of a good
strong voice. In the distance other voices were
taking up the cry.

In an earlier day, when a fire started in
town, the man who discovered it drew his pis-
tol if he were on the highway, or snatched it
up if he chanced to be at home, and pointing
its barrel at the sky emptied it into the air as
fast as the cylinder would turn. The man next
door followed suit and so on until volleys were

rattling all over the neighbourhood. Thus were
the townspeople aroused and, along with the
townspeople, the members of the volunteer fire
department. Now we had a paid department
and a regular electric-alarm system, predicated
on boxes and gongs and wires and things; but
in outlying districts the pistol-shooting fashion
of spreading the word still prevailed to a considerable extent, and more especially did it
prevail at nighttime. So it didn't take the late
dreamer longer than the shake of a sheep's tail
to separate what was fancy from what was
reality.

As Judge Priest, yet half asleep but waking
up mighty fast, shoved his stout legs into his
trousers and tucked the tails of his nightshirt
down inside the waistband, he decided it must
be his barn and not his house that was afire.
The smoke which filled the room seemed to be
eddying in through the side window, from
across the end of the ell structure. He thought
of his old white mare, Mittie May, fast in her
stall under the hay loft, and of Jeff, who was
one of the soundest sleepers in the world, in his
room right alongside the mow. There was need
for him to move, and move fast. He must
awaken Jeff first, and then get Mittie May out
of danger. Barefooted, he felt his way across
the room and along the ha" and down the
stairs, mending his gait as he ,ent. And then,
as he jerked the front door open and stumbled
out upon the porch, he came into violent colli-

sion with Ed Tilghman, Junior, who lived across the street, and who had just bounded up the porch steps with the idea of hammering on the front-door panels. Tilghman was a young man and the judge an old one; it was inevitable the judge should suffer the more painful consequences of the sudden impact of their two bodies together. He went down sideways with a great hard thump, his forehead striking against a sharp corner of the door jamb. He was senseless, and a little stream of blood was beginning to trickle down his face as Tilghman dragged him down off the porch into the yard and stretched him on his back in the grass, and then ran to fetch water.

In that same minute the big bell in the tower of fire headquarters, half a mile away, began sounding in measured beats, and a small hungry-looking tongue of flame licked up across the sill and flickered for a moment through the smoke which was pouring forth out of the bathroom window and rolling across the flat top of the extension. The smoke gushed out still thicker, smothering down the red pennon, but in a second or two it showed again, and this time it brought with it two more like it. The bathroom window became a frame for a cloudy pink glare, and the purring note of the fire became a brisk and healthy crackle as it ate through the seasoned clapboards of the outer wall.

All of a sudden, so it seemed, the yard and the street were full of people. Promptly there began to happen most of the things that do happen at a fire. As for instance: Mr. Milus Miles, who arrived among the very first and who had a commandingly loud voice, mounted a rustic bench alongside the croquet ground and called for volunteers to form a bucket brigade. That his recruits would have no buckets to pass after they had enrolled themselves for service was with Mr. Miles a minor consideration. It was the spirit of the thing, the forethought, the responsibility, the aptitude for leadership in a work of succour—all these inspired him.

Mr. Ulysses Rice, who lived in the next street, climbed the side fence—under the circumstances it somehow to him seemed a more resolute thing to scale the fence than to enter by the gate in the regular way—and ran across the yard, inspired with a neighbourly and commendable desire to save something right away. He put his toe in a croquet wicket and fell headlong. This was to be expected of Mr. Rice. He had a perfect genius for getting into accidents. All Nature was ever in a conspiracy with all the inanimate objects in the world to do him bodily hurt. If he went skiff riding and fell overboard, as he customarily did, it was not because he had rocked the boat. The boat rocked itself. He was the only man in town who had ever succeeded in gashing his throat with a safety razor.

He now disentangled his foot from the wicket

and scrambled up and, still actuated by the
best motives imaginable, he dashed toward the
back of the Priest homestead, being minded to
seek entrance by a rear door. But a wire
clothesline, swinging at exactly the right height
to catch him just under the nose, did catch him
just under the nose and almost sawed the tip
of that useful organ off Mr. Rice's agonised
face. Coincidentally, citizens of various ages
and assorted sizes ran into the house and dragged out the furnishings of the lower floor, bestowing their salvage right where other citizens
might fall over it. Through all the joints between the shingles the roof of the ell leaked
smoke, until it resembled a sloped bed of slak-
ing lime. This fire was rapidly getting to be
a regular fire.

With a great clattering the department came
tearing up the street. Dropping down from
their perches on the running boards of the wag-
ons, certain of its members began unreeling
the hose, then ran back with it to couple it to
the nearest fire hydrant, nearly two blocks
away down Clay Street. Others brought a
ladder and reared it against the side of the
house, with its uppermost rounds projecting
above the low eaves. While many hands steadied the ladder in place, Captain Bud Gorman
of Station No. 1—there was also a Station No.
2, but Bud skippered Station No. 1—mounted
it and, with an axe, started chopping a hole in
the roof at a point where there seemed as yet

to be no immediate peril. Under his strokes
the shingles flew in showers. It was evident
that if the flames should spread to this immediate area Captain Bud Gorman would have a
rough but practicable flue ready for their egress
into the open air, against the moment when
they had burst through the ceiling and the
rafters below.

More people and yet more kept coming.
The rubber piping, which perversely had kinked
and twisted as it came off the spinning drum of
hose reel No. 1, was fairly straight now, and
from his station just inside the gate the fire
chief bellowed the command down the line to
turn 'er on! They turned her on, but somewhere in the coupled sections of hose a stricture
had developed. All that happened was that
from the brass snout of the nozzle a languid
gush of yellow water arose in a fan shape to an
elevation of perhaps fifteen feet, thence descending in a cascade, not upon the particular
spot at which the nozzle was aimed, but full
upon the ill-starred Mr. Rice as he tugged to
uproot a wooden support of the little grape
arbor which flanked the house on the endan-
gered side. Somewhat disfigured by the clothesline but still resolute to lend a helping hand
somewhere, Mr. Rice had but a moment before become possessed of an ambition to remove the grape vines, trellis and all, to a place
of safety. His reward for this kindly attempt
was a sudden soaking.

As though the hiss of the water had aroused him, Judge Priest sat up in the grass, where he had been lying during these tumultuous and crowded five minutes. He was still half dazed. As his eyesight cleared, he saw that the bath-room was as good as gone and that his bed-room was about to go. Some one helped him to his unsteady feet and kept him upright. He shook himself free from the supporting grasp of the person who held him, and advanced to-ward the porch steps, wavering a little on his legs as he went.

Then, before anybody sensed what he meant to do, before anybody could make a move to stop him, he had mounted the steps and was at the front door.

Out of the door, bumping into him, backed a coughing, gasping squad, their noses smart-ing and their eyes streaming from the acrid reek, towing after them the big horsehair sofa which was the principal piece of furniture in the judge's sitting room. The sofa had lost two of its casters in transit, and it took all their strength to drag it over the lintel.

"It's no use, Judge Priest," panted one of these workers, recognising him; "we've got pretty nearly everything out that was down-stairs and you couldn't get upstairs now if you tried."

Then seeing that the owner meant to disre-gard the warning, this man threw out an arm forcibly to detain the other. But for all his

age and size, the judge was wieldy enough when
he chose to be. With an agile twist of his
body he dodged past, and as the man, astound-
ed and horrified, glared across the threshold he
saw Judge Priest running down the murky hall
and, with head bent and his mouth and nose
buried in the crook of one elbow, starting up
the stairs into the thickest and blackest of the
smoke. To this man's credit, be it said, he
made a valiant effort to overtake the old man.
The pursuer darted in behind him, but at the
foot of the steps fell back, daunted and unable
to breathe. He staggered out again into the
open, gagging with the smoke that was in his
throat and down in his lungs.

"He's gone in there!" he shouted, pointing
behind him. "He's gone right in there! He's
gone upstairs!"

"Who is it? Who's gone in there?" twenty
voices demanded together.

"The judge—just a second ago! I tried to stop
him—he got by me! He ain't got a chance!"

Even as he spoke the words, a draught of
fire came roaring through the crater in the roof
which Captain Bud Gorman's axe had dug for
its free passage. An outcry—half gasp, half
groan—went up from those who knew what
had happened. They ran round in rings wasting precious time.

Sergeant Jimmy Bagby, half dressed, trotted
across the lawn. He had just arrived. He
grabbed young Ed Tilghman by the arm.

"How'd she start, boy?" demanded the sergeant. "Where's the judge? Did they git everything out?"

"Everything out—hell!" answered Tilghman, sobbing in his distress. "The old judge is in there. He got a lick on the head and it must have made him crazy. He just ran back in there and went upstairs. He'll never make it—and nobody can get him out. He'll smother to death sure!"

Down on his knees dropped Sergeant Bagby and shut his eyes, and for the first, last and only time in his life he prayed aloud in public.

"Oh, Lord," he prayed, "fur God's sake git Billy Priest out of there! Oh, Lord, that's all I'll ever ask You—fur God's sake git Billy Priest out of there! Ez a favour to me, Lord, please, Suh, git Billy Priest out of there!"

From many throats at once a yell arose—a yell so shrill and loud that it overtopped all lesser sounds; a yell so loud that the sergeant ceased from his praying to look. Through the smoke, and over the sloping peak of the roof from the rear, came a slim, dark shape on its all-fours. Treading the pitch of the gable as swiftly and surefootedly as a cat, it scuttled forward to the front edge of the housetop, swung downward at arms' length from the eaves, and dropped on a narrow ledge of tin-covered surface where the small ornamental balcony, which was like a misplaced wooden

moustache, projected from the face of the building at the level of the second floor, then instantly dived headfirst in at that window of
the judge's bedchamber which was farthest
from the corner next the bathroom.

For a silent minute—a minute which seemed
a year—those below stared upward, with starting eyes and lumps in their throats. Then, all
together, they swallowed their several throat
lumps and united in an exultant joyous yell,
which made that other yell they had uttered a
little before seem by comparison puny and
cheap. Through the smoke which bulged from
the balcony window and out upon the balcony
itself popped the agile black figure. Bracing
itself, it hauled across the window ledge a
bulky inert form. It wrestled its helpless burden over and eased it down the flat, tiny railed-
in perch just as a fire ladder, manned by many
eager hands, came straightening up from below,
with Captain Bud Gorman of Station No. 1
climbing it, two rounds at a jump, before it
had ceased to waver in the air.

Volunteers swarmed up the ladder behind
Bud Gorman, forming a living chain from the
earth to the balcony. First they passed down
the judge, breathing and whole but uncon-
scious, with his nightshirt torn off his back
and his bare right arm still clenched round a
picture of some sort in a heavy gilt frame. His
grip on it did not relax until they had carried
him well back from the burning house, and for

the second time that night had stretched him out upon the grass.

The judge being safe, the men on the ladder made room for Jeff Poindexter to descend under his own motive power, all of them cheering mightily. Just as Jeff reached solid ground the stoppage in the hose unstopped itself of its own accord and from the brazen gullet of the nozzle there sprang up, like a silver sword, a straight, hard stream of water which lanced into the heart of the fire, turning its exultant song from a crackle to a croon and then to a resentful hiss.

In that same instant Sergeant Bagby found himself, for the first time since he escaped from the kindly tyranny of a black mammy—nearly sixty years before—in close and ardent embrace with a member of the African race.

"Jeff," clarioned the sergeant, hugging the blistered rescuer yet closer to him and beating him on the back with hearty thumps—"Jeff, God bless your black hide, how did you come to think of it?"

"Well, suh, Mr. Bagby," wheezed Jeff, "hit wuz lak dis: I didn't wake up w'en she fust started. I got so much on my mind to do day-times 'at I sleeps mighty sound w'en I does sleep. Presen'ly, tho', I did wake up, an' I got my pants on, an' I come runnin' acrost de lot frum de stable, an' I got heah jes' in time to hear 'em all yellin' out dat de jedge is done went back into de house. I sees there ain't no

chanc't of goin' in after him de way he's done
went, but jes' about that time I remembers
dat air little po'ch up yonder on de front of
de house w'ich it seem lak ever'body else had
done furgot all 'bout hit bein' there a-tall. So
I runs round to de back right quick, an' I
clim' up de lattice-work by de kitchen, an' I
comes out along over de roof, an' I drap down
on de little po'ch, an' after that, I reckin, you
seen de rest of it fur you'self, suh—all but
whut happen after I gits inside dat window."

"What did happen?" From the ring of men
who hedged in the sergeant and Jeff five or six
asked the same question at once. Before an
all-white audience Jeff visibly expanded himself.

"W'y, nothin' a-tall happen," he said,
" 'ceptin' that I found de ole boss-man right
where I figgered I'd find him—in his own room
at de foot of his baid. He'd done fell down
dere on de flo', right after he grabbed dat air
picture offen de wall. Yas, suh, that's perzack-
ly where I finds him!"

"But, Jeff, how could you breathe up there?"

Still in the sergeant's cordial grasp, Jeff made
direct answer:

"Gen'l'mens, I didn't! Fur de time bein' I
jes' natchelly abandoned breathin'!"

Again that night Judge Priest had a dream
—only this time the dream lacked continuity
and sequence and was but a jumble of things—
and he emerged from it with his thoughts all in

confusion. In his first drowsy moment of consciousness he had a sensation of having taken
a long journey along a dark rough road. For
a little he lay wondering where he was, piecing
together his impressions and trying to bridge
the intervening gaps.

Then the light got better and he made out
the anxious face of Doctor Lake looking down
at him and, just over Doctor Lake's shoulder,
the face of Sergeant Bagby. He opened his
mouth then and spoke.

"Well, there's one thing certain shore," said
the judge: "this ain't heaven! Because ef
'twas, there wouldn't be a chance of you and
Jimmy Bagby bein' here with me."

Whereupon, for no apparent reason on earth
that Judge Priest could fathom, Doctor Lake,
with a huskily affectionate intonation, called
him by many profane and improper names;
and Sergeant Bagby, wiping his eyes with one
hand, made his other hand up into a fist and
shook it in Judge Priest's face, meanwhile emo-
tionally denouncing him as several qualified
varieties of an old idiot.

Under this treatment the fogginess quit
Judge Priest's brain, and he became aware of
the presence of a considerable number of persons about him, including the two Edward
Tilghmans—Senior and Junior—and the two
Tilghman girls; and Jeff Poindexter, wearing
about half as many garments as Jeff customarily wore, and with a slightly blistered appear-

ance as to his face and shoulders; and Mr.
Ulysses Rice, with a badly skinned nose and
badly drenched shoulders; and divers others of
his acquaintances. Indeed, he was quite surrounded by neighbours and friends. Also by
degrees it became apparent to him that he was
stretched upon a strange bed in a strange room
—at least he did not recall ever having been in
this room before—and that he had a bandage
across the baldest part of his head, and that
he felt tired all over his body.

"Well, I got out, didn't I?" he inquired after
a minute or two.

"Got out—thunder!" vociferated the sergeant with what the judge regarded as a most
unnecessary violence of voice and manner. "Ef
this here black boy of yourn hadn't a-risked his
own life, climbin' down over the roof and goin'
in through a front window and draggin' you
out of that fire—the same ez ef you was a sack
of shorts—you'd a-been a goner, shore. Ain't
you 'shamed of yourself, scarin' everybody half
to death that-a-way?"

"Oh, it was Jeff, was it?" said the old judge,
disregarding Sergeant Bagby's indignant inter-
rogation. He looked steadfastly at his grinning
servitor and, when he spoke again, there was a
different intonation in his voice.

"Much obliged to you, Jeff." That was all
he said. It was the way he said it.

"You is more'n welcome, thanky, suh," answered Jeff; "it warn't scursely no trouble

a-tall, suh—'cep'in' dem ole shingles on dat roof suttin'y wuz warm to de te'ch.''

"Did—did Jeff succeed in savin' anything else besides me?" The judge put the question as though half fearing what the answer might be.

"Ef you mean this—why, here 'tis, safe and sound," said Sergeant Bagby, and he moved aside so that Judge Priest might see, leaning against the footboard of the bed, a certain crayon portrait. "The glass ain't cracked even and the frame ain't dented. You three come out of there practically together—Jeff a-hangin' onto you and you a-hangin' onto your picture. So if that's whut you went chargin' back in there fur, I hope you're satisfied!"

"I'm satisfied," said the judge softly. Then after a bit he cleared his throat and ventured another query:

"That old house of mine—I s'pose she's all burnt up by now?"

"Don't you ever believe it," said the sergeant. "That there house of yourn 'pears to be purty nigh ez contrary and set in its ways ez whut you are. It won't burn up, no matter how good a chance you give it. Jest about the time Jeff here drug you out on that little balcony outside your window, the water works begun to work, and after that they had her under control in less'n no time. She must be about out by now."

"Your bathroom's a total loss and the extension on that side is pretty badly scorched up, but the rest of the place, excusing damage by the water and the smoke, is hardly damaged," added the younger Tilghman. "You'll be able to move back in, inside of a month, judge."

"And in the meantime you're going to stay right here, Judge Priest, and make my house your home," announced Mr. Tilghman, Senior. "It's mighty plain, but such as it is you're welcome to it, judge. We'll do our level best to make you comfortable. Only I'm afraid you'll miss the things you've been used to having round you."

"Oh, I reckin not," said Judge Priest. His glance travelled slowly from the crayon portrait at the foot of the bed to Jeff Poindexter's chocolate-coloured face and back again to the portrait. "I've got mighty near everything I need to make me happy."

"What I meant was that maybe you'd be kind of lonesome away from your own house," Mr. Tilghman said.

"No, I don't believe so," answered the old man, smiling a little. "You see, I taken the cure for lonesomeness to-night. You mout call it the smoke cure."

CHAPTER VI
THE FAMILY TREE

THE family tree of the Van Nicht family was not the sort of family tree you think I mean, although they had one of that variety too. This was a real tree. It was an elm—the biggest elm and the broadest and the most majestic elm in the entire state, and in the times of its leafage cast the densest shade of any elm to be found anywhere, probably. For more than one hundred years the Van Nicht family had lived in its shadow. That was the principal trouble with them—they did live in the shadow. I'll come to that later.

Every consequential visitor to Schuylerville was taken to see the Van Nicht elm. It was a necessary detail of his tour about town. Either before or after he had viewed the new ten-story skyscraper of the Seaboard National Bank, and the site for the projected Civic Centre, and the monument to Schuyler County's defenders of the Union — 1861 - '65 — with a dropsical bronze figure of a booted and whis-

THOSE TIMES AND THESE

kered infantryman on top of the tall column, and the Henrietta Wing Memorial Library, and the rest of it, they took him and they showed him the Van Nicht elm. So doing, it was incumbent upon them to escort him through a street which was beginning to wear that vacillating, uncertain look any street wears while trying to make up its mind whether to keep on being a quiet residential byway in an old-fashioned town or to turn itself into an important thoroughfare of a thriving industrial centre. You know the kind of street I aim to picture— with here an impudent young garage showing its shining morning face of red brick in a side yard where there used to be an orchard, and there a new apartment building which has shouldered its way into a line of ancient dwellings and is driving its cast-iron cornices, like rude elbows, into the clapboarded short ribs of its neighbours upon either side.

At the far, upper end of that street, upon the poll of a gentle eminence, uplifted the Van Nicht elm. It was for sundry months of the year a splendid vast umbrella, green in the spring and summer and yellow in the fall; and in the winter presented itself against the sky line as a great skeleton shape, without a blemish upon it, except for a scar in the bark close down to the earth to show where once there might have been a fissure in its mighty bole. No grass, or at least mighty little grass, grew within the circle of its brandishing limbs. It was as though the roots of the tree sucked up all the nourishment that the soil might hold, leaving none for the humble grass to thrive upon.

It was in the winter that the house, which stood almost directly under the tree, was most clearly revealed as a square, ugly domicile of grey stone, a story and a half in height, lidded over by a hip roof of weathered shingles; with a deeply recessed front door, like a pursed and proper mouth, and, above it, a row of queer little longitudinal windows, half hidden below the overhang of the gables and suggesting so many slitted eyes peering out from beneath a lowering brow. You saw, too, the mould that had formed in streaky splotches upon the stonework of the walls and the green rime of age and dampness that had overspread the curled shingles and the peeling paint, turning to minute scales upon the woodwork of the window casings and the door frames. Also you saw one great crooked bough which stretched across the roof like a menacing black arm, forever threatening to descend and crush its rafters in. This was in winter; in summertime the leaves almost completely hid the house, so that one who halted outside the decrepit fence, with its snaggled and broken panels, must needs stoop low to perceive its outlines at all.

The carriage or the automobile bearing the prominent guest and the chairman of the local reception committee would halt at the end of the street.

"That," the chairman would say, pointing up grade, "is the Van Nicht elm. Possibly you've heard about it? Round here we call it the Van Nicht family tree. It is said to be the largest elm in this part of the country. In fact, I doubt whether there are any larger than this one, even up in New England. And that's the famous old Van Nicht homestead there, just back of it.

"Its got a history. When Colonel Cecilius Jacob Van Nicht came here right after the Revolutionary War—he was a colonel in the Revolution, you know—he built the house, placing it just behind the tree. The tree must've grown considerably since then, but the house yonder hasn't changed but mighty little all these years. It's the oldest building in Schuyler County. As a matter of fact, the town, with this house for a starter, sort of grew up down here on the flat lands below. The old colonel raised a family here and died here. So did his son and his grandson. They were rich people once—the richest people in the county at one time.

"Why all the land from here clear down to Ossibaw Street—that's six blocks south—used to be included in the Van Nicht estate. It was a farm then, of course, and by all accounts a fine one. But each generation sold off some of the original grant, until all that's left now is that house, with the tree and about an acre of ground more or less. And I guess it's pretty well covered with mortgages."

This, in substance, was what the guide would tell the distinguished stranger. This, in substance, was what was told to young Olcott on the day after he arrived in Schuylerville to take over the editorial management of the Schuylerville *News-Ledger*. Mayor T. J. McGlynn was showing him the principal points of interest— so the mayor had put it, when he called that morning with his own car at the Hotel Brainard, where Olcott was stopping, and invited the young man to go for a tour of inspection of the city, as a sort of introductory and preparatory course in local education prior to his assuming his new duties.

While the worthy mayor was uttering his descriptive remarks Olcott bent his head and squinted past the thick shield of limbs and leaves. He saw that the door of the house, which was closed, somehow had the look of about always being closed, and that most of the windows were barred with thick shutters.

"Appears rather deserted, doesn't it?" said the newcomer, striving to show a proper appreciation of the courtesy that was being visited upon him. "There isn't any one living there at present, is there?"

"Sure there is," said Mayor McGlynn. "Old Mr. Cecilius Jacob Van Nicht, 4th, who's the present head of the family, and his two old-maid sisters, Miss Rachael and Miss Harriet— they all live there together. Miss Rachael is considerably older than Miss Harriet, but

THOSE TIMES AND THESE

they're both regular old maids—guess they always will be. The brother never married, either—couldn't find anybody good enough to share the name, I suppose. Anyhow he's never married. And besides I guess it keeps him pretty busy living up to the job of being the head of the oldest family in this end of the state. That's about all he ever has done."

"Then he isn't in any regular business or any profession?"

"Business!" Mayor McGlynn snorted. "I should say not! All any one of the Van Nichts has ever done since anybody can remember was just to keep on being a Van Nicht and upholding the traditions and the honours of the Van Nichts—and this one is like all his breed. The poorer he gets the more pompous and the more important acting he gets—that's the funny part of it."

"Apparently not a very lucrative calling, judging by the general aspect of the ancestral manor," said Olcott, who was beginning now to be interested. "How do they manage to live?"

"Lord knows," said the mayor. "How do the sparrows manage to live? I guess there're times when they need a load of coal and a market basket full of victuals to help tide 'em over a hard spell, but naturally nobody would dare to offer to help them. They're proud as Lucifer themselves, and the town is kind of proud of 'em. They're institutions with us, as you might say."

McGlynn, who, as Olcott was to learn later, was a product of new industrial and new political conditions in the community, spoke with the half-begrudged admiration which the self-made so often have for the ancestor-made.

"We ain't got so very many of the real aristocrats in this section any more, what with all this new blood pouring in since our boom started up; and even if they are as poor as Job's turkey, these Van Nichts still count for a good deal round here. Money ain't everything anyway, is it? . . . Well, Mr. Olcott, if you've seen enough here, we'll turn round and go see something else." He addressed his chauffeur: "Jim, suppose you take us by the new hosiery mills next. I want Mr. Olcott to see one of the most prosperous manufacturing plants in the state. Employs nine hundred hands, Mr. Olcott, and hasn't been in operation but a little more than three years. That's the way this town is humping itself. You didn't make any mistake, coming here."

As the car swung about, Olcott gave the Van Nicht place a backward scrutiny over his shoulder and was impressed by its appearance into saying this:

"It strikes me as having a mighty unhealthy air about it. I'd say offhand it was a first-rate breeding spot for malaria and rheumatism. I wonder why they don't trim up that big old tree and give the sunshine and the light a chance to get in under it."

"For heaven's sake and your own, don't you suggest that to the old boy when you meet him," said McGlynn with a grin. "He'd as soon think of cutting off his own leg as to touch a leaf on the family tree. It's sacred to him. It represents all the glory of his breed and he venerates it, the same as some people venerate an altar in a church."

"Then you think I will be likely to meet him? I'd like to—from what you tell me, he must be rather a unique personality."

"Yes, he's all of that—unique, I mean. And you're pretty sure to meet him before you've been in town many months. He seems to regard it as his duty to call on certain people, after they've been here a given length of time, and extend to them the freedom of the town that his illustrious great-granddaddy founded. If you're specially lucky—or specially unlucky —he may even invite you to call on him, although that's an honour that doesn't come to very many, even among the older residents. The Van Nichts are mighty exclusive and it isn't often that anybody sees what the inside of their house looks like—let alone a stranger. . . . Say, Jim, after we've seen the hosiery mills, run us on out past the County Feeble-Minded and Insane Asylum. Mr. Olcott will enjoy that!"

Within a month's time from this time, Mayor McGlynn's prophecy was to come true. On a morning in the early part of the summer Ol-

cott sat behind his desk in his office adjoining
the city room on the second floor of the *News-
Ledger* building, when his office boy announced
a gentleman calling to see Mr. Olcott personally.

"See who it is, will you, please, Morgan?"
said Olcott to his assistant. Morgan had arrived less than a week before, having been sent
on by the syndicate which owned a chain of
papers, the *News-Ledger* included, to serve
under the new managing editor. The syndicate
had a cheery little way of shuffling the cards
at frequent intervals and dealing out fresh exec-
utives for the six or eight dailies under its
control and ownership.

"I'm busy as the dickens," added Olcott as
Morgan got up to obey; "so if it's a pest that's
outside, give him the soft answer and steer him
off!"

In a minute Morgan was back with a cryptic
grin on his face.

"You'd better see him—he's worth seeing,
all right," said Morgan.

"Who is it?" asked Olcott.

"It's somebody right out of a book," answered Morgan; "somebody giving the name
of Something Something Van Nicht. I didn't
catch all the first name—I was too busy sizing
up its proprietor. Says he must see you privately and in person. I gather from his manner that if you don't see him this paper will
never be quite the same again. And honestly,
Olcott, he's worth seeing."

"I think I know who it is," said Olcott, "and I'll see him. Boy, show the gentleman in!"

"I'll go myself," said Morgan. "This is a thing that ought to be done in style."

Olcott reared back in his chair, waiting. The door opened and Morgan's voice was heard making formal and sonorous announcement: "Mr. Van Nicht." And Olcott, looking over his desk top, saw, framed in the doorway, a figure at once picturesque and pitiable.

The first thing, almost, to catch his eye was a broad black stock collar—the first stock collar Olcott had ever seen worn by a man in daytime. Above it was a long, close-shaven, old face, with a bloodless and unwholesome pallor to it, framed in long, white hair, and surmounted by a broad-brimmed, tall-crowned soft hat which had once been black and now was gangrenous with age. Below it a pair of sloping shoulders merging into a thin, meagre body tightly cased in a rusty frock coat, and below the coat skirts in turn a pair of amazingly thin and rickety legs, ending in slender, well-polished boots with high heels. In an instantaneous appraisal of the queer figure Olcott comprehended these details and, in that same flicker of time, noted that the triangle of limp linen showing in the V of the close-buttoned lapels had a fragile, yellowish look like old ivory, that all the outer garments were threadbare and shiny in the seams, and that the stock collar was decayed to a greenish tinge along its edges. Although the weather was warm, the stranger wore a pair of grey cotton gloves.

"Good morning," said Olcott, mechanically putting a ceremonious and formal emphasis into the words and getting on his feet.

"Good morning, sir, to you," returned the visitor in a voice of surprising volume, considering that it issued from so slight a frame. "You are Mr. Olcott?"

"Yes, that's my name." And Olcott took a step forward, extending his hand.

"Mine, sir, is Cecilius Jacob Van Nicht, 4th." The speaker paused midway of the floor to remove one glove and to shift it and his cane to the left hand. Advancing, with a slight limp, he gave to Olcott a set of fingers that were dry and chilly and fleshless. Almost it was like clasping the articulated bones of a skeleton's hand.

"I have come personally, sir, to pay my respects and, as one representing the—ah—the old régime of our people, to bid you welcome to our midst."

"Thank you very much," said Olcott, a bit amused inwardly, and a bit impressed also by the air of mouldy grandeur which the other diffused. "Won't you sit down, Mr. Van Nicht?"

"I shall be able to tarry but a short while." The big voice boomed out of the little dried-up body as the old man took the chair which

Olcott had indicated. He took only part of it. He poised himself on the forward edge of its seat, holding his spine very erect and dramatising his posture with a stiff and stately investure.

Olcott caught himself telling himself Morgan had been right: This personage was not really flesh and blood, but something out of a book— an embodied bit of fiction. Why even his language had the stilted shaping of the characters in most of these old-timey classical novels.

"He wasn't really born at all," Olcott thought. "Dickens wrote him and then Cruikshank drew him and now here he is, miraculously preserved to posterity. But Charlotte Brontë endowed him with his conversation." What Olcott said—aloud—was something fatuous and commonplace touching on the state of the weather.

"I have yet other motives in presenting myself to-day, in this, your sanctum," stated Mr. Van Nicht. "First of all, I wish to congratulate you upon what to me appears to be a very gratifying stroke of journalistic enterprise which has come to light in the columns of your valued organ since your advent into the community and for which, therefore, I assume you are responsible."

"Well," said Olcott, "we try to get out a reasonably live sheet."

"Pardon me," said Mr. Van Nicht, "but I do not refer to the aspect of your news columns.

I am speaking with reference to a feature lately
appearing in your Sunday edition, in what I
believe is known as your magazine section. I
have observed that, beginning two weeks ago,
you inaugurated a department devoted to the
genealogies of divers of our older and more distinguished American families. As I recall, the
subjects of your first two articles were the
Adams family, of Massachusetts, and the Lee
family, of Virginia. It may interest you to
know, sir—I trust indeed that it may please
you to know—that I, personally, am most
highly pleased that you should seek to inculcate in the minds of our people, through the
medium of your columns, a knowledge of those
strains of blood to which our nation is particularly indebted for much of its culture, much of
its social development, many of its gentler and
more graceful influences. It is a most worthy
movement indeed, a most commendable undertaking. I repeat, sir, that I congratulate you
upon it."

"Thank you," said Olcott. "This coming
Sunday we are going to run a yarn about the
Gordon family, of Georgia, and after that I
believe come the Clays, of Kentucky."

"Quite so, quite so," said Mr. Van Nicht.
"The names you have mentioned are names
that are permanently embalmed in the written
annals of our national life. But may I ask, sir,
whether you have taken any steps as yet to in-
corporate into your series an epitome of the

achievements of the family of which I have the
honour to be the head—the Van Nicht family?"

"Well, you see," explained Olcott apologetic-
ally, "these articles are not written here in the
office. They are sent to us in proof sheets as
a part of our regular feature service, and we run
'em just as they come to us. Probably—probably"—he hesitated a moment over the job of
phrasing tactfully his white lie—"probably a
story on your family genealogy will be coming
along pretty soon."

"Doubtlessly so, doubtlessly so." The assent was guilelessly emphatic. "In any such
symposium, in any such compendium, my family, beyond peradventure, will have its proper
place in due season. Nevertheless, foreseeing
that in the hands of a stranger the facts and
the dates might unintentionally be confused or
wrongly set down, I have taken upon myself
the obligation of preparing an accurate account of the life and work of my illustrious,
heroic and noble ancestor, Colonel Cecilius Jacob Van Nicht, together with a more or less
elaborate *résumé* of the lives of his descendants
up to and including the present generation.
This article is now completed. In fact I have
it upon my person." Carefully he undid the
top button of his coat and reached for an inner
breast pocket. "I shall be most pleased to accord you my full permission for its insertion in
an early issue of your publication." He spoke
with the air of one bestowing a gift of great value.

Olcott's practised eye appraised the probable length of the manuscript which this volunteer contributor was hauling forth from his bosom and, inside himself, Olcott groaned. There appeared to be a considerable number of sheets of foolscap, all closely written over in a fine, close hand.

"Thank you, Mr. Van Nicht, thank you very much," said Olcott, searching his soul for excuses. "But I'm afraid we aren't able to pay much for this sort of matter. What I mean to say is we are not in a position to invest very heavily in outside offerings. Er—you see most of our specials—in fact practically all of them except those written here in the office by the staff—come to us as part of a regular syndicate arrangement."

Here Mr. Cecilius Jacob Van Nicht, 4th, attained the physically impossible. He erected his spine straighter than before and stiffened his body a mite stiffer than it had been.

"Pray do not misunderstand me, sir," he stated solemnly. "I crave no honorarium for this work. I expect none. I have considered it a duty incumbent upon me to prepare it, and I regard it as a pleasure to tender it to you, gratis."

"But—I'd like to be able to offer a little something anyway——"

"One moment, if you please! Kindly hear me out! With me, sir, this has been a labour of love. Moreover, I should look upon it as an impropriety to accept remuneration for such work. To me it would savour of the mercenary—would be as though I sought to capitalise into dollars and cents the reputation of my own people and my own stock. I trust you get my viewpoint?"

"Oh, yes, indeed"—Olcott was slightly flustered—"very creditable of you, I'm sure. Er —is it very long?"

"No longer than a proper appreciation of the topic demands." The old gentleman spoke with firmness. "Also you may rely absolutely upon the trustworthiness and the accuracy of all the facts, as herein recited. I had access to the papers left by my own revered grandfather, Judge Cecilius Van Nicht, 2d, son and namesake of the founder of our line, locally. I may tell you, too, that in preparing this compilation I was assisted by my sister, Miss Rachael Van Nicht, a lady of wide reading and no small degree of intellectual attainment, although leading a life much aloof from the world —in fact, almost a cloistered life."

He arose, opened out the sheaf of folded sheets, pressed them flat with a caressing hand and laid them down in front of Olcott. He spoke now with authority, almost in the tone of a superior giving instructions regarding a delicate matter to an underling:

"I feel warranted in the assumption that you will not find it necessary to alter or curtail my statements in any particular. I have had some previous experience in literary endeavours. In all modesty I may say that I am no novice. A signed article from my pen, entitled The Influence of the Holland - Dutch Strain Upon American Public Life, From Peter Stuyvesant to Theodore Roosevelt, was published some years since in the New York *Evening Post*, afterward becoming the subject of editorial comment in the Springfield *Republican*, the Hartford *Courant* and the Boston *Transcript*. At present I am engaged in a brief history of one of our earlier presidents, the Honourable Martin Van Buren. I have the honour to bid you a very good day, sir."

Olcott ran the story in his next Sunday issue but one. It stretched the full length of two columns and invaded a third. It was tiresome and long-winded. It was as prosy as prosy could be. To make room for it a smartly done special on the commercial awakening of Schuyler County was crowded out. Olcott's judgment told him he did a sinful thing, but he ran it. He went further than that. Into the editorial page he slipped a paragraph directing attention to "Mr. Cecilius Jacob Van Nicht's timely and interesting article, appearing elsewhere in this number."

He had his reward, though, in the comments of sundry ones of his local subscribers. From these comments, made to him by letter and by word of mouth, he sensed something of

the attitude of the community toward the Van
Nicht family. As he figured, this sentiment
was a compound of several things. It appeared
to embody a gentle intolerance for the shell of
social exclusiveness in which the present bearers of the name had walled themselves up, together with a sympathy for their poverty and
their self-imposed state of lonely and neglected
aloofness, and still further down, underlying
these emotions and tincturing them, an understanding and an admiration for the importance
of this old family as an old family—an admiration which was genuine and avowed on the part
of some, and just as genuine but more or less
reluctantly bestowed on the part of others. It
was as Mayor McGlynn had informed Olcott
on their first meeting. The Van Nichts were
not so much individuals, having a share in the
life of this thriving, striving, overgrown town,
as they were historical fixtures and traditional
assets. Collectively, they constituted something to be proud of and sorry for.

Soon, too, he had further reward. One afternoon a small and grimy boy invaded his room,
without knocking, and laid a note upon his
desk.

"Old guy downstairs, with long hair and a
gimpy leg, handed me this yere and gimme fi'
cents to fetch it up here to you," stated the
messenger.

The note was from Mr. Van Nicht, as a
glance at the superscription told Olcott before

he opened the envelope. In formal terms Olcott was thanked for giving the writer's offering such prominence in the pages of his valu-
able paper and was invited, formally, to call
upon the undersigned at his place of residence,
in order that undersigned might more fully express to Mr. Olcott his sincere appreciation.

On the whole, Olcott was glad of the opportunity to view the inside of that gloomy old
house under the big tree out at the end of Putnam Street. He wanted to see more of Mr.
Cecilius Jacob Van Nicht, and to see something
of the other two dwellers beneath that ancient
roof. Olcott had dreams of some day writing a
novel; some day when he had the time. Most
newspaper men do have such dreams; or else
it is a play they are going to write. Meanwhile, pending the coming of that day, he was
storing up material for it in his mind. Assuredly the bleached-out, pale, old recluse in the
black stock would make copy. Probably his
sisters would be types also, and they might
make copy too. Olcott answered the note, accepting the invitation for that same evening.

It was a night of crystal-clear moonlight,
and Olcott walked up Putnam Street through
an alchemistic radiance which was like a path
for a Puck to dance along. But the shimmer-
ing aisle broke off short, when he had turned
in at the broken gate and had come to the edge
of the shade of the Van Nicht elm. Under
there the shadow lay so thick and dense that,

as he groped through it to the small entry
porch, finding the way by the feel of his feet
upon the irregular, flagged walk, he had the
conviction that he might reach out with his
hands and gather up folds of the darkness in
his arms, like ells of black velvet. The faint
glow which came through a curtained front
window of the unseen house was like a phos-
phorescent smear, plastered against a formless
background, and only served to make the adjacent darkness darker still. If the moonlight
yonder was a fit place for the fairies to trip it,
this particular spot, he thought, must be re-
served for ghosts to stalk in.

Fumbling with his hands, he searched out
the heavy door knocker. Its resounding thump
against its heel plate, as he dropped it back in
place, made him jump. At once the door
opened. Centred in the oblong of dulled light
which came from an oil lamp burning upon a
table, behind and within, appeared the slender,
warped figure of Mr. Cecilius Jacob Van Nicht,
4th. With much ceremony the head of the
house bowed the guest in past the portals.

Almost the first object to catch Olcott's eye,
as he stepped in, was a portrait which, with its
heavy frame, filled up a considerable portion of
the wall space across the back breadth of the
square hallway into which he had entered. Ex-
cepting for this picture and the table with the
oil lamp upon it and a tall hat-tree, the hall
was quite bare.

Plainly pleased that the younger man's attention had been caught by the painted square of canvas, Mr. Van Nicht promptly turned up the wick of the light, and then Olcott, looking closer, saw staring down at him the close-set black eyes and the heavy-jowled, foreign-looking face of an old man, dressed in such garb as we associate with our conceptions of Thomas Jefferson and the elder Adams.

"My famous forbear, sir," stated Olcott's host, with a great weight of vanity in his words, "the original bearer of the name which I, as his great-grandson, have the honour, likewise, of bearing. To me, sir, it has ever been a source of deep regret that there is no likeness extant depicting him in his uniform as a regimental commander in the Continental armies. If any such likeness existed, it was destroyed prior to the colonel's removal to this place, following the close of the struggle for Independence. This portrait was executed in the later years of the original's life—presumably about the year 1798, by order of his son, who was my grandfather. It was the son who enlarged this house, by the addition of a wing at the rear, and to him also we are indebted for the written records of his father's gallant performances on the field of honour, as well as for the accounts of his many worthy achievements in the lines of civic endeavour. Naturally this portrait and those records are our most precious possessions and our greatest heritages.

"The first Cecilius Jacob Van Nicht was by
all accounts a great scholar but not a practised
scribe. The second of the name was both. Hence
our great debt to him—a debt which I may say
is one in which this community itself shares."

"I'm sure of it," said Olcott.

"And now, sir, if you will be so good, kindly
step this way," said Mr. Van Nicht. "The
light, I fear, is rather indifferent. This house
has never been wired for electricity, nor was it
ever equipped with gas pipes. I prefer to use
lights more in keeping with its antiquity and
its general character."

His tone indicated that he did not in the
least hold with the vulgarised and common
utilities of the present. He led the way diagonally across the hall to a side door and ushered
Olcott into what evidently was the chief living
room of the house. It was a large, square room,
very badly lighted with candles. It was clut-
tered, as Olcott instantly perceived, with a
jumble of dingy-appearing antique furnishings,
and it contained two women who, at his appearance, rose from their seats upon either side
of the wide and empty fireplace. Simultaneously his nose informed him that this room was
heavy with a pent, dampish taint.

He decided that what it mainly needed was
air and sunshine, and plenty of both.

"My two sisters," introduced Mr. Van
Nicht. "Miss Rachael Van Nicht, Mr. Olcott.
Miss Harriet Van Nicht, Mr. Olcott."

Neither of the two ladies offered her hand to him. They bowed primly, and Olcott bowed back and, already feeling almost as uncomfortable as though he had invaded the privacy of a family group of resident shades in their resident vault, he sat down in a musty-smelling armchair near the elder sister.

Considered as such, the conversation which followed was not unqualifiedly a success. The brother bore the burden of it, which meant that at once it took on a stiff and an unnatural and an artificial colouring. It was dead talk, stuffed with big words, and strung with wires. There were semioccasional interpolations by Olcott, who continued to feel most decidedly out of place. Once in a while Miss Rachael Van Nicht slid a brief remark into the grooves which her brother channelled out. Since he was called upon to say so little, Olcott was the better off for an opportunity to study this lady as he sat there.

His first look at her had told him she was of the same warp and texture as her brother; somewhat skimpier in the pattern, but identical in the fabric. Olcott decided though that there was this difference: If the brother had stepped out of Dickens, the sister had escaped from between the hasped lids of an old daguerreotype frame. Her plain frock of some harsh, dead-coloured stuff—her best frock, his intuition told him—the big cameo pin at her throat, the homely arrangement of her grey hair, her

hands, wasted and withered-looking as they
lay on her lap, even her voice, which was lugubriously subdued and flat—all these things helped
out the illusion. Of the other sister, sitting
two-thirds of the way across the wide room
from him, he saw but little and he heard less.
The poor light, and the distance and the deep
chair in which she had sunk herself, combined
to blot her out as a personality and to efface
her from the picture. She scarcely uttered a
word.

As Olcott had expected beforehand, the talk
dealt, in the main, with the Van Nicht family,
which is another way of saying that it went
back of and behind, and far beyond, all that
might be current and timely and pertinent to
the hour. There was no substance to it, for it
dealt with what had no substance. As he
stayed on, making brave pretense of being interested, he was aware of an interrupting,
vaguely irritating sound at his rear and partly
to one side of him. Patently the sound was
coming from without. It was like a sustained
and steady scratching, and it had to do, he figured, with one of the window openings. He
took a glance over his shoulder, but he couldn't
make out the cause; the window was too heavily shrouded in faded, thick curtains of a sad,
dark-green aspect. The thing got on his nerves,
it persisted so. Finally he was moved to mention it.

"I beg your pardon," he said, taking advantage of a pause, "but isn't somebody or something fumbling at the window outside?"

"It is a bough of the family elm," explained Mr. Van Nicht. "One of the lower boughs has grown forward and downward, until it touches the side of the house. When stirred by the breeze it creates the sound which you hear."

Internally Olcott shivered. Now that the explanation had been vouchsafed the noise made him think of ghostly fingers tapping at the glass panes—as though the spirit of the tree craved admittance to the dismal circle of these human creatures who shared with it the tribal glory.

"Don't you find it very annoying?" he asked innocently. "I should think you would prune the limb back." He halted then, realising that his tongue had slipped. There was a little silence, which became edged and iced with a sudden hostility.

"No human hand has ever touched the tree to denude it of any part of its majestic beauty," stated Mr. Van Nicht with a frigid intonation. "Whilst any of this household survives to protect it, no human hand ever shall."

From the elder sister came a murmur of assent.

The conversation had sagged and languished before; after this it sank to a still lower level and gradually froze to death. After possibly ten minutes more of the longest and bleakest minutes he ever recalled having weathered,

Olcott, being mentally chilled through, got up and, making a show of expressing a counterfeit pleasure of having been accorded this opportunity of meeting those present, said really he must be going now.

In their places Miss Rachael Van Nicht and her brother rose, standing stiff as stalagmites, and he knew he was not forgiven. It was the younger sister who showed him out, preceding him silently, as he betook himself from the presence of the remaining two.

Close up, in the better light of the hall, Olcott for the first time perceived that Miss Harriet Van Nicht was not so very old. In fact, she was not old at all. He had assumed somehow that she must be sered and soured and elderly, or at least that she must be middle-aged. With this establishment he could not associate any guise of youth as belonging. But he perceived how wrong he had been. Miss Harriet Van Nicht most assuredly was not old. She could not be past thirty, perhaps she was not more than twenty-five or six. It was the plain and ugly gown she wore, a dun-coloured, sleazy, shabby gown, which had given her, when viewed from a distance, the aspect of age—that and the unbecoming way in which she wore her hair slicked back from her forehead and drawn up from round her ears. She had fine eyes, as now he saw, with a plaintive light in them, and finely arched brows and a delicate oval of a face; and she was small and dainty of figure. He could tell that, too, despite the fit of the ungraceful frock.

At the outer door, which she held ajar for his passage, she spoke, and instantly he was moved by a certain wistfulness in her tones.

"It was a pleasure to have you come to see us, Mr. Olcott," she said, and he thought she meant it too. "We see so few visitors, living here as we do. Sometimes I think it might be better for us if we kept more in touch with people who live in the outside world and know something of it."

"Thank you, Miss Van Nicht," said Olcott, warming. "I'm afraid, though, I made a rather unfortunate suggestion about the tree. Really, I'm very sorry."

Her face took on a gravity; almost a condemning expression came into it. And when she answered him it was in a different voice.

"A stranger could not understand how we regard the Van Nicht elm," she said. "No stranger could understand! Good night, Mr. Olcott."

At the last she had made him feel that he was a stranger. And she had not shaken hands with him either, nor had she asked him to call again.

He made his way out, through the black magic of the tree's midnight gloom, into the pure white chemistry of the moonlight; and having reached the open, he looked back. Except for that faint luminous blotch, like smeared phosphorus, showing through the blackness from beyond the giant tree, nothing testified that a habitation of living beings might be tucked away in that drear hiding place. He shrugged his shoulders as though to shake a load off them and, as he swung down the silvered street in the flawless night, his thoughts thawed out. He decided that assuredly two of the Van Nichts must go into the book which some day, when time served, he meant to write.

They belonged in a book—those two poor, pale, sapless creatures, enduring a grinding poverty for the sake of a vain idolatry; those joint inheritors of a worthless and burdensome fetish, deliberately preferring the shadow of a mouldy past for the substance of the present day. Why, the thing smacked of the Oriental. It wasn't fit and sane for white people—this Mongolian ancestor-worship which shut the door and drew the blind to every healthy and vigorous impulse and every beneficent impulse. Going along alone, Olcott worked himself into quite a brisk little fury of impatience and disgust.

He had it right—they belonged in a book, those two older Van Nichts, not in real life. And into a book they should go—into his book. But the younger girl, now. It was a pitiable life she must lead, hived up there in that musty old house under that terrific big tree with those two grim and touchy hermits. On her account he resented it. He tried to picture her in some more favourable setting. He succeeded fairly

well too. Possibly, though, that was because
Olcott had the gift of a brisk imagination. At
times, during the days which followed, the vision
of Harriet Van Nicht, translated out of her
present decayed environment, persisted in his
thoughts. He wondered why it did persist.

Nearly a month went by, during which he
saw no member of that weird household. One
day he encountered upon the street the brother
and went up to him and, rather against the
latter's inclination, engaged him in small talk.
It didn't take long to prove that Mr. Van
Nicht had very little small talk in stock; also
that his one-time air of distant and punctilious
regard for the newspaper man had entirely
vanished. Mr. Van Nicht was courteous
enough, with an aloof and stand-away cour-
teousness, but he was not cordial. Presently
Olcott found himself speaking, from a rather
defensive attitude, of his own ancestry. He
came of good New England stock—a circumstance which he rarely mentioned in company,
but which now, rather to his own surprise, he
found himself expounding at some length. Afterward he told himself that he had been merely casting about for a subject which might
prove congenial to Mr. Van Nicht and had, by
chance, hit on that one.

If such were the care, the expedient failed.
It did not in the least serve to establish them
upon a common footing. The old gentleman
listened, but he refused to warm up; and when

he bade Olcott good day and limped off, he left Olcott profoundly impressed with the conviction that Mr. Van Nicht did not propose to suffer any element of familiarity to enter into their acquaintanceship. Feeling abashed, as though he had been rebuked after some subtle fashion for presumption and forwardness, Olcott dropped into the handiest bar and had a drink all by himself—something he rarely did. But this time he felt that the social instinct of his system required a tonic and a bracer.

Within the next day or two chance gave him opportunity for still further insight into the estimation in which he was held by other members of the Van Nicht family. This happened shortly before the close of a cool and showery July afternoon. Leaving his desk, he took advantage of a lull in the rain to go for a solitary stroll before dinner. He was briskly traversing a side street, well out of the business district, when suddenly the downpour started afresh. He pulled up the collar of his light raincoat and turned back to hurry to the Hotel Brainard, where he lived. Going in the opposite direction a woman pedestrian, under an umbrella, met him; she was heading right into the slanting sheets of rain. In a sidelong glance he recognised the profile of the passer, and instantly he had faced about and was alongside of her, lifting his soaked hat.

"How d'you do, Miss Van Nicht?" he was saying. "I'm afraid you'll make poor headway against this rainstorm. Won't you let me see you safely home?"

It was the younger Miss Van Nicht. Her greeting of him and her smile made him feel that for the moment at least he would not be altogether an unwelcome companion. As he fell in beside her, catching step with her and taking the umbrella out of her hands, he noted with a small throb of pity that her cheap dark skirt was dripping and that the shoes she wore must be insufficient protection, with their thin soles and their worn uppers, against wet weather. He noted sundry other things about her: Seen by daylight she was pretty—undeniably pretty. The dampness had twisted little curls in her primly bestowed hair, and the exertion of her struggle against the storm had put a becoming flush in her cheeks.

"I was out on an errand for my sister," she said. "I thought I could get home between showers, but this one caught me. And my umbrella—I'm afraid it is leaky."

Undeniably it was. Already the palm of Olcott's hand was sopping where water, seeping through open seams along the rusted ribs, had run down the handle. Each new gust, drumming upon the decrepit cloth, threatened to make a total wreck of what was already but little better than the venerable ruin of an umbrella.

"You must permit me to see you home then," he said. He glanced up and down, hoping to see a cab or a taxi. But there was no hireable vehicle in sight and the street cars did not run through this street. "I'm afraid, though, that we'll have to go afoot."

"And I'm afraid that I am taking you out of your way," she said. "You were going in the opposite direction, weren't you, when you met me?"

"I wasn't going anywhere in particular," he lied gallantly; "personally I rather like to take a walk when it's raining."

For a bit after this neither of them spoke, for the wind all at once blew with nearly the intensity of a small hurricane, buffeting thick rain spray into their faces and spattering it up about their feet. She seemed so small—so defenceless almost, bending forward to brace herself against its rude impetuosity. He was mighty glad it was his hand which clasped her arm, guiding and helping her along; mighty glad it was he who held the leaky old umbrella in front of her and with it fended off some part of the rain from her. They had travelled a block or two so, in company, when the summer storm broke off even more abruptly than it had started. There was an especially violent spatter of especially large drops, and then the wind gave one farewell wrench at the umbrella and was gone, tearing on its way.

In another half minute the setting sun was doing its best to shine out through a welter of shredding black clouds. There were wide patches

of blue in the sky when they turned into Putnam Street and came within sight of the Van
Nicht elm, rising as a great, green balloon at
the head of it. By now they were chatting
upon the basis—almost—of a seasoned acquaintanceship. Olcott found himself talking
about his work. When a young man tells a
young woman about his work, and is himself
interested as he tells it, it is quite frequently a
sign that he is beginning to be interested in
something besides his work, whether he realises
it yet or not. And in Miss Van Nicht he was
pleased to discern what he took to be a sympathetic understanding, as well as a happy apt-
ness and alertness in the framing of her replies.
It hardly seemed possible that this was the
second time they had exchanged words. Rather
it was as though they had known each other
for a considerable period; so he told himself.

But as, side by side, they turned in at the
rickety gate of the ancestral dooryard and
came under the shadow of the ancestral tree,
her manner, her attitude, her voice, all about
her seemed to undergo a change. Her pace
quickened for these last few steps, and she cast
a furtive, almost an apprehensive glance toward the hooded windows of the house.

"I'm afraid I am late—my sister and my
brother will be worrying about me," she said a
little nervously. "And I am sorry to have put
you to all this trouble on my account."

"Trouble, Miss Van Nicht? Why, it was——"

"I shan't ask you in," she said, breaking in on him. "I know you will want to be getting back to the hotel and putting on dry clothes. Good-by, Mr. Olcott, and thank you very much."

And with that she had left him, and she was hurrying up the porch steps, and she was gone, without a backward look to where he stood, puzzled and decidedly taken aback, in the middle of the seamed flags of the walk.

He was nearly at the gate when he discovered that he had failed to return her umbrella to her; so he went back and knocked at the door. It was the elder sister who answered. She opened the door a scant foot.

"How do you do, sir?" she said austerely.

"I forgot to give your sister her umbrella," explained Olcott.

"So I perceive," she replied, speaking through the slit with a kind of sharp impatience, and she took it from him. "Thank you! We are most grateful to you for your thoughtfulness."

She waited then, as if for him to speak, providing he had anything to say—her posture and her expression meanwhile most forcibly interpreting the attitude in which he must understand that he stood here. It was plain enough to be sensed. She resented—they all resented—his reappearance in any rôle at the threshold of their home. She was profoundly out of tem-

per with him and all that might pertain and
appertain to him. So naturally there was nothing for him to say except "Good evening," and
he said it.

"Good evening," she said, and as he bowed
and backed away she closed the door.

Outside the fence he halted and looked about
him, then he looked back over the gapped and
broken palings. Everywhere else the little
world of Putnam Street had a washed, cleansed
aspect; everywhere else nearly the sun slid its
flattened rays along the refreshed and mois-
tened sod and touched the wayside weeds with
pure gold; but none of its beams slanted over
the side hill and found a way beneath the in-
terlaced, widespread bulk of the family tree.
He saw how forlornly the lower boughs, under
their load of rain water, drooped almost to the
earth, and how the naked soil round about the
vast trunk of it was guttered with muddy, yellow furrows where little torrents had coursed
down the slope, and how poisonously vivid was
the mould upon the trunk. The triangular
scar in its lower bark showed as a livid greenish patch. Still farther back in the shadow
the outlines of the old grey house half emerged,
revealing dimly a space of streaked walls and
the sodden, warped shingles upon one outjut-
ting gable of the peaked roof.

"It's not an honest elm," thought Olcott to
himself in a little impotent rage. "It's a
cursed devil tree, a upas tree, overshadowing

and blighting everything pleasant and wholesome that might grow near it. Bats and owls
and snails belong back there—not human beings. There ought to be a vigilance committee
formed to chop it down and blast its roots out
of the ground with dynamite. Oh, damn!"

In his pocket he had a letter from the pre-
siding deity of the organisation that owned the
string of papers of which the paper he edited
was a part. In that letter he was invited to
consider the proposition of surrendering his
present berth with the Schuylerville *News-
Ledger* and going off to Europe, as special war
correspondent for the syndicate. He had been
considering the project for two days now. All
of a sudden he made up his mind to accept.
While the heat of his petulance and disappointment was still upon him, he went that same
evening and wired his acceptance to headquarters. Two days later, with his credentials in
his pocket and a weight of sullen resentment
against certain animate and inanimate objects
in his heart, he was aboard a train out of Schuylerville, bound for New York, and thereafter,
by steamer, for foreign parts.

He was away, concerned with trenches, gas
bombs, field hospitals and the quotable opin-
ions of sundry high and mighty men of war-
craft and statecraft, for upwards of a year. It
was a most remarkably busy year, and the job
in hand claimed jealous sovereignty of his eyes,
his legs and his brain, while it lasted.

He came back, having delivered the goods to the satisfaction of his employers, to find himself promoted to a general supervision of the editorial direction of the papers in his syndicate, with a thumping good salary and a roving commission. He willed it that the first week of his incumbency in his new duties should carry him to Schuylerville. In his old office, which looked much the same as it had looked when he occupied it, he found young Morgan, his former assistant, also looking much the same, barring that now Morgan was in full charge and giving orders instead of taking them. Authority nearly always works a change in a man; it had in this case.

"Say, Olcott," said Morgan after the talk between them had ebbed and flowed along a little while, "you remember that old geezer, Van Nicht, don't you? You know, the old boy who wrote the long piece about his family, and you ran it?"

"Certainly I do," said Olcott. "Why—what of him?"

Instead of answering him directly, Morgan put another question:

"And of course you remember the old Van Nicht house, under that big, whopping elm tree, out at the end of Putnam Street, where he used to live with those two freakish sisters of his?"

"Where he used to live? Doesn't he—don't they—live there now?"

"Nope—tree's gone and so is the house."

"Gone? Gone where?"

"Gone out of existence—vamoosed. Here's what happened, and it's a peach of a tale too: One night about six months ago there came up a hard thunderstorm—lots of lightning and gobs of thunder, not to mention rain and wind a plenty. In the midst of it a bolt hit the Van Nicht elm—ker-flewie—and just naturally tore it into flinders. When I saw it myself the next day it was converted from a landmark into the biggest whisk broom in the world. The neighbours were saying that it rained splinters round there for ten minutes after the bolt struck. I guess they didn't exaggerate much at that, because——"

"Was the house struck too? Was anybody hurt?" Olcott cut in on him.

"No, the house escaped somehow—had a few shingles ripped off the roof, and some of its windows smashed in by flying scraps; that was all. And nobody about the place suffered anything worse than a stunning. But the fright killed the older sister—Miss Rachael. Anyhow, that's what the doctors think. She didn't have a mark on her, but she died in about an hour, without ever speaking. I guess it was just as well, too, that she did. If she had survived the first shock I judge the second one would just about have finished her."

"The second shock? You don't mean the lightning?"

"No, no!" Morgan hastened to explain.

"Lightning never plays a return date—never has need to, I take it. I mean the shock of what happened after daylight next morning.

"That was the queerest part of the whole thing—that was what made a really big story out of it. We ran two columns about it ourselves, and the A. P. carried it for more than a column.

"After the storm had died down and it got light enough to see, some of the neighbours were prowling round the place sizing up the damage. Right in the heart of the stump of the elm, which was split wide open—the stump, I mean—they found a funny-looking old copper box buried in what must have been a rotted-out place at one time, maybe ninety or a hundred years ago. But the hollow had grown up, and nobody ever had suspected that the tree wasn't solid as iron all the way through, until the lightning came along and just naturally reached a fiery finger down through all that hardwood and probed the old box out of its cache and, without so much as melting a hinge on it, heaved it up into sight, where the first fellow that happened along afterward would be sure to see it. Well, right off they thought of buried treasure, but being honest they called old Van Nicht out of the house, and in his presence they opened her up—the box I mean. —and then, lo and behold, they found out that all these years this town had been worshipping a false god!

"Yes, sir, the great and only original Cecilius Jacob Van Nicht was a rank fake. He
was as bogus as a lead nickel. There were
papers in the box to prove what nobody, and
least of all his own flesh and blood, ever suspected before. He wasn't a hero of the Revolution. He wasn't a colonel under George
Washington. He wasn't of Holland-Dutch
stock. His name wasn't even Van Nicht. His
real name was Jake Nix—that's what it was,
Nix—and he was just a plain, everyday Hes-
sian soldier—a mercenary bought up, along
with the other Hessians, and sent over here by
King George to fight against the cause of lib-
erty, instead of for it.

"As near as we can figure it out, he changed
his name after the war ended, before he moved
here to live, and then after he died—or anyhow when he was an old man—his son, the
second Cecilius Jacob, concocted the fairy tale
about his father's distinguished services and
all the rest of it. The son was the one, it
seems, who capitalised the false reputation of
the old man. He lived on it, and all the Van
Nichts who came after him lived on it too—
only they were innocent of practising any de-
ception on the community at large, and the
second Van Nicht wasn't. It certainly put the
laugh on this town, not to mention the local
aristocracy, and the D. A. R.'s and the Colonial
Dames and the rest of the blue bloods generally, when the news spread that morning.

"Oh, there couldn't be any doubt about it! The proofs were all right there and dozens of reliable witnesses saw them—letters and papers and the record of old Nix's services in the British army. In fact there was only one phase of the affair that has remained unexplained and a mystery. I mean the presence of the papers in the tree. Nobody can figure out why the son didn't destroy them, when he was creating such a swell fiction character out of his revered parent. One theory is that he didn't know of their existence at all—that the old man, for reasons best known to himself, hid them there in that copper box and that then the tree healed up over the hole and sealed the box in, with nobody but him any the wiser, and nobody ever suspecting anything out of the way, but just taking everything for granted. Why, it was exactly as if the old Nix had come out of the grave after lying there for a century or more, to produce the truth and shame his own offspring, and incidentally scare one of his descendants plumb to death."

"What a tragedy!" said Olcott. But his main thought when he said it was not for the dead sister but for the living.

"You said it," affirmed Morgan. "That's exactly what it was—a tragedy, with a good deal of serio-comedy relief to it. Only there wasn't anything very comical about the figure the old man Van Nicht cut when he came walking into this office here about half past ten o'clock that day, with a ragged piece of crêpe tied round his old high hat. Olcott, you never in your life saw a man as badly broken up as he was. All his vanity, all his bumptiousness was gone—he was just a poor, old, shabby, broken-spirited man. I'd already gotten a tip on the story and I'd sent one of my boys out to find him and get his tale, but it seemed he'd told the reporter he preferred to make a personal statement for publication. And so here he was with his statement all carefully written out and he asked me to print it, insisting that it ought to be given as wide circulation as possible. I'll dig it up for you out of the files in a minute and let you see it.

"Yes, sir, he'd sat down alongside his sister's dead body and written it. He called it A Confession and an Apology, and I ran it that way, just as he'd written it. It wasn't very long, but it was mighty pitiful, when you took everything into consideration. He begged the pardon of the public for unwittingly practicing a deceit upon it all through his life—for living a lie, was the way he phrased it—and he signed it 'Jacob Nix, heretofore erroneously known as Cecilius Jacob Van Nicht, 4th.' That signature was what especially got me when I read it—it made me feel that the old boy was literally stripping his soul naked before the ridicule of this town and the ridicule of the whole country. A pretty manly, straightforward thing, I called it, and I liked him better for

having done it than I ever had liked him before.

"Well, I told him I would run the card for
him and I did run it, and likewise I toned down
the story we carried about the exposure too.
I'm fairly well calloused, I guess, but I didn't
want to bruise the old man and his sister any
more than I could help doing. But, of course,
I didn't speak to him about that part of it. I
did try, in a clumsy sort of way, to express my
sympathy for him. I guess I made a fairly sad
hash of it, though. There didn't seem to be
any words to fit the situation. Or, if there
were, I couldn't think of them for the moment.
I remember I mumbled something about let-
ting bygones be bygones and not taking it too
much to heart and all that sort of thing.

"He thanked me, and then, as he started to
go, he stopped and asked me whether by any
chance I knew of any opening—any possible
job for a person of his age and limitations. I
remember his words: 'It is high time that I
was casting about to find honourable employ-
ment, no matter how humble. I have been
trading with a spurious currency for too long.
I have spent my life in the imposition of a
monumental deceit upon this long - suffering
community. I intend now, sir, to go to work
to earn a living with my own hands and upon
my own merits. I wish to atone for the rôle
I have played.'

"It may have been imagination, but I

thought there was a kind of faint hopeful
gleam in his eye as he looked at me and said
this; and he seemed to flinch a little bit when
I broke the news to him that we didn't have
any vacancies on the staff at present. I sort
of gathered that he rather fancied he had literary gifts. Literary gifts? Can't you just see
that poor, forlorn old scout piking round so-
liciting want ads at twenty cents a line or trying to cover petty assignments on the news
end? I told him, though, I'd be on the lookout for something for him, and he thanked me
mighty ceremoniously and limped out, leaving
me all choked up. Two days later, after the
funeral, he telephoned in to ask me' not to
trouble myself on his account, because he had
already established a connection with another
concern which he hoped would turn out to be
mutually advantageous and personally lucrative; or words to that effect.

"So I did a little private investigating that
evening and I found out where the old chap
had connected. You see I was interested. A
live wire named Garrison, who owned the state
rights for selling the World's Great Classics of
Prose and Poetry on subscriptions, had landed
here about a week before. You know the kind
of truck this fellow Garrison was peddling?
Forty large, hard, heavy volumes, five dollars
down and a dollar a month as long as you live;
no blacksmith's fireside complete without the
full set; should be in every library; so much

for the full calf bindings; so much for the half leather; give your little ones a chance to acquire an education at a trifling cost; come early and avoid the rush of those seeking to take advantage of this unparalleled opportunity; price positively due to advance at the end of a limited period; see also our great clubbing offer in conjunction with Bunkem's Illustrated Magazine—all that sort of guff.

"Well, Garrison had opened up headquarters here. He'd brought some of his agents with him—experts at conning the simple peasantry and the sturdy yeomanry into signing on the dotted line A and paying down the first installment as a binder; but he needed some home talent to fill out his crew, and he advertised with us for volunteers. Old Van Nicht —Nix, I mean—had heard about it, and he had applied for a job as canvasser, and Garrison had taken him on, not on salary, of course, but agreeing to pay him a commission on all his sales. That was what I found out that night."

Before Olcott's eyes rose a vision of a dried-up, bleak-eyed old man limping from doorstep to doorstep, enduring the rebuffs of fretful housewives and the insolence of annoyed householders—a failure, and a hopeless, predestined failure at that.

"Too bad, wasn't it?" he said.

"What's too bad?" asked Morgan.

"About that poor old man turning book

agent at his age, with his lack of experience with the ways of the world."

"Save your pity for somebody that needs it," said Morgan, grinning. "That old boy doesn't. Why, Olcott, he was a hit from the first minute. This fellow Garrison was telling me about him only last week. All that stately dignity, all that Sir Walter Raleigh courtesy stuff, all that faculty for using the biggest possible words in stock, was worth money to the old chap when he put it to use. It impressed the simple-minded rustic and the merry villager. It got him a hearing where one of these gabby young canvassers with a striped vest and a line of patter memorised out of a book would be apt to fail. Why, he's the sensation of the book-agent game in these parts. They sick him on to all the difficult prospects out in the country, and he makes good nine times out of ten. He's got four counties in his territory, with all expenses paid, and last month his commissions—so Garrison told me—amounted to a hundred and forty dollars, and this month he's liable to do even better. What's more, according to Garrison, the old scout likes the work and isn't ashamed of it. So what do you know about that?"

As Morgan paused, Olcott asked the question which from the first of this recital had been shaping itself in the back part of his head:

"The other sister—what became of her?" He tried to put a casual tone into his inquiry.

"You mean Miss Harriet? Well, say, in her case the transformation was almost as great as it was in her brother's. She came right out of her shell, too—in fact, she seemed downright glad of a chance to come out of it and quit being a recluse. She let it be noised about that she was in the market for any work that she could do, and a lot of people who felt sorry for her, including Mayor McGlynn, who's a pretty good chap, interested themselves in her behalf. Right off, the school board appointed her a substitute teacher in one of the lower grammar grades at the Hawthorne School, out here on West Frobisher Street. She didn't lose any time in delivering the goods either. Say, there must have been mighty good blood in that family, once it got a real chance to circulate. The kiddies in her classes all liked her from the start, and the other teachers and the principal liked her, too, and when the fall term begins in October she goes on as a regular.

"On top of that, when she'd got a little colour in her cheeks and had frizzed her hair out round her face, and when she'd used up her first month's pay in buying herself some good black clothes, it dawned on the town all of a sudden that she was a mighty good-looking, bright, sweet little woman instead of a dowdy, sour old maid. They say she never had a sweetheart before in her life—that no man ever had looked at her the second time; at least that's the current gossip. Be that as it may, she can't complain on that score any more, even if she is still in mourning for her sister."

"How do you know all this?" demanded Olcott suspiciously. "Are you paying her attentions yourself?"

"Who, me? Lord, man, no! I'm merely an innocent bystander. You see, we live at the same boarding house, take our meals at the same table in fact, and I get a chance to see what's going on. She came there to board—it's Mrs. Gale's house—as soon as she moved out of the historic but mildewed homestead, which was about a month after the night of the storm. The New Diamond Auto Company—that's a concern formed since you left—bought the property and tore down the old house, after blasting the stump of the family tree out of the ground with giant powder; they're putting up their assembling plant on the site. After the mortgage was satisfied and the back taxes had been paid up, there was mighty little left for the two heirs; but about that time Miss Harriet got her job of teaching and she came to Mrs. Gale's to live, and that's where I first met her. Two or three spry young fellows round town are calling on her in the evenings—nearly every night there's some fellow in the parlour, all spruced up and highly perfumed, waiting to see her—not to mention one or two of the unmarried men boarders."

"Morgan," said Olcott briskly, "do me a

favour!   Take me along with you to dinner to-night at your boarding place, will you?"

"Tired of hotels, eh?" asked Morgan.   "Well, Mrs. Gale has good home cooking and I'd be glad to have you come."

"That's it," said Olcott; "I'm tired of hotel life."

"You're on," said Morgan.

"Yes," said Olcott, "I am—but you're not on—at least not yet." But Morgan didn't hear that, because Olcott said it to himself.

CHAPTER VII

HARK! FROM THE TOMBS

FROM all the windows of Coloured Odd
Fellows' Hall, on the upper floor of the
two-story building at the corner of Oak
and Tennessee Streets, streamed Jacob's
ladders of radiance, which slanted outward and
downward into the wet night. Along with
these crossbarred shafts of lights, sounds as of
singing and jubilation percolated through the
blurry panes. It was not yet eleven o'clock,
the date being December thirty-first; but the
New Year's watch service, held under the auspices of Castle Camp, Number 1008, Afro-
American Order of Supreme Kings of the Universe, had been going on quite some time and
was going stronger every minute.

Odd Fellows' Hall had been especially engaged and partially decorated for this occasion.
Already it was nearly filled; but between now
and midnight it would be fuller, and at a still
later time would doubtlessly attain the super-
latively impossible by being fuller than fullest.

From all directions, out of the darkness, came belated members of the officiating fraternity, protecting their regalias under umbrellas, and accompanied by wives and families if married, or by lady and other friends if otherwise. With his sword clanking impressively at his flank and his beplumed helmet nodding grandly as he walked, each Supreme King of the Universe bore himself with an austere and solemn mien, as befitting the rôle he played—of host to the multitude—and the uniform that adorned his form.

Later, after the young year had appropriately been ushered in, when the refreshments were being served, he might unbend somewhat. But not now. Now every Supreme King was what he was, wearing his dignity as a becoming and suitable garment. This attitude of the affiliated brethren affected by contagion those who came with them as their guests. There was a stateliness and a formality in the greetings which passed between this one and that one as the groups converged into the doorway, set in the middle front of the building, and by pairs and by squads ascended the stairs.

"Good evenin', Sist' Fontleroy. I trusts things is goin' toler'ble well wid you, ma'am?"

"Satisfactory, Br'er Grider—thank de good Lawd! How's all at yore own place of residence?"

"Git th'ough de C'ris'mus all right, Mizz Hillman?"

"Yas, suh; 'bout de same ez whut I always does, Mist' Duiguid."

"Well, ole yeah's purty nigh gone frum us, Elder; ain't it de truth?"

"Most doubtless is. An' now yere come 'nother! We don't git no younger, sister, does we?"

"Dat we don't, sholy!"

The ceremonial reserve of the moment would make the jollifying all the sweeter after the clocks struck and the whistles began to blow.

There was one late arrival, though, who came along alone, wearing a downcast countenance and an air of abstraction, and speaking to none who encountered him on the way or at the portal. This one was Jeff Poindexter; but a vastly different Jeff from the customary Jeff. Usually he moved with a jaunty gait, his elbows out and his head canted back; and on the slightest provocation his feet cut scallops and double-shuffles and pigeonwings against the earth. Now his heels scraped and his toes dragged; and the gladsome raiment that covered his person gave him no joy, but only an added sense of resentment against the prevalent scheme of mundane existence.

An unseen weight bowed his shoulders down, and beneath the wide lapels of an almost white waistcoat his heart was like unto a chunk of tombstone in his bosom. For the current light of his eyes, Miss Ophelia Stubblefield, had accepted the company of a new and most formidable rival for this festive occasion. Wherefore an embodiment of sorrow walked hand in hand with Jeff.

After this blow descended all the taste of delectable anticipation in his mouth had turned to gall and to wormwood. Of what use now the costume he had been at such pains to accumulate from kindly white gentlemen, for whom Jeff in spare moments did odd jobs of valeting—the long, shiny frock coat here; the only slightly spotted grey-blue trousers there; the almost clean brown derby hat in another quarter; the winged collar and the puff necktie in yet a fourth? Of what value to him would be the looks of envy and admiration sure to be bestowed upon the pair of new, shiny and excessively painful patent-leather shoes, specially acquired and specially treasured for this event?

He had bought those shoes, with an utter disregard for expense, before he dreamed that another would bring Ophelia to the watch party. With her at his side, his soul would have risen exultant and triumphant above the discomfort of cramped-up toes and pinched-in heels. Now, at each dragging step, he was aware that his feet hurt him. Indeed, for Jeff there was at that moment no balm to be found throughout all Gilead, and in his ointment dead flies abounded thickly.

It added to his unhappiness that the lady might and doubtlessly would rest under a misapprehension regarding his failure to invite her to share with him the pleasures of the night. He had not asked her to be his company; had not even broached the subject to her. For this seeming neglect there had been a good and sufficient reason—one hundred and ninety pounds of a chocolate-coloured reason. Seven days before, on Christmas Eve, Jeff had been currying Mittie May, the white mare of Judge Priest, in the stable back of the Priest place, when he heard somebody whistle in the alley behind the stable and then heard his name called. He had stepped outside to find one Smooth Crumbaugh leaning upon the alley gate.

"Hello, Smoothy!" Jeff had hailed with a smart and prompt cordiality.

It was not that he felt any deep warmth of feeling for Smooth, but that it was prudent to counterfeit the same. All in Smooth's circle deported themselves toward Smooth with a profound regard and, if Smooth seemed out of sorts, displayed almost an affection for him, whether they felt it or not. 'Twere safer thus.

With characteristic brusqueness, Smooth entirely disregarded the greeting.

"Come yere to me, little nigger!" he said out of one corner of his lips, at the same time fixing a lowering stare upon Jeff. Then, as Jeff still stood, filled with sudden misgivings: "Come yere quick w'en I speaks! Want me to come on in dat yard after you?"

Jeff was conscious of no act of wrongdoing

toward Smooth Crumbaugh. With Jeff, discretion was not only the greater part of fighting valour but practically was all of it. Nevertheless, he was glad, as he obeyed the summons and, with a placating smile fixed upon his face, drew nearer the paling, that he stood on the sanctuary ground of a circuit judge's premises, and that a fence intervened between him and his truculent caller.

"Comin' right along," he said with an affected gaiety.

Just the same, he didn't go quite up to the gate. He made his stand three or four feet inside of it, ready to jump backward or sidewise should the necessity arise.

"I'se feared I didn't heah you call de fus time," stated Jeff ingratiatingly. "I wuzn't studyin' about nobody wantin' me—been wipin' off our ole mare. 'Sides, I thought you wuz down in Alabam', workin' on de ole P. and A. Road."

"Num'mine dat!" said Smooth. "Jes' lis'en to whut I got to say."

The hostile glare of his eye bored straight into Jeff, making him chilly in his most important organs. Smooth was part basilisk, but mainly hyena, with a touch of the man-eating tiger in his composition. "Little nigger," he continued grimly, "I come th'ough dis lane on puppus' to tell you somethin' fur de good of yore health."

"I's lis'enin'," said Jeff, most politely.

"Heed me clost," bade Smooth; "heed me clost, an' mebbe you mout live longer. Who wuz you at de Fust Ward Cullid Baptis' Church wid last Sunday night? Dat's de fust question."

"Who—me?"

"Yas; you!"

"Why, lemme see, now," said Jeff, dissembling. "Seem lak, ez well ez I reckerleck, I set in de same pew wid quite a number of folkses durin' de service."

"I ain't axin' you who you set wid. I's axin' you who you went wid?"

"Oh!" said Jeff, as though enlightened as to the real object of the inquiry, and still sparring for time. "You means who did I go dere wid, Smoothy? Well——"

"Wuz it dat Stubblefield gal, or wuzn't it? Answer me, yas or no!"

The tone of the questioner became more ominous, more threatening, with each passing moment.

"Yas—yas, Smoothy." He giggled uneasily. "Uh-huh! Dat's who 'twuz."

"Well, see dat it don't happen ag'in."

"Huh?"

"You heared whut I said!"

"But I—— But she——"

"See dat it don't happen nary time ag'in."

"But—but——"

"Say, whut you mean, interrup'in' me whilst I's speakin' wid you fur yore own good? Shut

up dat trap-face of your'n an' lis'en to me, whut
I'm sayin': Frum dis hour on, you stay plum'
away frum dat gal. Understan'?"

"Honest, Smoothy, I didn't know you wuz
cravin' to be prankin' round wid Ophelia!"

Jeff spoke with sincerity, from the heart out.
In truth, he hadn't known, else his sleep of
nights might have been less sound.

"Dat bein' de case, you better keep yore
yeahs open to heah de news, else you won't
have no yeahs. Git me mad an' I's liable to
snatch 'em right offen de sides of your haid an'
feed 'em to you. I's tuck a lay-off fur de
C'ris'mus. An' endurin' de week I spects to
spend de mos' part of my time enjoyin' dat
gal's society. I aims to be wid her to-night
an' to-morrow night an' de nex' night, an' ever'
other night twell I goes back down de road. I
aims to tek her to de C'ris'mus tree doin's at
de church on Friday night, an' to de festibul
at de church on Sad'day night, an' to de watch
party up at de Odd Fellers' Hall on New Yeah's
Eve. Is dat clear to you?"

"Suttinly is, seein' ez it's you," assented Jeff,
trying to hide his disappointment under a smile.
"Course, Smoothy, ef you craves a young lady's
company fur a week or so, I don't know nobody dat's mo' entitled to it'n whut you is.
Jes' a word frum you is plenty fur me. You
done told me how you feels; dat's ample."

"No, 'tain't!" growled Smooth. "I got
somethin' mo' to tell you. Frum now on, all

de time I's in dis town I don't want to heah of
you speakin' wid dat gal, or telephonin' to her,
or writin' her ary note, or sendin' ary message
to her house. Ef you do I's gwine find out
'bout it; an' den I's gwine lay fur you an' strip
a whole lot of dark meat offen you wid a razor
or somethin'. I won't leave nothin' of you but
jes' a framework. Now den, it's up to you!
Does you want to go round fur de rest of yore
days lookin' lak a scaffoldin', or doesn't you?"

"Smoothy," protested Jeff, "I ain't got no
quarrel wid you. I ain't aimin' to git in no
rookus wid nobody a-tall—let alone 'tis you.
But s'posen'"—he added this desperately—
"s'posen' now I should happen to meet up wid
her on de street. Fur politeness' sake I's
natchelly 'bleeged to speak wid her, ain't I—
even ef 'tain't nothin' more'n jes' passin' de
time of day?"

"Is dat so?" said Smooth in mock surprise. "Well, suit yo'se'f; suit yo'se'f. Only,
de words you speaks wid her better be yore
farewell message to de world. Ef anythin ' happen to you now, sech ez a fun'el, hit's yore own
fault—you done had yore warnin' frum headquarters. I ain't got no mo' time to be wastin'
on a puny little scrap of nigger sech ez you is.
I's on my way now. But jes' remember whut
I been tellin' you an' govern yo'se'f 'cordin'ly.''

And with that the bully turned away, leaving poor Jeff to most discomforting reflections
amid the ruins of his suddenly blasted romance.

The full scope of his rival's design stood so clearly revealed that it left to its victim no loophole of escape whatsoever. Not only was he to be debarred, by the instinct of self-preservation, from seeking the presence of Ophelia during the most joyous and the most socially crowded week of the entire year; not only were all his pleasant dreams dashed and smashed, but, furthermore, he might not even make excuses to her for what would appear in her eyes as an abrupt and unreasonable cessation of sentimental interest on his part, save and except it be done at dire peril to his corporeal well-being and his physical intactness.

Above all things, Jeff Poindexter coveted to stay in one piece. And Smooth Crumbaugh was one who nearly always kept his word—especially when that word involved threats against any who stood between him and his personal ambitions.

Jeff, watching the broad retreating back of Smooth, as Smooth swaggered out of the alley, fetched little moans of acute despair. To him remained but one poor morsel of consolation—no outsider had been a witness to his interview with the bad man. Unless the bad man bragged round, none need know how abject had been Jeff's capitulation.

Solitary, melancholy, a prey to conflicting emotions, Jeff Poindexter climbed the stairs leading up to Odd Fellows' Hall, at the heels of

a family group of celebrants. Until the last
minute he hadn't meant to come; but something drew him hither, even as the moth to the
flame is drawn. He paid his fifty cents to the
Most High Grand Outer Guardian, who was
stationed at the door in the capacity of ticket
taker and cash collector, and entered in, to
find sitting-down space pretty much all occupied and standing room rapidly being pre-
empted—especially round the walls and at the
back of the long assembly room.

Outside, the air was muggy with the cling-
ing dampness of a rainy, mild winter's night; a
weak foretaste of the heightened mugginess
within. Nearly always, in our part of the
South, the first real cold snap came with the
New Year; but, as yet, there were no signs of
its approach. Inside, thanks to a big pot-
bellied stove, choked with hot coals, and to the
added circumstance of all the windows being
closed, the temperature was somewhere up
round eighty; which was as it should be. When
the coloured race sets itself to enjoy itself, it
desires warmth, and plenty of it.

This crowd was hot and therefore happy.
Trickles of perspiration, coursing downward,
streaked the rice powder upon the cheeks of
many mezzotint damosels, and made to glisten
the faces of the chrome-shaded gallants who
squired them.

On the platform at the far end of the hall,
beneath crossed flags, sat the principal offi-

ciating dignitaries, three in number—first, the Imperial Grand Potentate of the lodge, holder of an office corresponding to president elsewhere, but invested with rather more grandeur than commonly appertains to a presidency; then the second in command, known formally as First Vice Imperial Grand Potentate; and thirdly, the Reverend Potiphar Grasty, pastor of First Ward Church.

Facing these three and, in turn, faced by them, sat on the front seats the Supreme Kings, temporarily detached from their kinspeople and well-wishers, who, with the populace generally, filled the serried rows of chairs and benches behind the uniformed ranks.

At the rear, near the main entrance, in a cleared space, stood two long trestles bearing the refreshments, of which, at a suitable moment, all and sundry would be invited to partake. The feast plainly would be a rich and abundant one, including, as it did, such items as cream puffs, ham sandwiches, Frankfurters, bananas, and soda pop of the three more popular varieties—lemon, sarsaparilla and strawberry—in seemingly unlimited quantities.

Sister Eldora Menifee, by title Queen Bee of the Ladies' Royal Auxiliary of the Supreme Kings, had charge of the collation, its arrangement and its decorations. She hovered about her handiwork, a mighty, black mountain, vigilant to frown away any who might undertake any clandestine poaching. The display of nap-

ery and table linen was most ample; and why
not? Didn't Sister Menifee do the washing for
the biggest white folks' boarding house in
town?

With an eye filmed and morose, Jeff Poindexter, pausing at the rear, comprehended this
festive scene. Then, as his gaze ran to and fro,
he saw that which he dreaded to see and yet
sought to behold. He saw Smooth Crumbaugh sitting with Ophelia on the right side of
the hall, well up toward the front. Their backs
were to him; their heads inclined sidewise toward a common centre.

The loose fold of flesh in Smooth's bull neck
pouched down over his glistening collar as he
slanted one shoulder to whisper sweet somethings in Ophelia's ear. They must have been
sweet somethings, and witty withal; for at
once the lady gave vent to a clear soprano gig-
gle. Her mirthful outburst rose above the babble of voices and, floating backward, pierced
Jeff Poindexter's bosom as with darts and jave-
lins; and jealousy, meantime, like the Spartan
boy's fox, gnawed at his inwards.

The sight and the sound, taken together,
made Jeff Poindexter desperate almost to the
point of outright recklessness—almost, but not
quite. He noted the fortuitous circumstance
of a vacant chair directly behind the pair he
watched. Surely now Smooth Crumbaugh
would start no disturbance here. Surely—so
Jeff reasoned it—time, place, occasion and the

present company, all would operate and co-operate to curb Smooth's chronic belligerency.

If only for a fleeting period, Jeff longed to venture within conversational distance of Ophelia; to bask for a spell in one of her brilliant smiles; to prove to her by covert looks, if not by whispered words, that there were no ill feelings; to give her an opportunity for visual appreciation of his housings; and, most of all, subtly to convey the suggestion that it was bodily indisposition which had caused him to absent himself from her presence throughout the Christmas. Under cover of his hand he rehearsed a deep cough, and simultaneously began to inch his way along an aisle toward the coveted seat in the adjacent rear of the couple.

The programme proper was well under way; it had begun auspiciously and it promised much. There had been a prayer and a welcoming address by the Imperial Grand Potentate, and now there was singing. Starting shortly, the annual memorial service for any member or members who had departed this life during the preceding twelve months would follow; this lasting until five minutes before midnight. Then all the lights would be turned out, and the gathering would sit in darkness, singing some lugubriously appropriate song as a vocal valedictory for the passing year until the first stroke of midnight, when the lights would flash on again. Thereafter would follow the strictly social phases of the watch party.

Almost until the last it had seemed that the memorial exercises would have to be foregone for lack of material to work on. But at the eleventh hour, as it were, Red Hoss Shackleford, who always heretofore had been a disappointment to everybody, had greatly obliged, and, at the same time, disproved the oft-repeated assertion that one born for hanging can never be drowned, by falling overboard off the tugboat *Giles C. Jordan*.

This tragedy had occurred at a late hour of the evening of December twenty-sixth, when the *Giles C. Jordan* was forty miles up Tennessee River on a crosstie-towing venture, and while Red Hoss Shackleford, who had shipped aboard her as cook and general roustabout, was yet overcome by the potent elements of his Christmas celebration, self-administered internally in liquid form.

At least such were the tidings borne by the captain and surviving crew upon their return to port on the twenty-ninth instant. Whereupon the Supreme Kings had seized upon the opportunity thus vouchsafed as a free gift of a frequently inscrutable Providence.

To be sure, the late Shackleford was not exactly a member in good standing. Two years before, in a fine fervour of enthusiasm induced by the splendour of the uniforms worn at the funeral turnout of a departed brother, Red Hoss had joined the lodge. He had fallen behind in his dues, and, to all intents and purposes, had been expunged from the rolls. Red Hoss generally was in arrears, anyhow, except for those obligations he owed the county chain gang. Those were debts he always paid—if they could catch him.

None the less, certain points were waived by acclamation, following the receipt of the news of his taking-off. It was agreed that one Red Hoss Shackleford dead at such time was worth ten Red Hoss Shacklefords living. His memory was to be perpetuated, thereby lending to the programme precisely that touch of seriousness which was needed to round it out and make of it a thing complete and adequate.

To add to the effect, his sole surviving relative, a half sister, by name Sister Rosalie Shackleford, had a prominent place at the front, flanking the low platform. It was conceivable, everything considered, that her loss had been no great one; nevertheless, with a fine theatric instinct for the unities and the verities, she now deported herself as one utterly devastated by a grief almost too great to be borne. There was no mistake about it—when this sister mourned, she mourned!

With her prevalent dark complexion enhanced by enshrouding ells of black crape, she half lay, half sat in a slumped attitude betokening utter and complete despondency, and at timely intervals uttered low moans and sobs. Two friends attended her in a ministering capacity. One fanned her assiduously. The other, who was of ample girth, provided commodious and billowy accommodations for her supine form when she slipped back after swooning dead away. It was expected of Sister Rosalie that she should faint occasionally and be revived; and so she did.

The ritualistic features of the night had been disposed of and the singing was in full swing as Jeff Poindexter edged along, pussyfooting like a house cat, toward the point he sought. Eventually he arrived there unobserved by the quarry he stalked.

Up to this point fortune had favoured him; none had pre-empted the one vacant chair, half concealed from general view as it had been by the adjacent bulk of a very fleshy black woman. With a whispered apology to her for intruding, Jeff wormed his way in alongside. He let himself softly down into the seat and began to cough the gentle cough of a quasi invalid now on the road to recovery.

Together, it would seem, the pair in front of him sensed his presence so near them. With one accord they swung their heads.

"Evenin', Miss Stubblefield. Evenin', Smoothy," said Jeff, smiling wanly, as a convalescent naturally would. "Seein' ez how dis yere cheer wuz onuccupied, I jes' taken it so's to be out of de draf'. I ain't been so well dis week—had a little tech of pneumonia, I think 'twuz; an' so——"

Ophelia's surprised murmur of sympathy was

cut short. Smooth Crumbaugh distorted his gingerbread-coloured countenance into a hideous war mask. He turned in his place, thrusting his face forward. "Git up outen dat seat!" he ordered in a low, forceful grumble.

"But de seat ain't taken, Smoothy," protested Jeff weakly. "I 'lowed I'd set yere jes' fur a minute or two, account of de draf'."

"Git up outen dat cheer!" repeated Smooth Crumbaugh in a louder tone.

His shoulders began to hunch and his hands to curl up into fists. Ophelia's rising agitation was tempered perhaps by the realisation of the fact that for her favour two persons, both well known and prominent in their respective spheres of activity, were about to have words —possibly to exchange threats, or even blows. To be the storm centre of such a sensation is not always entirely unpleasant, especially if one be young and personable. She spoke now in a voice clearly audible to several about her.

"Please, suzz, gen'lemen, both of you be nice an' quiet!" she implored. "I trusts there ain't goin' be no trouble 'cause of me."

"'Tain't goin' be no trouble, gal," stated Smooth, as Jeff sat dumb with apprehension. "'Tain't goin' be nothin' but a pleasure to me to haul off an' knock dis little nigger naiked." He addressed Jeff: "Git up outen dat cheer, lak I tells you! Start travellin', an' keep on travellin'. Git plum' out of dis yere buildin'!"

Daunted to the very taproots of his being,

Jeff nevertheless strove to save his face. He made pretense that his cough prevented the utterance of a defiant rejoinder as he rose and backed out into the aisle and worked his way toward the rear, with Smooth Crumbaugh's glower following after him. Perhaps the excellence of his acting may have deceived some, but in his own soul Jeff suffered amain.

Far back, hard by the refreshment stand, he wriggled himself in behind an intervening frieze of standees. His judgment warned him that he should heed Smooth Crumbaugh's wishes and entirely betake himself hence; but his crushed and bruised spirit revolted against a surrender so abject and so utter. He told himself he had given up his chair because he did not care to be sitting down, anyway. Even so, this was a free country and he would stay a while longer if he wanted to stay. Only, he meant to keep yards of space and plenty of bystanders between him and Smooth Crumbaugh. He would be self-effacive, but not absolutely absent.

With an ear dulled by chagrin, he hearkened as the Reverend Grasty rose and opened his discourse touching on the life and works of the late Red Hoss Shackleford. The speaker's very first words made it clear to all that he had come to bury Cæsar—not to praise him. Really, the only complimentary thing which might truthfully be said of Red Hoss was that always he had a good appetite. At once the Reverend Grasty manifested that he meant to

adopt no weak and temporising course in his
discussion of the subject in hand. Forthrightly
he launched into a stirring recital of the shortcomings of the deceased; and out of his topic's
sins, cut off in the midst of his impenitence, he
builded a vivid lesson to warn the living.

If one might judge by her behaviour, the
lorn half sister resented not the attitude and
the language of the orator. She forgot to faint
and she sat erect. Presently she was chanting
an accompaniment to his shouted illustrations.

"Oh, my pore lost brother, sunken in de cold
waters." She quavered in a fine camp-meeting
tremolo. "Oh, my pore onworthy brother,
whut we gwine do 'bout you now?"

Fervently deep amens began to arise from
other quarters, punctuating the laments of Sister Rosalie and the louder outpourings of the
Reverend Grasty. The memorial service was
turning out to be the high point of the watch
party.

In spite of personal distractions, Jeff was
carried away by the dramatic intensity of the
scene. Forgetting momentarily his own trouble,
he shoved forward, the better to see and hear.
A menacing growl in his off ear brought him
back to earth with a jolt. It was the dread
voice of Smooth Crumbaugh, speaking from a
distance not of yards but of inches. And now,
as Jeff turned his head, Smooth's outjutted
underlip was almost brushing the tip of his
nose.

"Thought I tole you to git plum' outen dis hall!" quoth Smooth; and his voice, more than before, was freighted with the menace of dire catastrophe, imminent and impending.

Jeff didn't dare reply in regular words. He muttered unintelligible sounds beneath his breath, seeking the while to draw away.

"Quit mumblin'!" ordered Smooth. "You's liable to mumble up somethin' I don't keer to heah, an' den I'll tek an' jes' natchelly mek a set of nigger shoestrings outen you. B'lieve I'll do hit anyway—right now!"

One of his hands—the left one—closed entwiningly in Jeff's coat collar. His right stole back toward his hip pocket—the pocket wherein Smooth was reputed to carry his razor. Jeff felt dark wings fanning his clammy brow.

"Speak up an' say whut you got to say whilst you is got de breath to say hit," said the bad man.

"I—I wus jes' fixin' to go, Smoothy," his voice squeaked.

"Naw, you wuzn't. Ain't I been watchin' you, hangin' round back yere whar you thought I couldn't see you. Now den——"

A uniformed and helmeted form bulged in between them, breaking Smooth's hold on Jeff. The disturbance had drawn the Most Hig Grand Outer Guardian away from his post at the door.

"Yere! Dat'll be 'bout all!" stated this functionary in a voice of authority. "Go on

outside, you two, ef you wants to argify wid
one nurr. Dis ain't no place to be 'sputin'."

He gave a violent start of surprise and his
voice trailed off to nothingness. Until now he
had not recognised Jeff's adversary.

"Who you talkin' to, Mistah Monkey
Clothes?"

Smooth swung on the officer, ready in his
present state of feeling to carve up one or a
dozen. An ingratiating smile split the nervous
countenance of the Most High Grand Outer
Guardian. Than to be flirting with disaster
nothing was farther from his desires.

"Scuse me, Mistah Crumbaugh. I didn't
know 'twuz you. I begs yore pardon!" he
stated hastily. "Please, ef you don't mind, I'll
settle dis matter fur you."

He swung round on Jeff, who was making
himself smaller by the second.

"Whut you mean," he demanded, "per-
vokin' Mistah Crumbaugh twell he's jes' about
to lose his temper? Ef yore presence yere irri-
tates him, w'y don't you go on 'way, lak a gen-
'leman? . . . Lis'en to dat! Don't you
see you's 'bout to break up de programme?"

From the rows of seats nearest them came
indignant Sh-h-hs! Jeff's popped eyes, glaring
about him, read in all visible looks only intense
disapproval of him. It was not healthy to hold
Smooth Crumbaugh responsible for the inter-
ruption; but poor Jeff stood in quite a different
attitude with the assemblage.

He shrank away, pawing out behind him with both hands for the door. Partly mollified, but still growling, Smooth started to return to his seat, all in his way making a clear path for him. Jeff vanished through the opening like a scared chipmunk.

The Reverend Grasty had not been discommoded by the disturbance in the rear. He was getting louder every minute. So was Sister Shackleford.

Outside on the landing, Jeff breathed again and paused to master a trembling tendency as regards his legs, at the same time telling himself he had not wanted to stay through their old watch party anyhow. It was a lie; but he kept on telling it to himself over and over again until he almost believed it. With a bitter smile, reflective of the intense bitterness in his heart, he looked backward at the blank panels of the door and reflected that, barring one fascinating exception, he didn't have a real friend in all that multitude.

Why, if they really wanted to put somebody out, hadn't they clubbed in and put that tough Smooth Crumbaugh out? Why hadn't twenty-five or thirty of them formed a volunteer committee on good order and removed Smooth by force? He would have been glad to enroll as a member of that committee—as the thirtieth member and in an advisory capacity purely.

Oh, well, what was the use of hanging round

a place where true gentility was neither recognised nor appreciated? These here Supreme
Kings couldn't possibly last much longer, anyway—running things the way they did. He
might as well go on about his business. Reluctantly, making compromise with his out-
raged dignity at every step, and rent between
a hankering to linger on and a conviction that
if he did linger a most evil thing surely would
befall him, Jeff limped in his creaking new
shoes down the empty stairs, descending yard
by yard into a Slough of Despond.

At the foot of the steps he stopped again,
fumbling in his pockets. The jangled state of
his nerves demanded the sooth of nicotine.
From one pocket he exhumed nearly half of a
cigar and from the other a box of matches. He
inserted the cigar between his lips and undertook to strike a light. These were a new kind
of matches—long, thick ones, with big white-
and-black heads. Judge Priest had brought
home a supply of them the day before, and Jeff,
attracted vaguely by their novelty of appearance and their augmented size, had been moved
to borrow a box of them off the dining-room
sideboard without mentioning the matter to
any one.

The misanthrope drew one of the big matches
down the plastered side of the entryway.
It sputtered and snapped under the friction of
the stroke, but declined to burst into flame.
Jeff cast it away and tried another, with no

different result, except that the stick part snapped off short. Either the prevalent dampness had adversely affected them or they were defective and untrustworthy by reason of some flaw in their manufacture. But he noted that both matches had left queer luminous streaks upon the dingy wall.

Morbidly reflecting that in this night of his bad luck he was to be denied even the small solace of a smoke, Jeff absently fingered a third match between his fingers, plucking at its bulbous tip with a thumb nail. Instantly the effect of this was such as mildly to startle him; for at once on his finger ends appeared a strange spectral glow, as though he had been fondling some new and especially well-illuminated breed of lightning bug in his naked hand.

At any other time, almost, this phenomenon, so simply accomplished, would have set Jeff's nimble fancy at work devising experimental means of entertainment to be derived therefrom; but now and here, in his existent frame of thought, the discovery gave him no pleasure whatsoever.

He pouched cigar butt and matches, and stepped forth from the stair passage into the drizzle. Out of the darkness a figure reeled unsteadily. It bumped into him with such violence as to drive him back into the doorway, and then caromed off, rocking on its heels to regain its balance. Jeff made out that the awkward one was a person of his own colour and sex.

"Whut's ailin' you, man?" he demanded irritably. "Ain't a whole sidewalk wide 'nuff fur you, widout you tryin' to knock folkses down?"

"Huh?"

The wavering pedestrian exhaled a thick grunt, which brought with it an aroma of stick gin. He tottered forward again, throwing out his clutching hands for some support.

"Go on 'way frum me!"

Jeff flung out an arm to fend the other off; but the gesture froze solid while yet his elbow was crooked, and Jeff cowered back, transfixed and limber with terror, too scared to run, too weak to cry out.

For there, centred in the dim half-light that streamed down from above, swaying on his legs and dripping moisture, as befitting one who had but lately met a watery end, stood the mortal remains of the late unlamented—whom even now they were most unkindly commemorating upstairs—Red Hoss Shackleford, deceased. There was no doubt about it. Red Hoss' embodied spirit, with the restless malignity of a soul accursed, had come back to attend its own memorial service!

Jeff's jaws opened and refused to close. His throat locked on a howl, and that howl emerged as a thin, faint wheeze. The filling inside his knee joints turned to a marrowy jelly. His scalp crawled on his skull.

The ghost grabbed him in a fumbling embrace; and even as Jeff, in an intensified spasm of terror, wrestled to be free of that awful clutch, he realised that this ghost was entirely too solid for a regular ghost. Besides, there was that smell of gin. Ghosts did not drink— or did they? He found his voice—part of it.

"Shacky, ain't you daid?" he pleaded in croaking accents. "Fur Gawd's sake, tell me de truth—ain't you sho-'nuff daid?"

"Who say I'm daid?" demanded Red Hoss with maudlin truculence. Then instantly his tone became plaintive: "How come ever'whars I goes to-night dey axes me is I daid? Does I look daid? Does I act daid?"

"Wait a minute, Shacky—lemme think." And now Jeff, well recovered, was holding the ex-apparition upright. "You sorter taken me by s'prise; but lemme think."

Already, as his self-possession came back to him, the germ of a splendid, dazzling idea took root and sprouted in his brain.

Still supporting the burden of the miraculously restored Red Hoss, he glanced over his shoulder up the hallway. There was no one visible; none other shared this marvellous secret with him. As quickly as might be, he guided the uncertain form of Red Hoss away from the doorway and round the corner into the black shadows at the side of the building, where rain dripped on them from the eaves above.

That made no difference. Red Hoss was wet through, and in this moment any slight damage from dampness to his own vanities of wardrobe meant nothing at all to Jeff. He propped Red Hoss against the brick wall and steadied him there. And when he spoke, he spoke low; but, also, he spoke fast. Time was a precious commodity right now.

"Red Hoss," he said, "I's yore friend, ez you knows full well. Now tell me: How come you didn't git drownded in de river?"

"Me? Huh! Dey ain't nary river ever been dug deep 'nuff to drownd me in," Red Hoss was replying with drunken boastfulness. "Here's de way 'twuz: Come de night after C'ris'mus, I finds myse'f a little bit overtuck wid licker. So I lays down on de b'iler deck of dat dere tugboat, takin' a little nap. I reckin I must 'a' roll over in my sleep, 'ca'se all of a sudden I 'scovers myse'f in de middle cf dat ole Tennessee River; an' dat tugboat, she's agoin' 'long upstream same ez ef de w'ite folks is sayin' to deyse'ves: 'Well, one nigger mo' or less don't make no diff'ence in good times lak dese.'

"I treads water an' I yells; but she keep right on movin'. So den I jes' swims an' swims, an' swims some mo'; an' dat river suttinly is cold to my skin. After a spell I lands ashore whar dey's some thick-kinder woods; an' I walks back an' fo'th th'ough dem woods, tryin' to keep frum freezin' to death.

"Long 'bout daylight I comes to a tie camp whar two w'ite men is got a gang of niggers gittin' out crossties, an' I yells an' knocks on de

THOSE TIMES AND THESE

do' of de shack twell I rousts 'em all up. Dey
lemme in; an' dey ax me a whole passel of fool
questions 'bout whar'bouts is I come frum, an'
whut is I doin' dar, an' dey kindle up a big fire
an' I dries myse'f out; an' den bimeby dey feeds
me a meal of vittles. W'en I gits ready to start
frum dar, 'long about de middle of de day, one
of de w'ite men gives me six bits to pay my way
back yere on de railroad.

"But jes' after I leaves de camp to walk to
de railroad, w'ich is eight miles 'way, I runs
into a bunch of de hands, hid out in de woods
a little piece, shootin' craps; an' I stops. So
presently my six bits is gone. So den I goes
on to de railroad afoot; an', not havin' no money
nor nothin', I has to beat my way home. I
rides on de brake beams a spell, an' den de
brakeman he spies me; an' he th'ows me off;
and de las' eighteen miles I has to walk all de
way—an' hit a-rainin'!"

"W'en did you git yere? I means w'en did
you hit town?"

"'Bout a hour ago—or mebbe 'twuz a hour
an' a half."

With usage, Red Hoss' powers for coherent
speech were improving.

"So, fust off, I goes down to de river whar
dat tugboat is tied up to see whut chance dey
is, dat time of night, of my drawin' whut
money is comin' to me. But de cabin is all
dark an' t'ain't nobody aboard her 'cep'in' de
nigger night watchman; an' he's settin' down

back in de ingine room, sound asleep. I walks
back to whar he is an' I says to him, I says:
'Hello, nigger!'—jes' lak dat. An' he open his
eyes an' gimme jes' one look; an' den he give
out one yell, an' den he ain't dere no mo'. I
kin heah his footsteps goin' up de levee, scat-
terin' gravels lak a ole hen scratchin'; but dat
nigger is plum' gone. He act lak he seen a
ha'nt, or somethin'.

"So den, de nex' thing I does, I goes up de
wharf to de house whar my ha'f sister, Rosalie
—you knows dat 'ooman?—does cookin' fur a
w'ite fambly; an' I goes round de house an'
knocks at de kitchen do', but t'ain't nobody
answers. I keeps on knockin', an' after a spell
de boss of de house, a w'ite man, name of Futrell, he come out on de back po'ch in his night-
clo'es, wid a lamp in his hand, an' he suttinly
do act 'stonished to see me standin' dar; an' he
ax me p'intedly ain't I drownded; an' I tells
him No, suh; suttinly I ain't drownded! An'
I ax him whar is Rosalie. An' he say, ef she
ain't in her cabin in de yard, he reckon she
must 'a' come on up yere to dis yere hall fur
some kind of nigger doin's. Dat's de fust I
knows 'bout her livin' on de Futrell place.

"So I goes out to de cabin in de yard; but
she done gone, leavin' de do' unlocked an' on
de jar. So I goes in an' meks a light an' looks
'bout me; an' I finds sixty cents under a mat on
de washstand, w'ich on my way yere I spends
dat sixty cents fur gin at de Bleedin' Heart Sa-

loon, 'ca'se I's wet to de skin, ez you kin see
fur yo'se'f. An' so den I meks my way to dis
hall, 'ca'se I p'intedly does aim to drag dat
dere 'ooman out an' ax her whut put it into her
fool haid to go all round town tellin' folkses I's
drownded w'en she know, her ownse'f, dey ain't
nary river ever been dug deep 'nuff to drownd
me in."

His voice became complaining now, rather
than indignant:

"Fur de las' ha'f hour, mo' or less, I been
tryin' to git up dem stepses. But seem lak
dem stepses is a heap mo' steeper'n whut dey
used to be. Whut mek 'em steepen dem stepses
fur, Jeff?"

A sudden drowsiness overcame the narrator
and he sought to slump down against the wall.
But Jeff upheld him, against his will; and a
minute later Jeff's words had roused him out
of his gin-born daze:

"Lis'en to me, Red Hoss; lis'en! I jes' come
down frum up dere. I come away; 'ca'se I's
yore friend, an' I jes' natchelly couldn't bear
to set dere no longer an' heah 'em scandalise
you de way dey's doin'."

"Scandalise me! Who's scandalisin' me?"

"Ever'body is; but specially de pastor of de
Fust Ward Church—yas, suh; he's de main
scandaliser. An' dat sister of your'n, she's
settin' there harkin' to him, same ez ef he wuz
tellin' her some good news."

"Lemme go! Lemme go! I lay I'll learn

dem niggers to be 'stroyin' my good name behine my back!"

The victim of calumny, all wide-awake now,
wrestled to be free of the detaining hands.
After a little, though, he suffered his form to
relax and his struggles to abate as Jeff poured
agreeable advice upon him.

"Wait a minute, Shacky—jes' wait a minute! I got a better scheme 'n whut dat one is.
'Sides, you couldn't git past de do'—whole
place up dere is jest jammed an' blocked off
wid people. Come on now wid me. We'll go
in by de back way, whar de stepses ain't so
steep ez dey is round yere in front. You an'
me'll go up dat way, tippytoe, so ez not to
mek no noise; and we'll wait in dat little hall
behine de flatform—you knows de hall I means
—de one whar dey perpares de candidates fur
'nitiation?"

Red Hoss nodded.

"I knows it full well. Been dere oncet. And
den whut?" he inquired.

"Den we'll wait twell dey turns de lights
out; dey's aimin' to turn 'em out in a mighty
few minutes to welcome in de New Yeah in de
darkness. An' jes' w'en dey does dat I'll open
de do', an' you step out on de flatform an' say:
'Heah I is!' At dat I'll switch on de lights
right quick; an' den—don't you see?—you'll be
standin' right dere in full view, up on de flatform, whar you kin tell dat preacher whut you
thinks of him."

"I ain't 'lowin' to tell him nothin'—I 'low to jes' haul off an' bust him one, an' peel his nappy haid fur him!" avowed Red Hoss.

"Suit yo'se'f about dat," conceded Jeff; "but how do de res' of de plan seem to strike you?"

"You's my friend—seem lak you's de onlies' friend whut I got lef' in de world," stated Red Hoss. "An' so I does lak you says—up to a suttin point; but frum den on I's gwine cut loose an' be rough. Come on, Jeff! Show me de way! Dat's all I axes you—jes' show me de way!"

"Hole still a minute—we got time yit to spare," counselled Jeff; on top of his first inspiration a second one had burgeoned forth. "Fust off, lemme wipe de rain an' de cinders offen you—yore face is powerful dirty."

Obediently Red Hoss offered his features for renovation. From his pocket Jeff hauled out a handkerchief; hauled something else out, too— only Red Hoss didn't see that. He made pretense of wrapping a forefinger in the handkerchief; but it was not a finger tip that carefully encircled both of Red Hoss' blinking eyes, pressing firmly against the moist black flesh, and then outlined his nose and passed in rings round his mouth, above the upper lip and below the lower one.

"Hole up!" protested Red Hoss. "You's rubbin' too hard. Yore finger nail hurts me."

"Stay still!" urged Jeff. "I's 'most th'ough."

Craftily, with a fresh match, he touched the

outer and the inner corners of Red Hoss' eyes
and the lobes of his ears; and then he drew off,
almost appalled himself by the ghastliness of
his own handicraft, as revealed in the dark.

"Come along, Red Hoss. An' don't furgit
whut you's goin' to say w'en I opens de hall
do' fur you."

"Ain't furgittin' nothin'," promised Red
Hoss.

Their two figures, closely interwoven—one
steering and supporting; the other being steered
and being supported—passed in the murk
round the back corner of Odd Fellows' Hall, to
bring up at the foot of a flight of rough wooden
stairs, built on against the wall for added protection and as an added means of exit from the
upper floor in case of fire, fight or flight. Here
the hardest part of Jeff's job began. He had
to boost Red Hoss up, step by step.

Above, the most successful watch party ever
conducted under the auspices of the Supreme
Kings of the Universe had progressed almost to
its apogee. It was now six minutes before the
hour when, according to no less an authority
than the late Bard of Avon, churchyards yawn
and graves give up their sheeted dead. The
principal orator, with his high collar quite wilt-
ed down and his face, behind his spectacles,
slick and shiny with sweat, reached his conclusion, following a burst of eloquence so powerful that his hearers almost could hear the

Tophet fires crackling beneath their tingling feet.

"An' now, my dearly beloved sistern an' brethern," he proclaimed, in a short peroration to his longer one—"an' now I commands you to think on the fix this pore transgressor must be in at this very minute, cut off ez he wuz in the midst of his sins an' his shortcomin'ses. Think on yore own sins an' yore own shortcomin'ses. Think, an' think hard! Think, an' think copious!"

His voice swung downward to the more subdued cadence of the semiconversational tone:

"The hour of midnight is 'most at hand. In acco'dance wid the programme I shell now turn off the lights, an' this gatherin' will set in the solemn communion of darkness fur five minutes, till the New Yeah comes."

He stepped three paces backward and turned a plug set in the wall close to the doorjam. All over the hall the bulbs winked out. Nothing was to be seen, and for a few seconds nothing was heard except the sound of the minister's shuffling movements as he felt his way back to his place at the front of the platform, and, below him, in the body of the hall, the nervous rustle of many swaying bodies and of twice as many scuffling feet.

On the far side of the closed rear door crouched Jeff, breathless from his recent exertions, panting whispered admonitions in the ear of his co-conspirator. Red Hoss was impatient to lunge forward. He wanted to surge in right now. But Jeff held fast to him. Jeff could sense a psychological moment, even if he could not pronounce one.

"Wait jes' one secont mo'—please, Red Hoss!" he entreated. "Wait twell I opens dis yere do' fur you. Den you bulge right in an' speak up de words 'Here I is!' loud an' clear. You won't furgit dat part, will you?"

"'On't furgit nothin'!" muttered Red Hoss. "Jes' watch my smoke—dat's all!"

With his ear against a thin panel, Jeff listened; listened—and smiled. Through the barrier he heard the preacher's voice saying:

"All present will now unite in singin' the hymn w'ich begins: Hark! From the Tombs a Doleful Soun'!"

Softly, oh, so softly, Jeff's fingers turned the doorknob; gently, very gently, he drew the door itself half open; with the whispered admonition "Now, boy, now!" he swiftly but silently propelled Red Hoss, face forward, through the opening.

The Reverend Grasty stood waiting for the first words of the hymn to uprise from below him in a mighty swing. But from that unseen gathering down in front a very different sound came—a sound that was part a gasp of stupefaction, part a groan of abject distress. For the rest saw what the minister, as yet, did not see, by reason of his back being to the wall, whereas they faced it. They saw, floating against a background of black nothingness, a face limned in wavering pulsing lines of a most ghastly witch fire—nose and brow and chin and ears, wide mouth and glaring eyes, all wreathed about by that unearthly graveyard glow.

In that same flash of space Jeff Poindexter's hand had found the switch, set in the wall hard by the door casing, and had flipped the lights on. And now before them they beheld the form of the late Red Hoss Shackleford, his face seamed with livid greyish streaks, his garments all adrip, his arms outspread, his eyes like balls of flame, and his lips agleam with a palish blush, as though he had hither come direct from feasting on the hot coals of Perdition, without stopping to wipe his mouth. And then he opened that fearsome scupper of a mouth, and in a voice thickened and muddy—the proper voice for one who had lain for days in river ooze—he spoke the words:

"Here I is!" That was all he said. But that was enough.

It is believed that the Reverend Grasty was the first to move. Naturally he would be among the first, anyhow, he being the nearest of all to the risen form of the dead. He spread himself like an eagle and soared away from there; and when he lit, he lit a-running. Indeed, so high did he jump and so far outward that, though he started with a handicap, few there were who beat him in the race to the door.

Smooth Crumbaugh was one who beat him. Smooth feared neither man nor beast nor devil; but ha'nts were something else! He took a flying start, spurning the floor as he rose up over chairs and their recent occupants. Without checking speed, he clove a path straight through the centre of Sister Eldora Menifee's refreshment department; and on the stairway, going down, he passed the Most High Grand Outer Guardian as though the Most High Grand Outer Guardian had been standing still.

It was after he struck the sidewalk, though, and felt the solid bricks beneath his winged feet, that Smooth really started to move along. For some ten furlongs he had strong competition, but he was leading by several lengths when he crossed Yazoo Street, eight blocks away, with the field tailing out behind him for a matter of half a mile or so.

I might add that Sister Rosalie Shackleford, hampered though she was by skirts and the trappings of woe, nevertheless finished inside the money herself.

Jefferson Poindexter, calm, smiling and debonair, picked his way daintily among overthrown chairs and through a litter of hats, helmets, umbrellas and swords across the hall to Ophelia, who, helpless with shock, was plastered, prone and flat on the floor, close up against the side wall, where Smooth had flung her as he launched himself in flight.

Right gallantly Jeff raised her to her feet and supported her; and right mainfully she clung to him, inclosing herself, all distracted and aquiver, within the circle of his comforting arms. Already they were almost alone and within a space of moments would be entirely so, except for one fat auntie, lying in a dead faint under the wrecked snack stand.

Also there still remained Red Hoss Shackleford, who wavered to and fro upon the platform, with a hand to his bewildered brow, trying foggily to figure out just how he had been thwarted of his just retribution upon the persons of those vanished arch-detractors of him. He had had his revenge—had it sugar-sweet and brimming over—only he didn't know it yet.

"Oh, Jeffy," gasped Ophelia, "wuzn't you skeered too?"

"Who—me?" proclaimed Jeff. "Me skeered of a wet nigger, full of stick gin? Fair lady, mebbe I don't keer so much fur gittin' my clothes all mussed up fightin' wid bully niggers, but I ain't never run frum no ghostes yit; an' I don't never aim to, neither—not 'thout waitin' round long 'nuff to find out fust w'ether hit's a real ghost or not. Dat's me!"

"Oh, Jeffy, you suttinly is de bravest man I knows!" she answered back in muffled tones, with her head on his white waistcoat.

At this moment precisely the town clock sounded the first stroke of twelve, and all the steam whistles in town let go, blasting out shrilly; and all the giant firecrackers in town began bursting in loud acclaim of the New Year. But what the triumphant, proud, conquering Jeff heard was his Ophelia, speaking to him soul to soul.

CHAPTER VIII

CINNAMON SEED AND
SANDY BOTTOM

MAJOR PUTNAM STONE is dead, but his soul goes marching on. Mainly it does its marching on at Midsylvania University. Every fall, down yonder, on the night of the day of the last game of the season, when the squad has broken training and many of the statutes touching on the peace and quiet of the community, there is a dinner. At the end of this dinner the captain of the team stands up at one end of the table and chants out: "Cinnamon Seed and Sandy Bottom!"—just like that. Whereupon there are loud cheers. And then, at the far end of the table from him, the chairman of the athletic community stands up in his place and lifts his mug and says, in the midst of a little silence: "To the memory of Major Putnam Stone!" Then everybody rises and drinks; and there are no heel-taps.

This ceremony is never omitted. It is a tradition; and they go in rather strongly for tradi-

tions at Midsylvania, and always have since
the days when there was not much else to Midsylvania except its traditions. The team may
have won that afternoon, or it may have lost.
The boys may be jubilating for the biggest victory of the whole year, or, over the trenches
and the tankards, consoling themselves and one
another for an honourable defeat at the hands
of their classic rival, Vanderbeck. It makes no
difference. Win or lose, they toast the shade
and the name of Major Stone.

So there is no danger that the Major will be
forgotten at the University, any more than
there is danger of such a thing coming to pass
in the *Evening Press* shop where the Major used
to work. Most of the old hands who worked
there with him once upon a time are gone elsewhere now. One or two or three are dead and
the rest of us, with few exceptions, have scattered over the country. But among the men
who are our successors on the staff the spirit of
the old man walks, and there is a tale of him
to be told to each beginner who comes on the
paper. It is as much a part of the history of
the city room as the great stories that Ike Webb,
who was our star man, wrote back in those latter nineties; as much a part as the sayings and
the doings of little Pinky Gilfoil, who passed
out last year, serving with the American ambu-
lance corps over in France.

The last time I was down that way I stopped
over between trains and went around on Jeffer-

son Street to look the old place over. It was late in the afternoon, after press time for the final edition, and the day force had all departed; but out of the press-room to greet me came limping old Henry, the black night watchman, who, according to belief, had been a fixture of the *Evening Press* since the corner stone of the building was laid.

"Yassuh," said Henry to me after this and that and the other thing had been discussed back and forth between us; "we still talks a mighty much about ole Majah. Dis yere new issue crop of young w'ite genelmens we got workin' 'round yere now'days gits a chanc't to hear tell about him frequent an' of'en. They's a picture of him hangin' upstairs in de big boss' room on de thud flo'. Big boss, he sets a heap of store by 'at air picture. An' they tells me 'at de mate to it is hangin' up in 'at air new structure w'ich they calls de Forbes Memorial, out at de Univussity."

If my recollection serves me aright I have once or twice before touched on sundry chapters in the life and works of the old Major, telling how, for him, nothing of real consequence happened in this world between the surrender of Lee at Appomattox and the day, nearly forty years later, when all his tidy property was wiped out in an unfortunate investment, and he moved out of his suite at the old Gault House and abandoned his armchair in a front window at the Shawnee Club, and, at the age of sixty-four and a salary of twelve dollars a week, took a job as cub reporter on the *Evening Press;* how because he would persist in gnawing at the rinds of old yesterdays instead of nosing into the things of the current day he was a most utter and complete failure at the job; how once through chance, purely, he uncovered the whoppingest scoop that a real reporter could crave for and then chucked it away again to save a woman who by the standards of all proper people wasn't worth saving in the first place; how by compassion of the owner of the paper and against the judgment of everybody else, he hung on all through the summer, a drag upon the organization and a clog on the ankle of City Editor Wilford Devore; how on the opening day of the famous Lyric Hall convention he finally rose to an emergency that was of his liking and with the persuasive aid of a brace of long-barrelled, ivory-handled cavalry revolvers stampeded the Stickney gang, when they tried by force to seize the party machinery, having first put that official bad man and deputy sub-leader of the opposition, Mink Satterlee, out of business, by love-tapping Mink upon his low and retreating forehead with the butt end of one of his shooting irons; and how then as a reward therefor, he was made war-editor of the sheet, thereafter fitting comfortably and snugly into a congenial berth especially devised and created for his occupancy. All this has elsewhere been told.

This present tale, which has to do in part with the Major and in part with the student body of Midsylvania, dates from sometime after the day when he became our war editor, and was writing those long and tiresome special articles of his, dealing favourably with Jackson's Campaign in the Valley, and unfavourably with Sherman's March to the Sea.

Midsylvania, those days, was a university with a long vista of historic associations behind it and a puny line of endowments to go forward on; so it went forward very slowly indeed. To get the most favourable perspective on Midsylvania you must needs look backward into a distinguished but mouldy past, and consider the list of dead-and-gone warriors and statesmen and educators and clergymen who had been graduated in the class of '49 or the class of '54, or some other class. Chief among its physical glories were a beech tree, under which Daniel Boone was said to have camped overnight once; an ancient chapel building of red brick, with a row of fat composition pillars, like broken legs in plaster casts, stretching across its front to uphold its squatty portico; and in the centre of the campus, a noseless statue of Henry Clay.

Sons of Old Families in the state attended it, principally, I suppose, because their fathers before them had attended it; sons of new families mostly went elsewhere for their education. With justice, you might speak of Midsylvania as being conservative, which was true; but when you said that, you said it all, and it let you out. There was nothing more to be said.

If poor shabby old Midsylvania lagged behind sundry of her sister schools in the matter of equipment, most certainly and most woefully did she lag behind them in the matter of athletics. In that regard, and perhaps other regards, she was an Old Ladies' Home. Eight governors of American commonwealths, six of them dead and two yet living, might be listed on the roster of her alumni—and were; but you sought in vain there for the name of a great pitcher or of a consistent winner of track events, or of a champion pole vaulter. If anybody mentioned Midsylvania in connection with college sports, it was to laugh. So there was a good deal of laughing one fall when, for the first time, she went in for football. The laughter continued, practically without abatement, through that season; but early the following season it died away altogether, to be succeeded by a wave of astonishment and of reluctantly conceded admiration, which ran from the Ohio River to the Gulf of Mexico, and from the Atlantic Seaboard to the Mississippi River. Other football teams began to respect Midsylvania's football team. They had to; she mauled it into their respective consciousness.

The worm had turned—and turned something besides the other cheek, at that; for in that second year she won her first game, which was her game with Exstein Normal. Now Exstein Normal came up proudly, like an army glorious with banners, and went down abruptly, like a scuttled ship: Score, thirty-one to nothing. Following on this, she beat Holy Mount's team of fiery Louisiana Creoles, with a red-headed demon of a New Orleans Irish boy for their captain; and, in succession, she took on and overcame Cherokee Tech., and Alabama State, and Bayless.

She held to a tie what was conceded to be the best team that Old Dominion had ever mustered; and Vanderbeck, the largest and, athletically considered, the strongest of them all, bested her only by the narrowest and closest of margins on Vanderbeck's own gridiron. It was one of the upsetting things that never can happen, but occasionally do, that Midsylvania should go straight through to Thanksgiving Day with a miraculous record of five victories, one tie and one defeat out of seven games played, and with not a man in the regular line-up seriously damaged. And yet not so miraculous either when you came to cast up causes to find results. Her men had steam and had speed and had strategy, which meant team-work; in fact, they had everything. Heaven alone knew where, within the space of one year they had got it, but they had it: that was the main point, the incontrovertible detail.

You know the old saying: Home folks are always the last ones to appreciate us. More or less I think this must have been true of us as regards our own University's football outfit. Undoubtedly a lot had been written and said in cities farther south about it, before the *Evening Press* and the other papers in town began fully to realise that Midsylvania was putting the town on the football map. But when we did realise it we gave her and her team front page space and sporting page space, and plenty of both. Before we had been content to bestow upon her a weekly column which one of the undergraduates turned in at space rates, and pretty poor space rates at that—departmental stuff, mostly dealing with faculty changes, and Greek letter society doings and campus gossip and such-like. Now though almost anything that anybody on the staff or off of it chose to grind out about the boys who wore the M on their sweater breasts found a warm welcome after it landed on the City Editor's desk. Local pride in local achievement had been roused and if anybody knows of anything stronger than local pride in a city of approximately a hundred and fifty thousand population, please tell me what it is. We covered the games that were played at home that year as fully as the limitations of a somewhat scanty staff permitted, and Ike Webb was detailed to travel with the squad when it played away from home. He sent back by telegraph, regardless of expense, stories on the games abroad, which were smeared all over the sheet under spread heads and signed as being "By Our Special Staff Correspondent." They were good stories—Ike was not addicted to writing bad ones, ever—and they made circulation.

There is no telling how many letters from subscribers came to the chief commending him for his journalistic enterprise. He ran a good many of them. The paper rode with the team on the crest of the popularity wave. Trust Devore for that. He had a sense for news-values which compensated and more than compensated for certain temperamental shortcomings as exhibited inside the plant.

One day in the tail end of November the old Major came stumping down the stairs from his sanctum—anyhow, he always called it his sanctum—upon the top floor in a little partitioned-off space adjoining the chief's office, where he had a desk of his own and where he did his work. He had a wad of copy paper in his hand. In dress and in manner he was the same old Major that he had been in the flush times two years back, when he used to come in daily, ostensibly to get some exchanges but really to sit and sit, and bore everybody who would listen with tiresome long accounts of things that happened between 1861 and 1865—not the shabby forlorn figure he became that first summer after he got his twelve-dollar-a-week job—but his former self, recreated all over again. His full-breasted shirt of fine linen jutted out above the unbuttoned top of his low waistcoat in pleaty, white billows and his loose black sailor's tie made a big clump at his throat where the ends of his Lord Byron collar came together. His cuffs almost covered his hands and his longish white hair was like silk floss lying on his coat collar behind. That little white goatee of his jutted out under his lower lip like a tab of carded wool. Altogether he was the Major of yore, rejoicing sartorially in his present state of comparative prosperity. The boys around the shop always said that if the Major had only ten dollars and fifty cents in the world he would spend five dollars of it for his club dues and five of it on his wardrobe and give the remaining fifty cents to some beggar. I guess he would have, too.

He came downstairs this day and walked up to Devore, and laid down his sheaf of pages at Devore's elbow. "A special contribution, sir," he said very ceremoniously.

Devore ran through the first page, which was covered with pencil marks—the Major always wrote his stuff out in long hand—and glanced up, a little bit astonished.

"Kind of out of your usual line, isn't it, Major Stone?" he asked.

"In a measure, sir—yes," stated the old man; and he rocked on his high heels as though he might be nervous regarding the reception his contribution would have in this quarter. "Under the circumstances I feel justified in a departure from the material I customarily indite. But if you feel——"

"Oh, that's all right!" said Devore, divining what the Major meant to say before the Major finished saying it. "There's always room for good stuff."

He laid the first sheet aside and shuffled through the sheets under it, picking out lines and appraising the full purport of the manuscript, as any skilled craftsman of a newspaper copy desk can do in half the length of time an outsider would be needing to make out the sense of it.

"About young Morehead, eh? I didn't know you knew him, Major?"

"Personally I do not. But, in his lifetime, I knew his gallant father well; in fact, intimately. For some months we served together on the staff of General Leonidas Polk. Accordingly I felt qualified by my personal acquaintance with his family to treat of the subject as I have treated it."

"Oh, I see!" Devore gave an involuntary smile quick burial in the palm of his cupped hand. "And so you've caught the fever too?"

"Fever, sir? What fever?"

"I mean you've got yourself all worked up about football, the same as everybody else in town?"

"Not at all, sir. Of the game of football I know little or nothing. In my college days we concerned ourselves in our sportive hours with very different pursuits and recreations."

The Major, as we knew from hearing him tell

about it a hundred times, had left the University of Virginia in his second year to enlist in the army. And we knew his views on the subject of sports. If a young person of the masculine gender could waltz with the ladies, and ride a horse well enough to follow the hounds without falling off at the jumps, and with a shotgun could kill half the birds he fired at—these, from the Major's standpoint, were accomplishments enough for any Southern gentleman, now that the use of duelling pistols had died out. We had heard him say so, often.

"Football, considered as a game, does not interest me," he went on now. "I have never seen it played. But on account of Mr. James Payne Morehead, Junior, I am interested. Being of the strain of blood that he is, I am constrained to believe he will acquit himself in a manner worthy of his ancestry, wheresoever he may be placed. In the article you have there before you I have said as much."

"So I notice," said Devore, keeping most of the irony out of his tone. "Thank you, Major — we'll stick the yarn in to‑morrow." And then, as the old man started out: "By the way, Major Stone, if you've never seen a game you might enjoy seeing the one next Saturday —against Sangamon. It'll be your last chance this season. I'll save you out a press ticket—if you don't mind sitting in the newspaper box with the boys that I'll have out there covering the story?"

"I am obliged to you, sir," said Major Stone. "I shall be pleased to avail myself of the courtesy, and nothing could afford me more pleasure than to have the company of my youthful compatriots in the field of journalistic endeavour on that occasion."

He talked like that. Talking, he made you think of the way some people write in their letters, not of the way anybody else on earth spoke in ordinary conversation.

Out he went then, all reared back and Devore read the copy through, chuckling to himself. It wasn't a malicious chuckle, though. Devore was not likely to forget what the Major did for him that day eighteen months before at the Lyric Hall convention when Bad Mink Satterlee tried to cave in Devore's skull with a set of brass knuckles and doubtlessly would have carried the undertaking through successfully if Major Stone hadn't been so swiftly deft with the ivory butt of one of his pair of cavalry pistols, nor to forget how nasty he, as City Editor, had been before that, during all the months of the Major's apprenticeship as a sixty-four-year-old cub reporter.

"Just like the old codger!" he said, tapping the manuscript with his hand affectionately. "Starts out to write about the kid; gives the kid a couple of paragraphs; and then uses up twenty pages more telling what great men the kid's father and grandfather were. Here, you fellows, just listen a minute to this."

He read a few sentences aloud.

"Get the angle, don't you? Major figures that any spunk and any sense the Morehead boy's got is a heritage from his revered ancestors, and that he'll just naturally have to make good because he had 'em for his ancestors. Well, at that, the Maje is probably right, without realising it. I'm thinking Captain James Payne Morehead, Junior, and his bunch of little fair-haired playmates are going to need something more than they've got now when they go up against that bunch of huskies from Sangamon next Saturday. How about it, eh?"

We knew about it, or at least we thought we knew about it, as surely as anyone may know in advance of the accomplished event. There was a note of foreboding in the answers we made to our immediate superior there in the city room. One of the boys summed it up:

"'Pride goeth before a fall,'" he said; "and biting off more than you can chaw is bad on the front teeth — provided the Midsylvania eleven have any front teeth left after the Sangamon eleven get through toying with their bright young faces on Saturday afternoon."

Which, differently expressed, perhaps, was the common sentiment. A chill of dread was descending upon the community at large; in fact, had been descending like a dark, dank blanket for upward of a week now. During the first few hours after the announcement came out that the team of Sangamon College, making their post-season tour, would swing downward across Messrs. Mason and Dixon's justly celebrated survey marks for the express purpose of playing against Midsylvania, there had been a flare-up of jubilation that was statewide.

It was no small honour for victorious Midsylvania that her football eleven should be the chosen eleven below the Line to meet these all-conquering gladiators from above it. So everybody agreed, at the outset. But on second thought, which so often is the better thought of the two, the opportunity seemed, after all, not so glorious. A hero may go down leading a forlorn hope—may die holding a last ditch—and posterity possibly will applaud him; but we may safely figure that he does not greatly enjoy himself while thus engaged; nor can his friends and well-wishers, looking on, be so very happy, either, over the dire and distressful outcome of the sacrificial deed. The nearer came the day of the game and the more people read about the strength of the invaders, the more dismal loomed the prospect for the defenders.

To begin with, Sangamon was one of the biggest fresh-water colleges on the continent, and one of the richest. Sangamon had six times as many students enrolled as Midsylvania, which meant, of course, six times the bulk of raw material from which to pick and choose for her team. Sangamon had a professional coach, paid trainers and paid rubbers; and Sangamon had a fat fund to support her in her athletic endeavours.

Midsylvania, it is almost needless to state, had none of these. Sangamon had gone through the fall, mopping up ambitious contenders, east and west, due north, north by east, and north by west. Sangamon had two players—not one, but actually two—that the experts of the New York dailies had nominated for the All-American—her fullback, Vretson, known affectionately and familiarly as the Terrible Swede; and her star end, Fay, who, in full football panoply of spiked shoes and padded knickers, had, on test, done a hundred yards in twelve seconds flat. It isn't so very often that the astigmatic Eastern sharps can see across the Appalachians when they come to make up the roster of nominees for the seasonal hall of football fame. This year, though, they had looked as far inland as Sangamon. At the peril of a severe eyestrain they had to, because Sangamon simply would not be denied.

This was what Midsylvania must go up against this coming Saturday afternoon. Wherefore the apprehension of disaster was that thick you could slice it with a knife.

They played the game out at Morehead Downs, where every year the Derby was run. Neither the baseball park nor the rutty common at the back of the University campus, where the Varsity scrubs and regulars did their stint at practise, could begin to hold the number that was due to attend this game, decent weather being vouchsafed. So Morehead Downs it was, with the lines blocked out in the turf on the inner side of the white fence that bounded the track, a little way up the home stretch, so that the judges' stand should not cut off the view of any considerable number of the spectators sitting across in the grand stand.

For the newspaper fellows they rigged up elbowroom accommodations of bench and table against the base of the judges' kiosk. There we sat—Ike Webb and the Major and Gil Boyd, who was our sporting editor, and myself, all in a row—and there we had been sitting for nearly an hour before the time for starting. Ike Webb was to do the introduction and Gil Boyd the running account of the game, play by play. My job was to keep tab of incidents and local-colour stuff generally. But the old Major was there as a spectator merely.

He certainly saw a sight. In that town we always measured multitudes by our Derby Day figures; yet even Derby Days did not often turn out a bigger crowd than the crowd that swarmed to the Downs that bright gusty December afternoon. The governor came down from the capital and most of the statehouse force came with him. There were excursions by rail in from out in the state, all of them mighty well patronised.

As for the local attendance—well, so far as

compiling a directory of the able-bodied adult white population and a fair sprinkling of the black was concerned, the enumerators could have simplified and expedited their task considerably by going up and down the aisles and jotting down the names as they went. They could have made a fairly complete census of our prominent families without straying beyond the confines of the reserved-seat section at the front, or fashionable, side of the grand stand. And if a single society girl in town was absent it was because her parents or her guardian kept her at home under lock and key.

Before two o'clock, the slanting floor beneath the high-peaked red roof of the structure made you think of a big hanging garden, what with the faces and the figures of all those thousands packed in together, row after row of them, with the finery of the women standing out from the massed background in brighter patches of colour, and the little red pennons that the venders had peddled in the audience all dancing and swaying, like the petals cf wind-blown flowers. That spectacle alone, viewed from our vantage place over across the race course, was worth the price of admission to anybody.

Carrying the simile a bit farther, you might have likened two sections of space in the stand to hothouses where noise was being brought into bloom, by both artificial and natural means. One of these forcing beds of sound was where Midsylvania grouped herself—faculty and students and old graduates. The other, a smaller area, held the visitors from Sangamon, two hundred strong and more, who had come down three hundred miles by special train, to root for the challengers, bringing with them a brass band and their own glee club—or a good part of it, anyhow—and their own cheer leader.

This cheer leader, being the first of a now common species ever seen in our parts, succeeded in holding the public eye mighty closely, as he stood, bareheaded and long-haired, down below on the track, with his gaudy blue-and-gold sweater on, and his big megaphone in his hand, jerking his arms and his body back and forth as he directed his chorus above in its organised cheering and its well-drilled singing of college songs.

Compared with this output, Midsylvania's cheering arose in larger volume, which was to be expected, seeing that Midsylvania so greatly excelled in numbers present, and had behind its delegations the favour of the onlookers almost to a unit; but, even so, it seemed to lack the force and fervour of those vocal volleys arising from the ranks of the enemy. Each time Sangamon let off a yell it was platoon firing, steady and rapid and brisk; and literally it crackled on the air. When this had died away, and Midsylvania had answered back, the result somehow put you in mind of a boy whistling to keep up his courage while passing a cemetery after dark.

It is hard to express the difference in words, but, had you been there that day, you would have caught it in a jiffy. One group was certain of victory impending and expressed its certainty; the other was doubtful and betrayed it. In the intervals between the whooping and the singing Sangamon's imported band would play snatches of some rousing air, or else Midsylvania's band would play; between the two of them pumping up the pulsebeats of all and sundry.

I was struck by one thing—the Major maintained calm and dignity through all the preliminary excitement. In the moment of the first really big outburst, which was when the Varsity's students and former students marched in behind their band, out of the tail of my eye I caught the Major with a pencil, checking off the names of the home squad on his copy of the official programme. Knowing the old fellow as I did, I guessed he was figuring up to see how many of the players were members of Old Families. Nearly all of them were, for that matter. He even held himself in when, at two-fifteen or thereabouts, first one of the teams and then the other trotted out from under opposite ends of the grand stand and crossed the track to the field to warm up.

He asked me to point out young Morehead to him; and when I did he nodded as if in affirmation of a previous decision of his own. On my own initiative I pointed out some of the other stars to him too.

In advance we knew Sangamon was going to have the advantage of beef on her side; but I do not think anybody realised just how great the advantage was until we saw the two teams on the same ground and had opportunity to compare and appraise them, man for man. Then we saw, with an added sinking of the spirit—at least I knew my spirit sank at the inequality of the comparison—that her front line outweighed ours by pounds upon pounds of brawn.

In another regard as well, and a more essential regard, too, she showed superiority. For these champions from the upper Corn Belt had what plainly their opponents always before during the season had likewise had, but now lacked: they had an enormous conceit of themselves, a mountainous and a monumental belief in their ability to take this game away from the rival team.

They had brought it with them—this assurance—and they had fed it stall-fat beforehand; and now, with the easy and splendid insolence of lusty, pampered youth, they exhibited it openly before all these hostile eyes upon the enemy's soil. It showed in them individually and as a unit. Almost as visibly as though words of defiance had been stencilled upon their tight-laced jerkins fore and aft, they flaunted forth their confidence in themselves, somehow expressing it in their rippling leg muscles and in their broad backs and in their hunched shoul-

ders as they bunched up into formidable close
formation, and in everything they did and said
in the few minutes of practice intervening before they should be at grips with their opponents.

They accepted the handclaps from the onlookers—a tribute of hospitality this was, extended by people to whom hospitality for the
stranger was as sacred as their religion and as
sincere as their politics—with an air which betokened, most evidently, that presently they
meant to repay those who greeted them for the
greeting, by achieving one of Sangamon's customary victories in Sangamon's customary
workmanlike fashion. Among them Vretson,
the much-advertised, loomed a greater giant
above lesser giants, justifying by bulk alone his
title of the Terrible Swede.

As for Midsylvania's players, upon the other
hand, it seemed to me, as I watched them, that
they, in turn, watched the young Gogs and Ma-
gogs who were to grapple with them in a half-
fearsome, half-furtive fashion. I marked that
they flinched nervously, like débutantes, before
the volleys of friendly applause from the crowd.
It occurred to me that their thoughts must be
studded with big black question marks; whereas we all could understand that no suggestion
of doubtfulness punctuated the anticipations of
the opposing eleven touching on the possibili-
ties of the next two hours.

The feeling of foreboding spread like a cold

contagion from the field to the press stand, af-
fecting the newspaper men; and, becoming generally epidemic, it reached the spectators. That
earlier lustiness was almost altogether lacking
from the outbreak signalling the beginning of
play. In the salvo there was nothing hearten-
ing. It appeared rather to be pitched in the
tone of sympathetic consolation for a predestined and an impending catastrophe; and even
the bark and roar of Midsylvania's yell, as all
Midsylvania gave it, seemed to have almost a
hollow daunted sound to it. Where we sat we
could sense this abatement of spirit with particular plainness; in fact, I rather think Major
Stone was the only person there who did not
sense it in its full effect and its full import.

I am not going to spend overmuch space in
describing the first half of that game; this was
in the days when games were divided into
halves, and not quartered up into periods.
Anyhow, I have forgotten a good many of the
details. The principal points are what stick
out in my memory. I remember that on the
toss of the coin Sangamon won and kicked off.
It was Vretson—no less—who drove his tal-
ented punting toe into the pigskin.

There was a sound as though some one had
smote a taut bladder with a slapstick, and the
ball soared upward and away, shrinking from
the size of a watermelon to the size of a gourd,
and from a gourd to a goose egg; and then it
came whirling downward again, growing big-

ger as it dropped. Woolwine, our quarter, caught it and took a flying start off his shoe hobs. Fay and the other Sangamon end, whose name I have forgotten, were after him like a pair of coursing beagles after a doubling hare; and together they nailed him before he had gone twenty yards, and down he went, with Fay on top of him and What'shisname on top of Fay. When they dug the three of them out of their heap little Woolwine still had the ball under him.

As the teams lined up, boring their heads forward to a common centre, billy-goat fashion, and Morehead, who was playing end, called out the signals, "Six—eight—twenty-eight—thirty-one"—or some such combination of figures—we caught the quaver in his voice. Ike Webb, sitting next to me, gave a little groan and laid down his pencil, and put his pessimistic face in his sheltering hands.

"Listen to that tremolo note, will you?" he lamented from between his fingers. "Licked, by golly, before they start! They won't play to win, because they're scared to death already. They'll play to keep from being licked by too big a score, and that means they won't have a chance. Just you fellows watch and see if I'm not right. Ah-h! There she goes!"

We watched all right; and we saw that our boys meant to try to carry the ball through for gains. There was not a chance of that, though. They butted their heads against a stone wall until they fairly addled the football instincts in their brains. In two attempts they did not advance the ball six feet; so they tried kicking it. Young Railey punted well into Sangamon territory and now Sangamon had the ball. She lost it on a fumble, but got it back a minute or two later on a fumble slip by the other side. In their respective shortcomings as regards fumbling it was even-Stephen between the teams; but Ike Webb couldn't view the thing in any such optimistic light. He had turned into a merciless critic of the Varsity outfit.

"Aha!" he muttered dolorously as a scrimmaging tangle of forms disentangled and showed that Sangamon, by a smart bit of strategy, had gained three yards. "What did I tell you not five minutes back? Those boys lost their hearts before they even began, and now they're due to lose their heads too."

It really looked as though Ike Webb was qualifying for clairvoyant honours, for promptly Midsylvania's defence became more and more inefficient, more and more uncertain. Sangamon had a smart field commander, and he took leeway of the advantage. He set his men to the job of jamming through; and jam through they did. It took time, though, because Midsylvania, of course, offered a measure of resistance. To me, however, it appeared to be the mechanical resistance of bodies in action rather than anything guided by a spiritual determination—if you get what I mean. It took a good deal of time; but after a while, by dint of shoving ahead with all her tonnage against Midsylvania's slighter and lighter displacement, the visitors forced the ball along to Midsylvania's thirty-yard line.

At this point, Sangamon suddenly changed her tactics. Collop, her captain, made a gesture with his arms and the Blue tackles dropped back a little. From the centre of the massed wedge of shapes a signal was barked out. So swiftly that the spectacle made you think of a pyramid of pool balls scattering over a pool table when the cue ball hits it hard on the nose, the visiting players shifted positions.

For ten seconds we lost sight of the ball altogether. When we saw it again it was cuddling in Vretson's vast, outspread paws. Who had passed it, or how it got there after being passed, I never knew. Magically it had materialised in his grasp in the same way that a prestidigitator's china egg is produced from a countryjake's whiskers. He tucked it into the bight of his left arm and, with his mighty right arm swinging behind him as a rudder and before him as a flail, he tore down the field, going away out to the right.

He was fast for his size—wonderfully fast, and besides, he had perfect interference to help him along. His mates, skirmishing out on his flank, threw back and bowled over the men who bored in to tackle him. In his flight he himself accounted for at least two Varsity players who sprang round the wings of his protecting line, hoping to intercept the big sprinter. One he dodged, the other he flung aside; and then he kept on and on until after a run of thirty-five yards, he flung himself through the air; and, with Cabell, of Midsylvania, clutching at the wideness between his shoulder blades, he dropped flat across Midsylvania's goal line. A groan went up from the grand stand.

There wasn't a sound from any quarter, though, as Vretson squared off to kick for a goal; but whoops of relief arose when the ball, after soaring high and straight, veered off under pressure of a puff of air and, instead of passing over the bar, struck one of the goal posts with a mellow smack and dropped back. So the score, by the rules of those times, stood four to naught.

Nearly everybody there, I guess, figured that Sangamon would promptly buttress her lead by at least four additional points, and very possibly more; but she didn't. True, she played all round and all over and all through Midsylvania during the remaining portion of the first half, but she did not score again. This was due not so much to the rebuttal fight the defenders offered, for now their playing sagged more woefully weak than ever, but to small misplays and slip-ups and seeming overconfidence on the part of Sangamon.

It may have been they were cocksure of their power to score again when they chose. Maybe

they were a trifle tired. Maybe they were satisfied to postpone the slaughter-house work until toward the end of the game and make a
spectacular, overwhelming finish of it. Anyhow, it struck us, in the press stand, that the
reason behind their failure to push their advantage still farther, during the next ten minutes or so, was rather because of their own dis-
inclination than because of any strategy or
strength Midsylvania's plainly despondent
eleven presented against them.

Along here I became aware, subconsciously
at first, and then in a minute or so with a fuller
sense of realisation, that Major Stone had
waked up. I felt him wriggling on the bench,
joggling me in the side with his elbow; and
when I looked at him his face was an indignant
pink and his little white goatee was bristling
like a thistle pod.

He was saying something to himself, and by
listening, I caught from his muttered words the
purport of the change that had come into the
old man's emotions, which change, as I speed-
ily divined, was exactly what might have been
expected of him. He did not have the attitude
of the average spectator over in the grand
stand, for his bump of local pride was not being
bruised, as theirs was, by this exhibition. Nor
had he grasped and assimilated the feelings of
those two groups of youngsters whose cleated
feet ripped up the turf in front of him.

It did not lie within his capabilities to share

their youthful and, therefore, profound conviction that all which was desirable in life, here or
hereafter, centred on the results of this struggle; and that the youth who failed now to acquit himself to the greater glory of his comrades and his class and his college—and, most
of all, himself—would droop an abased and
shameful head through all the years to come.
For, as I may have remarked before, Major
Stone was not a bright person, but rather a
stupid one; and his viewpoint on most subjects
had not altered materially since Appomattox.

That was it—it had not altered since Appomattox; and because it had not he was viewing
the present event as a struggle between North
and South—as a conflict into which Civil War
causes and Civil War effects directly entered.
Possibly you cannot understand that. But you
could if you had known Major Stone and men
like him, most of whom are now dead and
gone. His face turned from a hot pink to a dull
brick-dust red, and he gnawed at his moustache.

"It is monstrous!" I heard him say. "It is
incredible! Southern sons of Southern sires,
every damned one of them! And because the
odds are against them they have weakened! I
myself can see that they are weakening every
minute. Why, the thing's incredible—that's
what it is! Incredible!"

Just then the whistle blew, and the teams,
which had been in a mix-up, unsnarled themselves. The Sangamon eleven came off the

field; some of them were briskly trotting to prove their fitness, and some were swaggering a little as their band hit up the tune of Marching Through Georgia to play them into their quarters under the stand. But the Varsity eleven passed out of sight with shoulders that drooped and with no spring in their gaits.

Back at the tail end of their line went little Morehead, wiping his damp eyes with the dirty sleeve of his jersey. Morehead was no young Saint Laurence, to expire smilingly on a gridiron. He was not of the stuff that martyrs are made of; he was a creature, part man and part boy, and the man part of him made him furious with self-reproach, but the boy in him made him cry. I take it, some of the spectators felt almost like crying too; certainly their cheering sounded so.

One of the Red tackles—Rodney—had been disabled just before the breakaway, and I ran over to Midsylvania's quarters to find out for the paper whether he was injured to the degree of being definitely incapacitated for further participation in the game. In what, during race meets, was a refreshment establishment, under the grand stand, I obtruded upon a veritable grand lodge of sorrow.

Gadsden, the coach, who had played with the team the year before, which was his graduating year, was out in the centre of the floor making a brave pretense at being hopeful; but I do not think anybody present suffered himself to be deceived thereby. His pleas to the team to buck up and to brace up, and to go back in and fight for every point, lacked sincerity. He appeared to be haranguing them because that was the ordained thing for him to do, and not because he expected to infuse into them any part of his make-believe optimism. Lying on their backs upon blankets, with limbs relaxed, some of his hearers turned dejected faces upward. Others, sitting upright or squatted on their knees, kept their abashed heads on their breasts, staring down steadfastly at nothing at all.

Morehead was sulking by himself in a corner, winking his eyelids and wrinkling his face up to hold back the tears of his mortification. He blamed himself, I take it, for what was the fault of all. Cabell was a tousled heap, against a wall. He was flexing a bruised wrist, as though that small hurt was just now the most important thing in the world to him. Even the darky rubbers and the darky water carrier showed their sensations by their dejected faces. There was enough of downcastness in that room to supply half a dozen funerals with all the gloom they might require; the whole place exhaled the essence of a resentful depression that was as plainly to be sniffed up into the nostrils as the smells of alcohol and arnica and liniment which burdened the air and gave the accompaniment of a drug-store smell to the picture.

As I halted at the door on my way out of
this melancholy spot to the scarcely less melancholy atmosphere of the open, having learned
that Rodney was not really injured, somebody
bumped into me, jostling me to one side; and,
to my astonishment, I saw that the impetuous
intruder was Major Stone. I had not known
until then that he had followed me here, and I
did not know now what errand could have
brought him along. But he did not keep me
wondering long; in fact, he did not keep me
wondering at all. He burst in on them with a
great "Woof!" of indignation.

Before scarcely any one there had realised
that a newcomer, arriving unheralded and all
unexpected, was in their midst, he stood in the
middle of the littered floor, glaring about him
and snorting loudly. His first words, too, were
calculated not only to startle them but deeply
to profane the semi-privacy of their grief and
their humiliation.

"Young gentlemen," he fairly shouted, "I
am ashamed of you! And I have come here to
tell you so, and to tell you why I am ashamed."

By sight, even, he was probably a stranger to
most of those who, with one accord, now stared
at the little, old-fashioned figure of this invader.
They straightened up. There was a rustle and
a creaking of their harnessed and padded bodies. Perhaps surprise held them dumb; or perhaps they were in a humour to take a scolding,
even from an outsider, feeling that they de-

served it. At any rate, only one of them spoke.
I think it was the voice of Gadsden, the coach,
that answered back.

"Who the devil are you?" he asked. "And
who the devil let you in here, anyhow?"

"You may not know me," snapped the Major; "but I know you." He wheeled on his
heels, aiming a jabbing forefinger at this man
and that. "And I know you—and I know
you—and I know you—and you, and you, too,
young sir, over there in the corner. What is
more, I knew your fathers before you."

"Well, what of it?"

"What of it? This much of it: Your fathers before you were gallant Southern gentlemen—the bearers of honoured names; names
revered in this state and in the Southern armies. That is what your fathers were. And
what have you, their sons, proved yourselves
to be this day? Cravens—that is the word.
Cravens! Out of all the South you were chosen
to represent your native land against these
Northerners; and how have you repaid the trust
imposed in you? By quitting—by showing the
white feather, like a flock of dunghill cockerels
—by raising the white flag at the first attack!"

A babble of resentful voices arose:

"Say, look here; now——"

"What do you know about football?"

"Who gave you any license to butt in here?"

"Say, that's pretty rough!"

He broke into the confused chorus of their

protests, silencing the interrupters by the stormy blare of his rejoinder.. He was so terribly in earnest that they just had to hearken.

"I know nothing of this game you have essayed to play. Before to-day I never saw it played; and if this miserable exhibition by you is a sample of the game I hope never to see it played again. But I know courage when I see it and I know cowardice when I see it."

He levelled his condemning finger at little Morehead and focused his glare upon that unhappy youth.

"Your name is Morehead! Your grandfather was a great governor of this great state. Your father was my companion in arms upon the field of battle—and no braver man ever breathed, sir. This historic inclosure bears the honoured name of your honoured line—Morehead Downs. You are the chosen leader of these companions of yours. And how have you led them to-day? How have you acquitted yourself of your trust? I ask you that—how?"

He halted, out of breath.

"The other team is stronger. They've got us outclassed. Look—why, look at the reputation they've got all over this country! What —what chance have we against them?"

The confession came from little Morehead haltingly, as though he spoke against his own will in his own defence.

"Damn their reputation!" shouted Major Stone. "Your very words are an admission of the things I allege against you, and against all of you here. Concede that your antagonists are stronger than you, man for man. Concede that they outclass you in experience. Is that any reason why they should outclass you in courage and in determination? Your father and the fathers of more than half of the rest of you served in an army that for four years defended our beloved country against a foe immensely stronger than they were—stronger in men, in money, in munitions, in food, in supplies, in guns—stronger in everything except valour.

"Suppose, because of the odds against them, your people had lost heart from the very outset, as you yourselves have lost heart here today. Would that great war have lasted for four years? Or would it have lasted for four months? Would the Southern Confederacy have endured until it no longer had the soldiers to fill the gaps and hold the lines; or food for the bellies of those soldiers who were left; or powder and lead for their guns? Or would it have surrendered after the first repulse, as you have surrendered? Answer me that, some of you!

"These Northerners are game clear through; I can tell that. Their ancestors before them were brave men—the Southern Confederacy could never have been starved out and bled white by a breed of cowards. And these young men here—these splendid young Americans

from up yonder in that Northern country—
have the same gallant spirit their people showed
forty years ago against your people. But you
—you have lost the spirit of your race, that
surely must have been born in you. You are
going to let these Yankees run right over you
— your behaviour proves it — and not fight
back. That is what I charge against you.
That is what I am here to tell you."

"How about me?" put in one of the blan-
keted contingent of his audience. "My people
were all Unionists."

"Your name?" demanded the Major of him.

"Speedman."

"A son of the late Colonel Henry T. Speedman?"

"His nephew."

"I knew your uncle and your uncle's brothers and your grandfather. They were Union-
men from principle; and I admired them for it,
even though we differed, and even though they
took up arms against their own kinsmen and
fought on the opposite side. They wore the
blue from conviction; but when the war was
over your uncle, being a Southerner, helped to
save his native state from carpetbaggery and
bayonet rule. That was the type of man your
uncle was. I regret to note that you did not
inherit his qualities. I particularly observed
your behaviour out there on that field yonder a
while ago. You quit, young man—you quit
like a dog!"

"Say, look here; you're an old man, and that's enough to save you!" Speedman suddenly was sobbing in his mortification. "But —but you've got no right to say things like that to me. You've—you've——" A gulp cut the miserable youngster's utterance short. He choked and plaintively tried again: "If we can't win we can't win—and that's all there is to it! Isn't it, fellows?"

He looked to his companions in distress for comfort; but all of them, as though mesmerised, were looking at Major Stone. It dawned on me, watching and listening across the threshold, that some influence—some electric appeal to an inner consciousness of theirs—was beginning to galvanise them, taking the droop out of their spines, and making their frames tense where there had been a sag of nonresistance, and putting sparks of resentment into their eyes. The transformation had been almost instantaneously accomplished, but it was plainly visible.

"I am not expecting that you should win," snapped the Major, turning Speedman's words into an admonition for all of them. "I do not believe it is humanly possible for you to win. There is nothing disgraceful in being fairly defeated; the disgrace is in accepting defeat without fighting back with all your strength and all your will and all your skill and all your strategy and all your tactics. And that is exactly what I have just seen you doing. And that, judging by all the indications, is exactly what you will go on doing during the remaining portion of this affair."

There were no more interruptions. For perhaps two or three minutes more, then, the old Major went steadily on, saying his say to the end. Saying it, he wasn't the Old Major I had known before; he was not pottering and ponderous; he did not clothe his thoughts in cumbersome, heavy phrases. He fairly bit the words off—short, bitter, scorching words—and spat them out in their faces. He did not plead with them; nor—except by indirection—did he invoke a sentiment that was bound to be as much a part of them as the nails on their fingers or the teeth in their mouths.

And, somehow, I felt—and I knew they felt —that here, in this short, stumpy white-haired form, stood the Old South, embodied and typified, with all its sectional pride and all its sectional devotion—yes, and all its sectional prejudices. All at once, in the midst of a sentence, he checked up; and then, staring hard at them through a pause, he spoke his final message:

"You are of the seed of heroes. Try to remember that when you go back out yonder before that great crowd. You are the sons of men who had sand, who had bottom, who had all the things a fighting man should have. Try —if you can—to remember it!"

Out from behind the group that had clustered before the speaker, darted a diminutive

darky — Midsylvania's self - appointed water
carrier:

"He done jest said it!" whooped the little
negro, dancing up and down in frenzy. "He
done jest said it! 'Cinnamon Seed an' Sandy
Bottom!' Dat's it! 'Cinnamon Seed an' Sandy
Bottom!'—same ez you sez it w'en you sings
Dixie Land. Dem's de words to win by! W'ite
folks, youse done heared de lesson preached
frum de true tex'. Come on! Le's us go an'
tear dem Sangamonders down! 'Cinnamon
Seed an' Sandy Bottom!' Oh, gloree, gloree,
hallelujah!"

He rocked back on his splay feet, his knees
sprung forward, his mouth wide open, and his
eyes popping out of his black face.

The Major did not look the little darky's
way. Settling his slouch hat on his head, he
faced about and out he stalked; and I, following along after him, was filled with conflicting
emotions, for, as it happened, my father was a
Confederate soldier, too, and I had been bred
up on a mixed diet of Robert E. Lee, N. B.
Forrest and Albert Sidney Johnston.

I followed him back to our post, he saying
nothing at all on the way and I likewise silent.
I scrouged past him to my place alongside Ike
Webb and sat down, and tried in a few words
to give Ike and Gil Boyd a summary of the
sight I had just witnessed. And when I was
done I illustrated my brief and eager narrative
by pointing with a flirt of my thumb to Major

Stone, stiffly erect on my left hand, with his chest protruded and his head held high in a posture faintly suggestive of certain popular likenesses of the late Napoleon Bonaparte; and on his elderly face was the look of one who, having sowed good seed in receptive loam, confidently expects an abundant and a gratifying harvest.

It was a different team which came out for the second half of that game; not exactly a jaunty team, nor yet a boisterous one, but rather a team that were grimly silent, indicating by their silence a certain preparedness and a certain resolution for the performance of that which is claimed to speak louder than words—action.

The onlookers, I judged, saw the difference almost instantly and realised that from some source, somehow, Morehead's men had gathered unto themselves a new power of will, which presently they meant to express physically. And three minutes later Sangamon found herself breasted by a mechanism that had in its composition the springiness of an earnest desire and a sincere determination, whereas before, in emergencies, it had expressed no more than sullen and downhearted desperation.

Now from the very outset there was resilience behind its formations and active intelligence behind its movements, guiding and shaping them. The confronting line might give under the pressure of superior weight, but it bounced

right back. At once it was made manifest that
the Red eleven would not thenceforward be
content merely to defend, but would have the
effrontery actually to attack, and attack again,
and to keep on attacking. No longer was it a
case of hammer falling on anvil; two hammers
were battering against one another, nose to nose
now, and in one stroke there was as much
buoyancy as in the other.

In my eagerness to reach my climax I am
getting ahead of my story. Let's go back a
bit: The whistle blew. The antagonists having swapped goals, Midsylvania now had what
benefit was to be derived from the wind, which
blew out of the West at a quartering angle
across the field. Following the kick-off an in-
terchange of punts ensued. Midsylvania apparently elected to continue these kicking operations indefinitely; whereupon it is probable the
Sangamon strategists jumped at the conclusion
that, realising the hopelessness of overcoming
the weight presented against them, the locals
meant to make a kicking match of it. Be that
as it may, they accepted the challenge, if challenge it was, and a punting duel ensued, with
no noteworthy fortunes falling to either eleven.

I think it was early in this stage of the pro-
ceedings, after some mighty brisk scrimmaging,
when the strangers, by coming into violent
physical contact with their opponents, discovered that a new spirit inspired and governed
the others, and began to apprehend that, after

all, this would not be a walkover for them; but that they must fight, and fight hard, to hold their present lead, and fight even harder if they expected to swell that lead.

When, at the first opportunity for a forward push, the Red line came at the Blue with an impetuosity theretofore lacking from its frontal assaults, you could almost see the ripple of astonishment running down the spines of the Northerners as they braced themselves to meet and stay the onslaught. Anyhow, you could imagine you saw it; certainly there were puzzled looks on the faces of some of them as they emerged from the mêlée.

With appreciative roars, the crowd greeted these evidences of a newer and more comforting aspect to the situation. Each time some Midsylvania player caught the booted ball as it came tumbling out of the skies the grand stand rocked to the noise; each time Midsylvania sent it flying back to foreign ground it rocked some more; each time the teams clashed, then locked together, it was to be seen that the Midsylvanians held their ground despite the efforts of their bulkier rivals to uproot and overthrow them.

And, at that, the air space beneath the peaked roof was ripped all to flinders by exultant blares from sundry thousands of lungs. Under the steady pounding feet the floor of the grand stand became a great bass drum, which was never silent; and all the myriad red flags danced together. Into the struggle an element of real dash had entered and mightily it uplifted the spectators. They knew now that, though the Varsity team might be beaten, and probably would be, they would not be disgraced. It would be an honourable defeat before overpowering odds, and one stoutly resisted to the end by all that intelligence, plus pluck, could do.

There was no fault now to be found with Midsylvania's captain. Little Morehead, with his face a red smear, was playing all over the lot. The impact of a collision with a bigger frame than his, had slammed him face down against the ground, skinning one cheek and bloodying his nose. He looked like a mad Indian in streaky war paint, and he played like one. He seemed to be everywhere at once, exhorting, commanding, leading; by shouted precept and by reckless example giving the cue to his teammates.

I suppose the latter half was about half over when the Sangamon team changed their tactics and, no longer content to play safe and exchange punts, sought to charge through and gain ground by sheer force. Doubtlessly their decision was based on sound principles of reason; but by reason of certain insurmountable obstacles, personified in eleven gouging, wrestling, panting, sweating youths, they were effectually deterred, during a breathless period of minutes, from so doing.

It was inevitable that a break must come sooner or later. It was not humanly possible for any team or any two teams to maintain that punishing pace very long without giving way somewhere.

The ball, after various vicissitudes, was in the middle of the field, and the Northerners had it. As the Blue tackles slipped back of their comrades stealthily, and Vretson, stealing forward, poised himself to take the catch, we on the press benches realised that Sangamon meant to undertake a repetition of the device that had won her lone goal for her. Thirty minutes earlier it would have seemed the logical move to try. Now, in view of everything, it was audacious.

At that, though, I guess it was Sangamon's best card, even though Midsylvania would be forewarned and forearmed by their earlier disastrous experience to take measures for combating the play. Everything depended on getting Vretson away to a flying start and then keeping his interference intact.

The captain chanted the code numbers. The Blue press shifted in quick shuttlelike motions, and the ball, beautifully and faultlessly handled, was flipped back, aiming straight for Vretson's welcoming grasp. Simultaneously something else happened. That something else was Morehead.

As the ball was passed he moved. There was a hole in Sangamon's breastworks, made by the spreading out of her men. It was a little hole and a hole which instantaneously closed up again, being stoppered by an interposing torso; but in that flash of space Morehead saw the opening and, without being touched, came whizzing straight through it like a small, compact torpedo. Head in and head down, he crashed into Vretson in the same tenth-second when the ball reached Vretson's fingers. With his skull, his shoulders, his arms, and his trunk he smashed against the giant.

Vretson staggered sideways. The ball escaped from his grip; and, striking the earth, it took one lazy bound, and then another; but no more. As it bounced the second time, Morehead, bending double from his hips, slid under it with outspread arms, scooped it up to his breast, and was off, travelling faster, I am sure, than Morehead in all his life had ever travelled. He was clear and away, going at supertopspeed, while Vretson still spun and rocked on his heels.

Obeying the signal for the play the majority of the Sangamon team already had darted off to their right to make a living barrier upon the threatened side of the imaginary lane their star was due to follow. It behooved them to reverse the manœuvre. Digging their heels into the earth for brakes they wheeled round, scuttling back and spreading out to intercept the fugitive; but he was already past and beyond Vretson, and nearing the line of cross-angle along which the nearest of his pursuers must go to encounter him. Before him, along the eastern boundary of Sangamon's territory, was a clear stretch of cross-marked turf.

Vretson recovered himself and made a stern chase of it, and Vretson could run, as I said before; but it would have been as reasonable to expect a Jersey bull to overtake a swamp rabbit when the swamp rabbit had the start of the bull, and was scared to death besides, as to expect Vretson to catch Morehead. The Red captain travelled three feet for every two the bigger man travelled. Twenty yards—thirty, forty—he sped, and not a tackler's hand was laid on him. With the pack of his adversaries tagging out behind him like hounds behind a hare, he pitched over the goal line and lay there, his streaming nose in the grass roots, with the precious ball under him, and the Sangamon players tumbling over him as they came tailing up. Single-handed, on a fluky chance, Morehead had duplicated and bettered what Vretson, with assistance, had done.

The crowd simply went stark, raving crazy and behaved accordingly. But the Varsity section in the grand stand and the clump of blanketted Varsity substitutes and scrubs on the side lines were the craziest spots of all.

After this there isn't so very much to be told. Midsylvania kicked for a goal, but failed, as Sangamon had done. The ball struck the crossbar between the white goal posts and flopped back; and during the few remaining minutes of play neither side tallied a point, though both tried hard enough and Sangamon came very near it once, but failed—thanks to the same inspired counterforces that had balked her in similar ambitions all through this half.

So, at the end, with the winter sun going down red in the west, and the grand stand all red with dancing flags to match it, the score stood even—four to four.

Officially a tie, yes; but not otherwise—not by the reckoning of the populace. That Midsylvania, outmanned and outweighted as she was, should have played those Middle West champions to a standstill was, in effect, a victory—so the crowd figured—and fitting to be celebrated on that basis, which promptly it was.

Out from the upstanding ranks of the multitude, down from the stand, across the track and into the field came the Varsity students, clamouring their joy, and their band came with them, and others, unattached, came trailing after them. Some were dancing dervishes and some were human steam whistles, and all the rest were just plain lunatics. They fell into an irregular weaving formation, four or six abreast, behind the team, with Morehead up ahead, riding upon the shoulders of two of his fellows; and round the gridiron they started, going first between one pair of goal posts and then between the other pair. Doubtlessly the band played; but what tune they elected to play nobody knew, because nobody could hear it—not even the musicians themselves.

As the top of the column, completing its first circuit, swung down the gridiron toward the judges' stand, Morehead pointed toward where we sat and, from his perch on their shoulders, called down something to those who bore him. At that, a deputation of about half a dozen broke out of the mass and charged straight for us. For a moment it must have seemed to the crowd that this detachment contemplated a physical assault upon some obnoxious newspaper man behind our bench, for they dived right in among us, laying hands upon one of our number, heaving him bodily upward, and bearing him away a prisoner.

Half a minute later Major Putnam Stone, somewhat dishevelled as to his attire, was also mounted on a double pair of shoulders and was bobbing along at the front of the procession, side by side with young Morehead. Judging by his expression, I should say the Major was enjoying the ride. Without knowing the whys and the wherefores of it, the spectators derived that in some fashion this little, old, white-haired man was esteemed by Midsylvania's representatives to have had a share in the achieved result.

As this conviction sank home, the exultant yelling mounted higher and higher still. I think it was along here the members of the band quit trying to be heard and stopped their playing, and took their horns down from their faces.

Immediately after this still another strange figure attained a conspicuous place in the parade: A little darky, mad with joy, and wearing a red-and-gray sweater much too roomy for him, came bounding across the field, with an empty water bucket in one hand. He caught up with the front row of the marchers; and, scuttling along backward, directly in front of them, he began calling out certain words in a sort of slogan, repeating them over and over again, until those nearest him detected the purport of his utterances and started chanting them in time with him.

Presently, as the chorus of definite sounds and the meaning of the sounds spread along down the column, the Varsity boys took up the refrain, and it rose and fell in a great, thundering cadence. And then everybody made out its substance, the words being these:

"Cinnamon Seed and Sandy Bottom! *Cinnamon Seed and Sandy Bottom!* CINNAMON SEED AND SANDY BOTTOM!"

The sun, following its usual custom, continued to go down, growing redder and redder as it went; and Midsylvania, over and above the triumph it had to celebrate and was celebrating, had also these three things now added unto her: A new college yell, in this perfectly meaningless line from an old song; a new cheer leader—her first, by the way—in the person of a

ragged black water boy; and a new football idol
to take to her heart, the same being an elderly
gentleman who knew nothing at all of the
science of football, and doubtlessly cared less—
an idol who in the fullness of time would become a tradition, to be treasured along with
the noseless statue of Henry Clay and the beech
tree under which Daniel Boone slept one night.

So that explains why, each year after the
main game, when the team of a bigger and
stronger Midsylvania have broken training,
they drink a rising toast to the memory of Major Putnam Stone, deceased; whereat, as afore-
stated, there are no heel-taps whatsoever.

CHAPTER IX

A KISS FOR KINDNESS

AS WILL be recalled, it was from the lips of His Honour, Judge Priest, that I heard the story relating to those little scars upon the legs of Mr. Herman Felsburg. It was from the same source that I gleaned certain details concerning the manner of Mr. Felsburg's enlistment and services as a private soldier in the Army of the Confederate States of America; and it is these facts that make up the narrative I would now relate. As Judge Priest gave them to me, with occasional interruptions by old Doctor Lake, so now do I propose giving them to you.

This tale I heard at a rally in the midst of one of the Bryan campaigns, back in those good days before the automobile and the attached cuff came in, while Bryan campaigns were still fashionable in the nation. It could not have been the third Bryan campaign, and I am pretty sure it was not the first one; so it must have been the second one. On second thought, I am certain it was the second one—when the candidate's hair was still almost as long in front as behind.

By reason of the free-silver split four years earlier, and bitter dissensions within the party organization subsequently, our state had fallen into the doubtful column; wherefore, campaigns took on even a more hectic and feverish aspect than before. Of course there was no doubt about our own district. Whatever might betide, she was safe and sound—a Democratic Rock of Ages. "Solid as Gibraltar!" John C. Breckinridge called her once; and, taking the name, a Gibraltar she remained forever after, piling up a plurality on which the faithful might mount and stand, even as on a watch-tower of the outer battlements, to observe the struggle for those debatable counties to the eastward and the northward of us. It was not a question whether she would give a majority for the ticket, but a question of how big a majority she would give. Come to think about it, that was not much of a question, either. We had sincere voters and competent compilers of election returns down our way then; and still have, for that matter.

Nevertheless and notwithstanding, it was to be remembered that, four years before, the bulk of the state's votes in the Electoral College, for the first time in history, had been recorded for a Republican nominee; and so, with a possibility of a recurrence of this catastrophe staring us in the face, the rally that was held

on that fine Indian summery day at Cold
Springs, five miles out from town on the road
to Maxon's Mills, assumed a scope and an importance beyond the rallies of earlier and less
uncertain times. It was felt that by precept
and deed the Stalwarts should set an example
for all wavering brethren above the river. So
there was a parade through town in the morning and burgoo and a barbecue in the woods at
noon, and in the afternoon a feast of oratory,
with Congressman Dabney Prentiss to preside
and a United States Senator from down across
the line in Tennessee to deliver the principal
address. There was forethought in the shaping of the programme thus: those who came to
feast would remain to hear.

Time waits on no man, but has an accommodating way of checking up occasionally, while
the seed pod of reminiscence sprouts beneath
the warm, rich humus of a fellow's memory;
and, because time does do just this, I yet can
visualise, with sufficient clarity for my present
purposes, some of the things which happened
that day. Again is my blood quickened by
sweet strains of music as Dean's Brass Band
swings up Franklin Street, leading the procession of the forenoon.

Without serious mental strain I re-create the
picture of the prominent guests riding in open carriages with members of the reception committee
and, behind them, the Young Men's Democratic
Marching Club going afoot, four hundred strong.

I see a big four-horse wagon, used ordinarily for such prosaic purpose as moving household goods, but now with bunting and flags converted into a tableau car, and bearing pretty girls, badged and labelled with the names of the several states of the Union. And the prettiest, stateliest girl of all stands for Kentucky. At her side is a little dark girl who represents the Philippines, and accordingly she wears upon her wrists a dangling doubled loop of ironmongery. This hardware is very new and very shiny, and its links jangle effectively as the pageant moves onward, thereby causing the captive sister to smile a gratified smile not altogether in keeping with the lorn state of servitude here typified by these trace-chain manacles of hers.

It seems a long time—doesn't it?—since Expansion was a cardinal issue and Imperialism a war cry, and we were deeply concerning ourselves with the fate and future of the little brown brother, and warmly debating among ourselves whether we should continue to hold him as a more or less unwilling ward of the nation or turn him and his islands loose to fend for themselves. But really, when we cast up the tally of the intervening years, it isn't so very long ago after all. It is as though this might have happened yesterday, isn't it?

So it is with me—abiding as one of those yesterdays that stand out from the ruck and run of yesterdays. Perhaps that is why I can

almost taste the dust which is winnowed up
from beneath the hoofs of the teams and the
turning wheels as the crowds stream off out
the gravel turnpike, bound for Cold Springs.
Nearly everybody of consequence, politically
or socially, joins in that hurrying pilgrimage.
Like palmers of old, Judge Priest and Commonwealth's Attorney Flournoy and Sheriff Giles
Birdsong and all our district and county and
city officials attend, to attest by their presence
the faith that is in them. I attend, too; but in
the capacity of scribe. I go to report the doings for the *Daily Evening News*. I am the
principal reporter and, by the same token, one-
half of the local staff of that dependable jour-
nal, the remaining half being its editor in chief.

Time in its flight continuing to turn backward, we are now at Cold Springs. Mint-mas-
ter Jack Frost has been busy there these last
few nights, so that the leaves of the hickories
are changing from summer's long green to
swatches of the crisp yellow-backed currency
of October. On the snake fence, which sepa-
rates the flanks of the woodland from the
cleared lands beyond, the trumpet vine and the
creeper blaze in clumps so red that one almost
wonders the dried rails do not catch fire too.

The smells of fall are in the air—of corn in
the shock; of bruised winesaps dropping, dead
ripe, from the orchard trees; of fox grapes turning purple in the vine canopies away up in the
tops of the trees. From the fringes of the grove

come the sounds of the stamping of horses' feet and the restless swishing of horses' tails. Off in quiet places a hundred flat flasks have been uncorked; in each thicket rendezvous forethoughted citizens are extending the hospitalities of the occasion to such as forgot to freight their hip pockets before journeying hither. There have been two fights and one runaway.

And now it is noon time; and now it is half an hour past it, and the county committee, with the aid of the only known Republicans present—all these latter being of African descent and all, or nearly all, camp cooks of high repute in Red Gravel County—is about to play host to the multitude.

In retrospect I smell the burgoo a-cooking, and sympathetically my mouth waters. Do you know burgoo? If not your education has been sadly neglected—most woefully neglected. It is a glorified gumbo, made in copper caldrons over open fires; and it contains red meats and white meats, and ducks and chickens, and young squirrels, and squabs, and all the fresh green vegetables in season. And into it with prodigal black hands the cooks put plenty of tomatoes for color and potatoes for body and red peppers for seasoning and onions for flavour. And all these having stewed together for hours and hours, they merge anon into a harmonious and fragrant whole. So now the product is dipped up in ladles and bestowed upon the assemblage in tin cups, to be drunk after a fashion said to have been approved of by Old Hickory Jackson himself. A Jeffersonian simplicity likewise governs the serving out of the barbecued meats, following afterward. You eat with the tools Nature has given you, and the back of your hand is your napkin. And when everybody is as full of victuals as a good Democrat should be—which is another way of saying so full he cannot hold another bite or another sup—the band plays and the speaking starts on a plank platform under a brush arbour, with the audience sitting or standing—but mostly sitting—on a fragrant thick matting of faded wild grasses and fallen red and yellow leaves.

The programme of events having progressed to this point, I found my professional duties over for the day. The two principal speeches were already in type at the *Daily Evening News* office, advance copies having been furnished by Congressman Prentiss and the visiting Senator from Tennessee, the authors of the same. By special messenger I had transmitted brief dispatches touching on the complete and unqualified success of the burgoo, the barbecue, the two fist fights and the runaway.

Returning from the fringes of the woodland, after confiding my scribbled advices to our courier, my way led me under the shoulder of the bluff above Cold Springs. There, right where the water came seeping out through the bank of tawny gravel, I came upon a picture

which is one of the pictures that have endured
in reasonably vivid colours on the background
of my mind.

The bole of an uptorn gum tree spanned a
half-moon depression at the verge of the spring.
Upon the butt end of the log, where an up-
ended snag of root made a natural rest for his
broad back, was perched Judge Priest. His
plump legs hugged the rounded trunk. In one
hand he held a pint flask and in the other a tin
cup, which lately must have contained burgoo. A short distance down the tree from him
sat old Doctor Lake, without any bottle, but
with the twin to Judge Priest's tin cup poised
accurately upon one of his bony knees.

Behind these two, snugly screening them in,
was a wall of green and yellow grape leaves.
Through the vines the sunlight filtered in, to
make a mellow flood about them. Through
the leaves, also, came distantly the sound of
the present speaker's voice and, at frequent intervals, cheering. There was to be heard a
gentle tinkling of cracked ice. A persuasive
odour of corn distillations perfumed the languid air. All through the glade nuts were
dropping from the hickories, with sharp little
reports. It was a picture, all right enough!

My feet made rustlings in the leaves. Judge
Priest squinted over his glasses to see who the
intruder upon their woodland privacy might be.

"Why, howdy, son!" he hailed. "How's
everything with you?"

He didn't offer to share his store of refreshment with me. I never knew him to give a very young man a drink or to accept a drink from such a one. Doctor Lake raised his cup to stir its contents and nodded in my direction over it.

"The big speech of the day has just got started good, gentlemen," I said. "Didn't you-all know it?"

"Yes; we knowed it," answered the old Judge; "in fact, we heared the beginnin' of it. That's one reason why me and Lew Lake come on away. The other reason was that Lew run acrost a little patch of late mint down here by the spring. So we slipped off frum the crowd and come on down here to sort of take things nice and easy till it gits time to be startin' back toward the city."

"Why, I thought he was a mighty fine speaker, from what I heard right after Mr. Prentiss introduced him," I said.

"He's all of that," assented the old Judge; "he's a regular Cicero—seems to know this here oratory business frum who laid the rail. He don't never jest plain ast somebody to do somethin'. He adjures 'em by the altars of their Sunny Southland, and he beseeches 'em by the memories of their sires; but he don't ast 'em. And I took notice, durin' the few minutes I lingered on—spellbound, ez you mout say, by the witchery of his voice—that when he gits holt of a good long word it ain't a word

no more. He runs her as a serial and every
syllable is a separate chapter.

"Oh, no; I ain't got a word to say ag'inst
the distinguished gentleman's style of delivery.
I only wisht I had his gift of melodious expression. I reckin ef I did, I'd talk in public part
of the day and sing the rest of the time. But
the p'int is, son, that me and Lew Lake have
heared consid'able of that particular brand of
oratory in our day, and after a little spell of lis-
tenin' we decided betwixt ourselves that we
favoured the quiet of the sylvan dell to the
heat and dust of the forum. So here we are,
ez you behold us.

"One speech more or less won't make much
difference in the gineral results, noways, I reckin. Down here in the pennyrile country we'll
all vote the regular ticket the same ez we always do; and the Republikans will vote their
ticket, bein' the stubborn unreasonable creatures that they are; and then our boys'll hold
back the returns to see how many Democrat
votes are needed, and up in the mountains the
Republikans will hold theirn back to see how
many Republikan votes are needed—and that'll
be the whole upshot of it, onless the corrupt
scoundrels should succeed in outcounting the
party of the people.

"Of course there's a great crisis hoverin'
over our country at present. There's a crisis
hoverin' every four years, regular—to hear the
orators tell it. But I've took notice that, after

the votin' is over, the crisis always goes back
in its hole to stay till the next presidential
election, and the country remains reasonably
safe, no matter which side gits in; though I admit it's purty hard to convince the feller who's
already got a government job, or hopes to git
one, that the whole nation won't plumb go to
thunder onless his crowd wins."

"Still, Billy," put in Doctor Lake, "there
was a time when all these high - sounding
phrases about duty and patriotism meant more
to us than they do now—back in the spring
and summer of Sixty-one—eh?"

Behind the Judge's spectacle lenses sparks of
reminiscence burned in his faded blue eyes. He
lifted his cup ceremoniously and Doctor Lake
lifted his, and I knew they were drinking to the
memory of olden days.

"Now you're shoutin'!" Judge Priest assented. "Say, Lew, do you call to mind them
speeches Hector Dallas used to utter 'way back
yonder, when Sumter was bein' fired on and
the Yankee Government was callin' fur troops
to put down the Rebellion, ez they seen fit to
term it? Heck Dallas was our champion home-
grown orator in those times," he vouchsafed in
an aside for my better enlightenment. "Somethin' about that young feller yonder, that's
speakin' so brilliantly and so fluently now, puts
me right smartly in mind of him. Heck was
plenty copious with language himself. When it
come to burnin' words he was jest the same

ez one of these here volcanoes. Remember,
don't you, Lew, how willin' Heck was to bleed
and die fur his native land?"

"But he didn't," stated Doctor Lake
grimly.

"Well—since you mention it—not to any
noticeable extent," said Judge Priest. "Least-
wise, any bleedin' that he done was done internally, frum the strain of utterin' all them
fiery remarks." Again he included me with a
gesture. "You see, son, Heck didn't go off to
the war with the rest of us. Nearly everybody
else did—this town was purty near emptied of
young fellers of a suitable courtin' age after
we'd gone down to Camp Boone to begin drillin'. But Hecky didn't go.

"Ez I recollect, he felt called upon to put
out first fur Richmond to give President Davis
and the Cabinet the benefit of his advice or
somethin'; and aimed to join us later. But he
didn't—somehow, somethin' always kept inter-
ferin' with his ambition to bleed and die, until
after a while it seemed like he jest got discouraged and quit tryin'. When we got back home,
four years later—sech ez was left of us—Heck
had done been entirely reconstructed and was
fixin' to run fur office on the Black Radical
ticket."

"The cat had to jump mighty brisk to beat
Hector," said Doctor Lake; "or else, when she
landed on the other side, she'd find him already
there, warming a place for her. I've known a

good many like Hector—and some of them prospered fairly well—while they lasted."

"Well, the spring of Sixty-one was a stirrin' period, and I reckin oratory helped along right smartly at the start," said Judge Priest; "though, to be sure, later on it came to pass that the boys who could go hongry and ragged, and still keep on fightin' the Yankees, were the ones that really counted.

"Take Meriwether Grider now: He went in as our company commander and he come out with the marks of a brigadier on his coat collar; but I'll bet you a ginger cookie Meriwether Grider never said a hundred words on a stretch in his life without he was cussin' out some feller fur not doin' his duty. Meriwether certainly learned to cuss mighty well fur a man whose early trainin' had been so turribly neglected in that respect."

"Recall how Meriwether Grider behaved the night we organised Company B?" inquired Doctor Lake.

"Jest the same ez ef it was yistiddy!" assented Judge Priest.

He half turned his chubby body so as to face me. By now I was sitting on the log between them. I had scented a story and I craved mightily to hear it, though I never dreamed that some day I should be writing it out.

"You see, boy, it was like this: Upstate the sentiment was purty evenly divided betwixt stayin' in the Union and goin' out of it; but down here, in Red Gravel County, practically everybody was set one way—so much one way that they took to callin' our town Little Charleston, and spoke of this here Congressional District as the South Carolina of the West. Ez state after state went out, the feelin' got warmer and warmer; but the leaders of public opinion, all except Heck Dallas, counselled holdin' off till the legislature could act. Heck, he was for crossin' over into Illinois some nice pleasant dark night and killin' off the Abolitionists, though at that time of speakin' there weren't many more Abolitionists livin' on that side of the river than there were on this. That was merely Heck's way of expressin' his convictions.

"In spite of his desires, we kept on waitin'. But when word come from Frankfort that the legislature, by a mighty clost vote, had voted down the Secession Ordinance and had declared fur armed neutrality—which was in the nature of a joke, seein' ez everybody in the state who was old enough to tote a fusee was already armed and couldn't be a neutral—why, down in this neck of the woods we didn't wait no longer.

"Out of the front window of his printin' office old Colonel Noble h'isted the first Confederate flag seen in these parts; and that night, at the old market house, there was the biggest mass meetin' that ever had been held in this here town up to then. A few young fellers had already slid down acrost the border into Ten-

nessee to enlist, and a few more were already
over in Virginia, wearin' the grey; but everybody else that was anybody was there.

"Right away Heck took the platform.
They'd 'a' had to lock it up somewheres to keep
him frum takin' it. He was up on one of them
market benches, wavin' his arms and spoutin'
about the mudsills and the nigger lovers, and
jest darin' the accursed invader to put one heel
upon the sacred soil of the grand old Commonwealth—not both his heels, but ary one of 'em
—when all of a sudden Meriwether Grider
leaned over and kissed his wife—he hadn't been
married but a little more'n a year and they
had a baby about three weeks old at home.
And then he stepped forward and climbed up
on the bench and sort of shoved Heck to one
side, and called out that there'd been enough
talk, and that it was about time for action; and
said, ef somebody had a piece of paper handy,
he'd like mightily to put his name down as a
volunteer fur the Southern Army. And in another second every woman there was cheerin'
with one side of her mouth and cryin' with the
other.

"And Colonel Noble had fetched his flag up
and was wavin' it with both hands; and old
Doctor Hendrickson, the Presbyterian preacher, had made a prayer—a heap shorter one
than whut he ginerally made—and had yanked
a little pocket Testament out frum under his
coattails fur the boys to take the oath on. And

in less'n no time Heck Dallas was back down
in the crowd, in consider'ble danger of being
trompled to death in the rush of young fellers
to git up there and sign their names to the
roll."

Doctor Lake slid off the log and stood up,
with his black hat crumpled in one gnarled old
hand. In the emotion of the moment he forgot his grammar:

"You remember, Billy—don't you?—how you
and me and Peter J. Galloway and little Gil
Nicholas went up together to sign?"

"I ain't exactly liable to furgit it, ever,"
said Judge Priest. "That was the night I jest
natchelly walked off and left my little law office
flat on its back. I'd been advertisin' myself to
practise law fur about a year, but whut I'd
mainly practised up to that time was economy
—that and checkers and old sledge, to help pass
away the time. No, suh; I didn't leave no
clients behind me, clamourin' fur my professional services. Clients were something I'd
heared a lot of talk about, but hadn't met face
to face. All I had to do when I quit was jest
to put out the fire and shut the door, and come
on away."

"And the last one of all to sign that night
was Herman Felsburg," stated Doctor Lake, as
though desirous of rounding out a recital.

"Yes—that's right too, Lew," agreed the old
Judge. "Herman was the very last one. I remember how some of the crowd begun snick-

erin' when he come stumpin' up on them crook-
etty little laigs of hisn; but the snickerin' died
out when Meriwether Grider grabbed Herman's
hand and shook it, and Doctor Hendrickson
held out the Book fur him to swear on it to be
true and faithful to the cause of the Southern
Confederacy. A person don't snicker so very
well that's got a lump in his throat at the moment.

"You see, son, Herman was a kind of town
joke them days," stated Judge Priest, again
digressing for my benefit. "There weren't
many furreign-born people in this section back
yonder in Sixty-one. Ef a feller come along
that was frum Greece or Italy or Spain, or
somewheres else down that way, we jest called
him a Dago, dry-so—and let it go at that.
But ef he hailed from Germany or Holland or
Russia, or anywhere in Northern Europe, he
was a Dutchman to us.

"There were just two exceptions to the rule:
An Irishman was an Irishman, of course; and a
Jew was a Jew. We had a few Irish families in
town, like the Galloways and the Hallorans;
and there was one Jewish family livin' here—
the Liebers; but they'd all been born in this
country and didn't speak nothin' but English,
and, exceptin' that old man Lieber used to close
up his hide-and-pelt store of a Sad'day, instid
of Sunday, it never occurred to anybody that
the Liebers practised a different religion frum
the rur of folks.

"Herman had been here about a year, off
and on. He didn't seem to know nobody, and
he didn't have any friends. He wasn't more'n
nineteen years old—or maybe twenty; and he
was shy and awkward and homely. He used
to go out through the county with a pack on
his back, sellin' gimcracks to country people.
He could make change all right—I reckin he
jest natchelly inherited that ez a gift—and he
was smart enough at drivin' a bargain; but
somehow it seemed like he jest couldn't learn
to talk English, or to understand it, neither, exceptin' when the subject was business. Understand, that was thirty-odd years back; but
sometimes, even now, when old Herman gits
excited, you'd think, to hear him, that he didn't
know much English yit. His language matches
the shape of his laigs then."

I nodded understandingly, Mr. Felsburg's
conversational eccentricities being a constant
fount of material for the town humourists of
my own generation. The Judge went on:

"Well, anyway, he signed up that night,
along with all the rest of us. And after that,
fur a few days, so many things was happenin'
that I sort of forgot about him; and I reckin
nearly everybody else did too. It seemed like
the whole town sort of went crazy fur a spell,
whut with the first company, which was our
company, electin' its officers, and the County
Battery formin', and a troop of cavalry organisin', and the older men enrollin' fur home de-

fence, and a lot of big-mouth fellers standin'
round on street corners 'lowin' as how it was
goin' to be only a ninety-day picnic, anyway,
and that any Southern man could whip five
Yankees—and so forth and so on.

"And then we'd go home at night and find
our mothers and sisters settin' round a coal-oil
lamp, makin' our new grey uniforms, and sew-
in' a tear in with every stitch. And every feller's sweetheart was makin' him a silk sash to
wear round his waist. I could git a sash round
my waist then, but I s'pose if I felt called on
to wear one now I'd have to hire old man Dil-
lon, the mattress maker, to make one fur me
out of a roll of bedtickin'." And the speaker
glanced downward toward the bulge of his
girth.

"My mother kept telling me that it would
kill her for me to go—and that she'd kill me if
I didn't go," interpolated Doctor Lake.

"I reckin no set of men on this earth ever
went out to fight with the right sort of spirit in
'em onless their womenfolk stood behind 'em,
biddin' 'em to go," said the old Judge. "That's
the way it was with us, anyway—I know that
much. Well then, right on top of everything
else, along come the big ball they gave us at
the Richland House the night before we left
fur Camp Boone to be mustered in, regular
fashion. There wasn't any absentees there that
night—not a single solitary one. They'd 'a'
had to tie me hand and foot to keep me frum

comin' there to show off my new grey suit and my red-striped sash and all my brass buttons.

"Fur oncet, social lines didn't count. That night the best families mixed with all the other families that was mebbe jest as good, but didn't know it. Peter Galloway's old daddy drove a dray down on the levee and his mother took in washin', but before the ball broke up I seen old Mrs. Galloway with both her arms round Mrs. Governor Trimble, and Mrs. Governor Trimble had her arms round Mrs. Galloway, and both of 'em cryin' together, the way women like to do. The Trimbles were sending three sons; but old Mrs. Galloway was givin' up Peter, and he was all the boy she had.

"We danced till purty near sunup, stoppin' only oncet, and then jest long enough fur 'em to present Captain Meriwether Grider with his new gold-mounted sword. You remember, Lew, we buried that sword in the same coffin with him fifteen years later?

"About four o'clock in the mornin', when the first of the daylight was beginnin' to leak in at the winders, the nigger string band in the corner struck up Home, Sweet Home! We took partners, but that was one dance which never was finished.

"All of a sudden that sassy little red-headed Janie Thornbury stopped dead-still out in the middle of the floor, and she flung both arms round the neck of Garrett Hinton, that she was engaged to marry, but didn't—on account

of her marryin' somebody else while Garry
was off soldierin'—and, before everybody, she
kissed him right smack on the mouth!

"And then, in less'n no time at all, every feller in the company had his arms round his
sweetheart or his sister, or mebbe his mother,
and kisses were goin' off all over that old ball
room like paper bags a-bustin'. I fergit now-
who 'twas I kissed; but, to the best of my
recollection, I jest browsed round and done
quite a passel of promiscuous kissin'."

"I'll never forget the one I kissed!" broke in
Doctor Lake. "With the exception of the en-
suing four years, I've been kissing the same
girl ever since. She hefts a little more than she
did then—those times you could mighty near
lock a gold bracelet round her waist, and many's
the time I spanned it with my two hands—and
she's considerably older; but her kisses still
taste mighty sweet to me!"

"Go 'way, Lew Lake!" protested Judge
Priest gallantly. "Miss Mamie Ellen is jest ez
young ez ever she was; and she's sweeter, too,
because there's more of her to be sweet. I
drink to her!"

Two tin cups rose in swinging circles; and I
knew these old men were toasting a certain ma-
tron of my acquaintance who weighed two hundred and fifty if she weighed a pound, and had
white hair and sizable grandchildren.

"And so then"—Judge Priest was resuming
his narration—"and so then, after a spell, the

epidemic of kissin' began to sorter die down, though I reckin some of the boys would 'a' been willin' to keep it up plumb till breakfast time. I mind how I was standin' off to one side, fixin' to make my farewells to Miss Sally Machen, when out of the tail of my off eye I seen little Herman Felsburg, over on the other side of the ballroom, lookin' powerful forlorn and lonesome and neglected.

"Doubtless he'd been there all night, without a soul to dance with him, even ef he'd knowed how, or a soul to speak with him, even ef he could have understood whut they said to him. Doubtless he wasn't exactly whut you'd call happy. Jest about then Miss Sally Machen must 'a' seen him too; and the same thought that had jest come to me must 'a' come to her too.

" 'It's a shame!' she said—jest like that— under her voice. And in another minute she was walkin' acrost the floor toward Herman.

"I remember jest how she looked. Why, ef I was an artist I could draw a picture of her right now! She was the handsomest girl in town, and the proudest and the stateliest—tall and slender and dark, with great big black eyes, and a skin like one of these here magnolia buds —and she was well off in her own name; and she belonged to a leadin' family. Four or five boys were beauin' her, and it was a question which one of 'em she'd marry. Sometimes, Lew, I think they don't raise very many girls like Miss Sally Machen any more.

"Well, she kept right on goin' till she came to where Herman was scrouged up ag'inst the wall. She didn't say a word to him, but she took him by the hand and led him right out into the middle of the floor, where everybody could see; and then she put those white arms of hers round his neck, with the gold bracelets on her wrists jinglin', and she bent down to him—she had to bend down, bein' a whole head taller than whut he was—and she kissed him on the lips; not a sweetheartin' kiss, but the way his own mother might 'a' kissed him good-bye, ef he'd had a mother and she'd been there.

"Some few started in to laugh, but stopped off short; and some started to cheer, but didn't do that, neither. We-all jest stood and watched them two. Herman's face turn't ez red ez blood; and he looked up at her sideways and started to smile that funny little smile of hisn —he had one front tooth missin', and that made it funnier still. But then his face got serious, and frum clear halfway acrost the hall I could see his eyes were wet. He backed off frum her and bowed purty near to the ground before her. And frum the way he done it I knowed he was somethin' more than jest a lit-tle, strange Jew pedlar in a strange land. You have to have the makin's of a gentleman in you to bow like that. You mout learn it in time, with diligent practice, but it comes a sight easier ef you're born with it in you."

From his flat flask the old Judge toned up the contents of their julep cups. Then, with pauses, during which he took delicate but prolonged sips, he spoke on in the rambling, contemplative fashion that was as much a part of him as his trick of ungrammatical speech or his high bald forehead was, or his wagging white chin-beard:

"Well, purty soon after that we were all down yonder at old Camp Boone, and chiefly engaged, in our leisure hours—which we had blamed few leisure hours, at that—in figurin' out the difference between talkin' about soldierin' and braggin' about it, and actually doin' of it. There wasn't no more dancin' of quadrilles with purty girls then. We done our grand right-and-left with knapsacks on our backs and blisters on our feet. Many and many a feller that had signed up to be a hero made the distressin' discovery that he'd really j'ined on to do day labour fur mighty small pay in paper money, and monstrous slim pickin's in the way of vittles. Whut with drillin', and foragin' round fur enough to eat, and gittin' seasoned, and fallin' sick and gittin' well ag'in, and learnin' how to use our guns—such of us ez had 'em, because there wasn't more'n half enough muskets to go round and we used to have to take turns usin' 'em—we kept real busy fur about sixteen to eighteen hours a day, includin' week days and Sundays.

"All this time little old Herman was doin'

his share like a major. Long before he could
make out the words of command, he'd picked
up the manual of arms, jest frum watchin' the
others in the same awkward squad with him.
He was peart enough that-a-way. Where he
was slow was learnin' how to talk so ez you
could make out whut he was aimin' to say. It
seemed like that was the only slow thing about
him.

"Natchelly the boys poked a heap of fun at
him. They kept prankin' with him constantly. But he taken it all in good part and grin-
ned back at 'em, and never seemed to lose his
holt on his temper. You jest couldn't help
likin' him—only he did cut such funny mon-
keyshines with the Queen's English when he
tried to talk!

"Because he was so good-natured, some of
the boys took it into their heads, I reckin, that
he didn't have no real grit; or mebbe they
thought he wasn't spunky because he was a
Jew. That's a delusion which a good many
suffer frum that don't know his race.

"I remember one night, about three weeks
or a month after we went into camp, Herman
was put on post. The sergeant mighty near
lost his mind, and did lose his disposition, drillin' the countersign and the password into Herman's skull. So a couple of boys out of the
Calloway County company—they called themselves the Blood River Tigers, and were a
purty wild and devilish lot of young colts

ginerally—they took it into their heads that after it got good and dark they'd slip down to the lines and sneak up on Herman, unbeknownst to him, and give him a good skeer, and mebbe take his piece away from him—sort of play hoss with him, ginerally. So, 'long about 'leven o'clock they set out to do so."

He paused and looked at Doctor Lake, grinning. I couldn't hold in.

"What happened?" I asked.

"Oh, nothin' much," said Judge Priest—"exceptin' that presently there was a loud report and consider'ble many loud cries; and when the corporal of the guard got there with a squad, one of them Calloway County boys was layin' on the ground with a hole through his right shoulder, and the other was layin' alongside of him right smartly clubbed up with the butt end of a rifle. And Herman was standin' over 'em, jabberin' in German—he'd forgot whut little English he knowed. But you could tell frum the way he carried on that he was jest double-dog darin' 'em to move an inch. I don't believe in my whole life I ever seen two fellers that looked so out of the notion of playin' practical jokes as them two Blood River Tigers did. They were plumb sick of Herman, too—you could tell that frum a mere glance at 'em ez we toted 'em in and sent for the surgeon to patch 'em up.

"So, after that, the desire to prank with Private Felsburg when he was on duty sort of languished away. Then, when Herman took down sick with camp measles, and laid there day after day in the hosspital tent under an old ragged bedquilt, mighty sick, but never complainin'—only jest grinnin' his gratitude when anybody done a kind turn fur him—we knowed he was gritty in more ways than one. And there wasn't a man in Company B but whut would have fit any feller that ever tried ag'in to impose on him.

"He was sick a good while. He was up and round ag'in, though, in time to do his sheer in the first fight we were in—which was at Belmont, over acrost the Mississippi River frum Columbus—in the fall o' that year. I seem to recall that, ez we went into action and got into fire, a strange pair of laigs took to tremblin' mightily inside the pair of pants I was wearin' at the time; and most of my vital organs moved up into my throat and interfered some with my breathin'.

"In fact I made a number of very interestin' discoveries in the openin' stages of that there fight. One was that I wasn't never goin' to be entirely reconciled to the idea of bein' killed on the field of battle; and another was that, though I loved my native land and would die fur her if necessary—only hopin' it wouldn't be necessary to go so fur ez all that—still, ef I lived to git out of this particular war I wasn't goin' to love another native land ez long ez I lived."

"Shucks, William!" snorted Doctor Lake. "Try that on somebody else, but don't try to come such stuff on me. Why, I was right alongside of you when we went into that charge, and you never faltered!"

"Lew," stated Judge Priest, "you might ez well know the truth. I've been waitin' fur nearly forty years to make this confession. The fact of the matter was, I was so skeered I didn't dare to stop goin' ahead. I knowed ef ever I did slow up, and give myself a chance to think, I'd never quit runnin' the other way until I was out in the Gulf of Mexico, swimmin'.

"And yit another thing I found out that day was that the feller back home who told me one Southerner could whip five Yankees, single-handed, made a triflin' error in his calculations; or else the Yankees he had in mind when he uttered the said remark was a different breed frum the bunch we tackled that day in the backskirts of the thrivin' little community of Belmont, Missoury. But the most important thing of all the things I discovered was about Herman Felsburg—only that come later.

"In the early stages of that little battle the Federals sort of shoved us back a few pegs; but about three o'clock in the evenin' the tide swung the other way, and shortly thereafter their commandin' general remembered some pressin' business back in Cairo, Illinois, that needed attendin' to right away, and he started back there to do so, takin' whut was left of his army along with him. So we claimed it ez a victory for us, which it was.

"Along toward dusk, when the fightin' had died down, our company was layin' alongside a country road jest outside the town, purty well tuckered out, and cut up some. We were all tellin' each other how brave we'd been, when along down the road toward us come a file of prisoners, under guard, lookin' mighty forlorn and low-sperrited. They was the first prisoners any of us had ever seen; so we jumped up from where we was stretched out and crowded up round 'em, pokin' fun at 'em. The guards halted 'em to let 'em rest and we had a good chance to exchange the compliments of the season with 'em. Right in the front rank of the blue-bellies was one big furreign-lookin' feller, with no hat on, and a head of light yaller hair. He ripped out somethin' in German—a cuss word, I take it. Doubtless he was tellin' us to go plum' to hell. Well, suh, at that, Herman jumped like he'd been stung by one of these here yaller jackets. I reckin he was homesick, anyway, fur the sound of his own language.

"He walked over and begun jabberin' in Dutch with the big sandy-haired Yank, and the Yank jabbered back; and they talked together mighty industrious until the prisoners moved on—about fifteen minutes, I should say, offhanded. And ez we went back to lay down ag'in I took notice that Herman had the fun-

niest look on his face that ever I seen on almost any human face. And he kept scratchin'
his head, like there was somethin' on his mind,
troublin' him, that he jest simply couldn't make
out noway. But he didn't say nothin' to nobody
then—jest kept on scratchin' and studyin'.

"In fact, he held in till nearly ten o'clock
that night. We made camp right there on the
edge of the battleground. I was fixin' to turn
in when Herman got up frum where he'd been
squattin', over by a log fire, lookin' in the
flames; and he come over to me and teched me
on the shoulder.

"'Pilly Briest,' he says in that curious way
of hisn, 'I should like to speak mit you. Please,
you gecomin' mit me.'

"So I got up and follered him. He led me
off into a little thicket-like and we set down
side by side on a log, same ez we three are settin' here now. There was a full moon that
night, ridin' high, and no clouds in the sky;
and even there in the shadders everythin' was
purty nigh ez bright ez day.

"'Well, old hoss,' I says, 'whut seems to be
on your mind?'

"I ain't goin' to try very hard to imitate his
accent—you-all kin imagine it fur yourselves.
And he says to me he's feared he's made a big
mistake.

"'Whut kind of a mistake?' I says.

"'Ven I j'ined dis army,' he says—or words
to that effect.

" 'How so?' I says.

"And then he starts in to tell me, talkin' ez fast ez his tongue kin wag, and makin' gestures with both his hands, like a boy tryin' to learn to swim dog-fashion. And after a little, by piecin' together ez much of his talk ez I kin ketch, I begin to make out whut he's drivin' at; and the shock is so great I come mighty near fallin' right smack off that log backward.

"Here's the way the thing stands with him: That night at the old market house, when the company is bein' formed, he happens along and sees a crowd, and drops in to find out, ef he kin, whut's afoot. Presently he makes out that there's a war startin' up ag'inst somebody or other, and, sence he's made up his mind he's goin' to live in America always and make it his country, he decides it's his bounden duty to fight fur his country. So he jest up and signs, along with the rest of us.

"Of course from that time on he hears a lot of talk about the Yankee invader and the Northern vandal; but he figgers it that the enemy comes frum somewhere 'way up North— Canada or Greenland, or the Arctic regions, or the North Pole, or some of them other furreign districts up in that gineral vicinity. And not fur a minute—not till he talked with the big Dutch prisoner that day—had it ever dawned on him fur a single minute that a Yankee mout possibly be an American, too.

"When he stops I sets and looks at him a

minute, takin' it all in; and he looks back. Finally I says:

"'And so you went and enlisted, thinkin' you was goin' to fight fur the United States of America, and you're jest findin' out now that all these weeks you've been organisin' yourself to fight ag'inst her? Is that it?'

"And he says, 'Yes, that's it.' And I says: 'Well, I wisht I might be dam'!' And he says, well, he wishes he might be dam' too, or in substance expresses sech a sentiment. And fur another spell we two merely continues to set there lookin' one another in the face.

"After a little I asts him whut he's aimin' to do about it; and he says he ain't decided yit in his own mind. And then I says:

"'Well, Herman, it's purty tough on you, anyway you take it. I don't rightly know all the rules o' this here war business yit, myself; but I reckin ef it was made clear to the higher authorities that you was sort of drug into this affair under false pretenses, ez it were, why, mebbe they mout muster you out and give you an honourable discharge—providin', of course, you pledged yourself not to take up arms fur the other side, which, in a way of speakin', would make you a deserter. We-all know you ain't no coward, and we'll all testify to it ef our testimony is needed. I reckon the rest of the boys'll understand your position in the matter; in fact, I'll undertake to make 'em understand.'

"He asts me then: 'Whut iss false pretenses?' And I explains to him the best I kin; and he thinks that p'int over fur a minute or two. Then he looks up at me sideways frum under the brim of his cap, and I kin see by the moonlight he's blushin' ez red ez a beet, and grinnin' that shy little snaggle-teethed grin of hisn.

"'Pilly,' he says, 'mebbe so you remember dot young lady vot put her arms round me dot night—de von vot gif to me a kiss fur kindness? She iss on de Deexie side—yes?—no?'

"And I says to him: 'You kin bet your sweet life she is!'

"'All right!' he says. 'I am much lonesome dot night—and she kiss me! All right, den. I fights fur her! I sticks mit Deexie!' And when he says that he makes a salute, and I notice he's quit grinnin'."

"And did he stick?" I asked.

Before he answered, the old Judge drained his tin cup to the bottom.

"Did he stick? Huh! Four long hard bitter years he stuck—that's all! Boy, you mout not think it, to see old Herman waddlin' acrost that Oak Hall Clothin' Store to sell some young buck from the country a pair of twenty-five-cent galluses or a celluloid collar; but I'm here to tell you he's one of the stickin'est white men that ever drawed the breath of life. Lew Lake, here, will tell you the same thing. Mebbe it's because he is sech a good sticker that he's one

of the wealthiest men in this county to-day. I
only wisht I had to spend on sweetenin' drams
whut he lays by every year. But I don't be-
grudge it to him.'

Through the grove ran an especially loud
outburst of cheering, and on top of it we heard
the scuffling of many yeomen feet. Judge
Priest slid off the log and stood up and stretched
his pudgy legs.

"That must mean the speakin's over and the
rally's breakin' up," he said. "Come along,
son, and ride on back to town with us in my
old buggy. I reckin there's room fur you to
scrouge in between me and Doctor Lake, ef
you'll make yourself small."

The October sun, slanting low, made long
stippled lanes between the tree trunks, so that
we waded waist-deep in a golden haze as we
made for the place where Judge Priest's Mittie
May was tethered to a sapling. The old white
mare recognised her master from afar, and
whinnied a greeting to him, and I was moved
to ask another question. To me that tale stood
uncompleted:

"Judge, what ever became of that young
lady who kissed him that night at the Richland House?"

"Oh, her? She died a long, long time ago—
before you was born. Her folks lost their
money on account of the war, and she married
a feller that wasn't much account; they moved

out to Arkansaw and the marriage turned out bad, and she died when her first baby was born. There ain't none of her family livin' here now—they've purty much all died out too. But they shipped her body back here, and she's buried out in Ellum Grove Cemetery, in the old Machen lot.

"Some of these days, when you are out there in the cemetery foolin' round, with nothin' much else to do, you look for her grave—you kin find it. Bein' a Christian woman, she had a Christian burial and she's restin' in a Christian buryin' ground; but, in strict confidence, I'll tell you this much more while we're on the subject: It wasn't no Christian that privately paid the bill fur the tombstone that marks the place where she's sleepin'. I wonder ef you could figger out who it was that did pay fur it? I'll give you two guesses.

"And say, listen, sonny: your first guess will be the right one."

CHAPTER X

LIFE AMONG THE ABAN-
DONED FARMERS

I WISH to say I have given up all intention
of buying an abandoned farm. This decision on my part is fixed and irrevocable.
I arrived at it after a long period of study
and investigation. Much as I regret to state
it, I shall never live on an abandoned farm
and be an abandoned farmer.

For years it has been the dream of our life
—I should say our lives, since my wife shared
this vision with me—to own an abandoned
farm; but now I know this can never be. The
idea first came to us through reading articles
that appeared in the various magazines and
newspapers telling of the sudden growth of
what I may call the abandoned-farm industry.

It seemed that New England in general—
and the state of Connecticut in particular—was
thickly speckled with delightful old places
which, through overcultivation or illtreatment,
had become for the time being sterile and non-
productive; so that the original owners had

moved away to the near-by manufacturing towns, leaving their ancestral homesteads empty and their ancestral acres idle. As a result there were great numbers of desirable places any one of which might be had for a song. That was the term most commonly used by the writers of these articles—abandoned farms going for a song.

Now singing is not my forte. People would be more apt to go away from a song of mine than to go for it; still, I made up my mind that if such indeed was the case I would sing a little, accompanying myself on my bank balance, and win me an abandoned farm.

The formula as laid down by the authorities was simple in the extreme: Taking almost any Connecticut town for a starting point, you merely meandered along an elm-lined road until you came to a desirable location, which you purchased for the price of the aforesaid ditty, lullaby or roundelay. This formality being completed, you spent a trivial sum in restoring the fences, and so on, and modernising the interior of the house; after which it was a comparatively easy task to restore the land to productiveness by processes of intensive agriculture—procurable from any standard book on the subject or through easy lessons by mail. And so presently, with scarcely any trouble or expense at all, you were the possessor of a delightful country estate upon which to spend your declining years. It made no difference

whether you were one of those persons who
had never to date declined anything of value;
there was no telling when you might start in.

I could shut my eyes and see the whole delectable prospect: Upon a gentle eminence
crowned with ancient trees stood the rambling
old manse, filled with marvellous antique furniture, grandfather's clocks dating back to the
whaling days, spinning wheels, pottery that
came over on the *Mayflower*, and all those sorts
of things. Round about were the meadows,
some under cultivation and some lying fallow,
the latter being dotted at appropriate intervals
with the grazing fallow deer.

At one side of the house was the orchard,
the old gnarly trees crooking their bent limbs
as though inviting one to come and pluck the
sun-kissed fruit from the burdened bough; at
the other side a purling brook wandering its
way into a greenwood copse, where through all
the golden day sang the feathered warblers
indigenous to the climate, including the soft-
billed Greenwich thrush, the Peabody bird, the
Pettingill bird, the Phelps-Stokes bird, the
albatross, the flamingo, and others of the com-
moner varieties too numerous to mention.

At the back were the abandoned cotes and
byres, with an abandoned rooster crowing
lustily upon a henhouse, and an abandoned
bull calf disporting himself in the clover of the
pasture. At the front was a rolling vista un-
dulating gently away to where above the tree-

tops there rose the spires of a typical New England village full of old line Republicans and characters suitable for putting into short stories. On beyond, past where a silver lake glinted in the sunshine, was a view of either the distant Sound or the distant mountains. Personally I intended that my establishment should be so placed as to command a view of the Sound from the east windows and of the mountains from the west windows. And all to be had for a song! Why, the mere thought of it was enough to make a man start taking vocal culture right away.

Besides, I have been waiting impatiently for a long time for an opportunity to work out several agricultural projects of my own. For example, there is my notion in regard to the mulberry. The mulberry, as all know, is one of our most abundant small fruits; but many have objected to it on account of its woolly appearance and slightly caterpillary taste. My idea is to cross the mulberry on the slippery elm—pronounced, where I came from, ellum—producing a fruit which I shall call the mulellum. This fruit will combine the health-giving qualities of the mulberry with the agreeable smoothness of the slippery elm; in fact, if my plans work out I shall have a berry that will go down so slick the consumer will not taste it at all unless he should eat too many of them and have indigestion afterward.

Then there was my scheme for inducing the

common chinch bug to make chintz curtains. If the silk worms can make silk why should not the chinch bug do something useful instead of wasting his energies in idle pursuits? This is what I wish to know. And why should this man Luther Burbank enjoy a practical monopoly of all these propositions? That was the way I looked at it; and I figured that an abandoned farm would make an ideal place for working out such experiments as might come to me from time to time.

The trouble was that, though everybody wrote of the abandoned farms in a broad, general, alluring way, nobody gave the exact location of any of them. I subscribed for one of the monthly publications devoted to country life along the Eastern seaboard and searched assiduously through its columns for mention of abandoned farms. The owners of most of the country places that were advertised for sale made mention of such things as fourteen master's bedrooms and nine master's baths— showing undoubtedly that the master would be expected to sleep oftener than he bathed— sunken gardens and private hunting preserves, private golf links and private yacht landings.

In nearly every instance, also, the advertisement was accompanied by a halftone picture of a structure greatly resembling the new county building they are going to have down at Paducah if the bond issue ever passes. This seemed a suitable place for holding circuit court in, or even fiscal court, but it was not exactly the kind of country home that we had pictured for ourselves. As my wife said, just the detail of washing all those windows would keep the girl busy fully half her time. Nor did I care to invest in any sunken gardens. I had sufficient experience in that direction when we lived in the suburbs and permanently invested about half of what I made in our eight-by-ten flower bed trying to make it produce the kind of flowers that the florists' catalogues described. You could not tell us anything about that subject—we knew where a sunken garden derives its name. We paid good money to know.

None of the places advertised in the monthly seemed sufficiently abandoned for our purposes, so for a little while we were in a quandary. Then I had a bright thought. I said to myself that undoubtedly abandoned farms were so cheap the owners did not expect to get any real money for them; they would probably be willing to take something in exchange. So I began buying the evening papers and looking through them in the hope of running across some such item as this:

To Exchange—Abandoned farm, centrally located, with large farmhouse, containing all-antique furniture, barns, outbuildings, family graveyard—planted—orchard, woodland, fields—unplanted—for a collection of postage stamps in album, an amateur magician's outfit, a guitar with book of instructions, a safety bicycle, or anything useful. Address ABANDONED, South Squantum Center, Connecticut.

I found no such offers, however; and in view of what we had read this seemed stranger still. Finally I decided that the only safe method would be by first-hand investigation upon the spot. I would go by rail to some small but accessible hamlet in the lower part of New England. On arriving there I would personally examine a number of the more attractive abandoned farms in the immediate vicinity and make a discriminating selection. Having reached this conclusion I went to bed and slept peacefully—or at least I went to bed and did so as soon as my wife and I had settled one point that came up unexpectedly at this juncture. It related to the smokehouse. I was in favour of turning the smokehouse into a study or workroom for myself. She thought, though, that by knocking the walls out and altering the roof and building a pergola on to it, it would make an ideal summer house in which to serve tea and from which to view the peaceful landscape of afternoons.

We argued this back and forth at some length, each conceding something to the other's views; and finally we decided to knock out the walls and alter the roof and have a summer house with a pergola in connection. It was after we reached this compromise that I slept so peacefully, for now the whole thing was as good as settled. I marvelled at not having thought of it sooner.

It was on a bright and peaceful morning that I alighted from the train at North Newburybunkport. Considering that it was supposed to be a typical New England village, North Newburybunkport did not appear at first glance to answer to the customary specifications, such as I had gleaned from my reading of novels of New England life. I had expected that the platform would be inhabited by picturesque natives in quaint clothes, with straws in their mouths and all whittling; and that the depot agent would wear long chin whiskers and say "I vum!" with much heartiness at frequent intervals. Right here I wish to state that so far as my observations go the native who speaks these words about every other line is no longer on the job. Either I Vum the Terrible has died or else he has gone to England to play the part of the typical American millionaire in American plays written by Englishmen.

Instead of the loafers, several chauffeurs were idling about the station and a string of automobiles was drawn up across the road. Just as I disembarked there drove up a large red bus labelled: Sylvan Dale Summer Hotel, European and American Plans. The station agent also proved in the nature of a disappointment. He did not even say "I swan" or "I cal'late!" or anything of that nature. He wore a pink in his buttonhole and his hair was scal-

loped up off his forehad in what is known as the
lion tamer's roach. Approaching, I said to
him:

"In what direction should I go to find some
of the abandoned farms of this vicinity? I
would prefer to go where there is a good assortment to pick from."

He did not appear to understand, so I repeated the question, at the same time offering
him a cigar.

"Bo," he said, "you've sure got me wing-
ing now. You'd better ask Tony Magnito—
he runs the garage three doors up the street
from here on the other side. Tony does a lot
of driving round the country for suckers that
come up here, and he might help you."

To reach the garage I had to cross the road,
dodging several automobiles in transit, and
then pass two old-fashioned New England
houses fronting close up to the sidewalk. One
had the sign of a teahouse over the door, and
in the window of the other, picture postcards,
birch-bark souvenirs and standard varieties of
candy were displayed for sale.

Despite his foreign-sounding name, Mr.
Magnito spoke fair English—that is, as fair
English as any one speaks who employs the
Manhattan accent in so doing.

Even after he found out that I did not care
to rent a touring car for sightseeing purposes
at five dollars an hour he was quite affable and
accommodating; but my opening question ap-

peared to puzzle him just as in the case of the
depot agent.

"Mister," he said frankly, "I'm sorry, but
I don't seem to make you. What's this thing
you is looking for? Tell me over again slow."

Really the ignorance of these villagers regarding one of their principal products—a
product lying, so to speak, at their very doors
and written about constantly in the public
prints—was ludicrous. It would have been
laughable if it had not been deplorable. I saw
that I could not indulge in general trade terms.
I must be painfully explicit and simple.

"What I am seeking"—I said it very slowly
and very distinctly—"is a farm that has been
deserted, so to speak—one that has outlived
its usefulness as a farm proper, and everything
like that!"

"Oh," he says, "now I get you! Why didn't
you say that in the first place? The place
you're looking for is the old Parham place, out
here on the post road about a mile. August'll
take good care of you—that's his specialty."

"August?" I inquired. "August who?"

"August Weinstopper—the guy who runs
it," he explained. "You must have known
August if you lived long in New York. He used
to be the steward at that big hotel at Broad-
way and Forty-second; that was before he
came up here and opened up the old Parham
place as an automobile roadhouse. He's clean-
ing up about a thousand a month. Some class

to that mantrap! They've got an orchestra, and nothing but vintage goods on the wine card, and dancing at all hours. Any night you'll see forty or fifty big cars rolling up there, bringing swell dames and——"

I judge he saw by my expression that he was on a totally wrong tack, because he stopped short.

"Say, mister," he said, "I guess you'd better step into the post-office here—next door—and tell your troubles to Miss Plummer. She knows everything that's going on round here—and she ought to, too, seeing as she gets first chance at all the circulars and postal cards that come in. Besides, I gotter be changing that gasoline sign—gas has went up two cents a gallon more."

Miss Plummer was sorting mail when I appeared at her wicket. She was one of those elderly, spinsterish-looking, kittenish females who seem in an intense state of surprise all the time. Her eyebrows arched like croquet wickets and her mouth made O's before she uttered them.

"Name, please?" she said twitteringly.

I told her.

"Ah," she said in the thrilled tone of one who is watching a Fourth of July skyrocket explode in midair. The news seemed to please her.

"And the initials, please?"

"The initials are of no consequence. I do not expect any mail," I said. "I want merely to ask you a question."

"Indeed!" she said coyly. She said it as though I had just given her a handsome remembrance, and she cocked her head on one side like a bird—like a hen-bird.

"I hate to trouble you," I went on, "but I have experienced some difficulty in making your townspeople understand me. I am looking for a certain kind of farm—a farm of an abandoned character."

At once I saw I had made a mistake.

"You do not get my meaning," I said hastily. "I refer to a farm that has been deserted, closed up, shut down—in short, abandoned. I trust I make myself plain."

She was still suffering from shock, however. She gave me a wounded-fawn glance and averted her burning face.

"The Prewitt property might suit your purposes—whatever they may be," she said coldly over her shoulder. "Mr. Jabez Pickerel, of Pickerel & Pike, real-estate dealers, on the first corner above, will doubtless give you the desired information. He has charge of the Prewitt property."

At last, I said to myself as I turned away, I was on the right track. Mr. Pickerel rose as I entered his place of business. He was a short, square man, with a brisk manner and a roving eye.

"I have been directed to you," I began. He seized my hand and began shaking it warmly. "I have been told," I continued, "that you

have charge of the old Prewitt farm somewhere near here; and as I am in the market
for an aban——" I got no farther than that.

"In one minute," he shouted explosively—
"in just one minute!"

Still clutching me by the hand, he rushed me
pellmell out of the place. At the curbing stood
a long, low, rakish racing-model roadster, looking something like a high-powered projectile
and something like an enlarged tailor's goose.
Leaping into this machine at one bound, he
dragged me up into the seat beside him and
threw on the power. Instantly we were streak-
ing away at a perfectly appalling rate of speed
—fully forty-five to fifty-five miles an hour I
should say. You never saw anything so sudden in your life. It was exactly like a kidnap-
ping. It was only by the exercise of great self-
control that I restrained myself from screaming for help. I had the feeling that I was being
abducted—for what purpose I knew not.

As we spun round a corner on two wheels,
spraying up a long furrow of dust, the same as
shown in pictures of the chariot race in Ben-
Hur, a man with a watch in his hand and wearing a badge—a constable, I think—ran out of a
house that had a magistrate's sign over it and
threw up his hand authoritatively, as though
to stop us; but my companion yelled something the purport of which I could not distinguish and the constable fell back. Glancing
rearward over my shoulder I saw him halting

another car bearing a New York license that did not appear to be going half so fast as we were.

In another second we were out of town, tearing along a country highway. Evidently sensing the alarm expressed by my tense face and strained posture, this man Pickerel began saying something in what was evidently intended to be a reassuring tone; but such was the roaring of the car that I could distinguish only broken fragments of his speech. I caught the words "unparallelled opportunity," repeated several times—the term appeared to be a favourite of his—and "marvellous proposition." Possibly I was not listening very closely anyhow, my mind being otherwise engaged. For one thing I was surmising in a general sort of way upon the old theory of the result when the irresistible force encounters the immovable object. I was wondering how long it would be before we hit something solid and whether it would be possible afterward to tell us apart. His straw hat also made me wonder. I had mine clutched in both hands and even then it fluttered against my bosom like a captive bird, but his stayed put. I think yet he must have had threads cut in his head to match the convolutions of the straw and screwed his hat on, like a nut on an axle.

I have a confused recollection of rushing with the speed of the tornado through rows of trees; of leaping from the crest of one small hill to the crest of the next small hill; of passing a truck patch with such velocity that the lettuce and tomatoes and other things all seemed to merge together in a manner suggestive of a well-mixed vegetable salad. Then we swung off the main road in between the huge brick columns of an ornate gateway that stood alone, with no fence in connection. We bumpily traversed a rutted stretch of cleared land; and then with a jar and a jolt we came to a pause in what appeared to be a wide and barren expanse.

As my heart began to throb with slightly less violence I looked about me for the abandoned farmhouse. I had conceived that it would be white with green blinds and that it would stand among trees. It was not in sight; neither were the trees. The entire landscape presented an aspect that was indeed remarkable. Small numbered stakes, planted in double lines at regular intervals, so as to form aisles, stretched away from us in every direction. Also there were twin rows of slender sticks planted in the earth in a sort of geometric pattern. Some were the size of switches. Others were almost as large as umbrella handles and had sprouted slightly. A short distance away an Italian was steering a dirtscraper attached to a languid mule along a sort of dim roadway. There were no other living creatures in sight. Right at my feet were two painted and lettered boards affixed at cross angles to a wooden upright. The

legend on one of these boards was: Grand Con-
course. The inscription on the other read:
Nineteenth Avenue West. Repressing a gasp,
I opened my mouth to speak.

"Ahem!" I said. "There has been some
mistake——"

"There can be no mistake!" he shouted
enthusiastically. "The only mistake possible
is not to take advantage of this magnificent
opportunity while it is yet possible to do so.
Just observe that view!" He waved his arm
in the general direction of the horizon from
northwest to southeast. "Breathe this air! As
a personal favour to me just breathe a little of
this air!" He inhaled deeply himself as though
to show me how, and I followed suit, because
after that ride I needed to catch up with my
regular breathing.

"Thank you!" I said gratefully when I had
finished breathing. "But how about——"

"Quite right!" he cried, beaming upon me
admiringly. "Quite right! I don't blame you.
You have a right to know all the details. As
a business man you should ask that question.
You were about to say: But how about the
train service? Ah, there spoke the true business man, the careful investor! Twenty fast
trains a day each way—twenty, sir! Remember! And as for accessibility—well, accessibility is simply no name for it! Only two or
three minutes from the station. You saw how
long it took us to get here to-day? Well, then,

what more could you ask? Right here," he went on, pointing, "is the country club—a magnificent thing!"

I looked, but I didn't see anything except a hole in the ground about fifty feet from us.

"Where?" I asked. "I don't see it."

"Well," he said, "this is where it is going to be. You automatically become a member of the country club; in fact, you are as good as a member now! And right up there at the corner of Lincoln Boulevard and Washington Parkway, where that scraper is, is the public library—the site for it! You'll be crazy about the public library! When we get back I'll let you run over the plans for the public library while I'm fixing up the papers. Oh, my friend, how glad I am you came while there was yet time!"

I breasted the roaring torrent of his pouring language.

"One minute," I begged of him—"One minute, if you please! I am obliged to you for the interest you take in me, a mere stranger to you; but there has been a misunderstanding. I wanted to see the Prewitt place."

"This is the Prewitt place," he said.

"Yes," I said; "but where is the house? And why all this—why all these——" I indicated by a wave of my hand what I meant.

"Naturally," he explained, "the house is no longer here. We tore it away—it was old; whereas everything here will be new, modern

and up to date. This is—or was—the Prewitt
place, now better known as Homecrest Heights,
the Development Ideal!" Having begun to
capitalise his words, he continued to do so.
"The Perfect Addition! The Suburb Superb!
Away From the City's Dust and Heat! Away
From Its Glamour and Clamour! Into the
Open! Into the Great Out-of-Doors! Back to
the Soil! Villa Plots on Easy Terms! You
Furnish the Birds, We Furnish the Nest! The
Place For a Business Man to Rear His Family!
You are Married? You Have a Wife? You
Have Little Ones?"

"Yes," I said, "one of each—one wife and
one little one."

"Ah!" he cried gladly. "One Little One—
How Sweet! You Love Your Little One—Ah,
Yes! Yes! You Desire to Give Your Little
One a Chance? You Would Give Her Con-
genial Surroundings — Refined Surroundings?
You Would Inculcate in Her While Young the
Love of Nature?" He put an entire sentence
into capitals now: "GIVE YOUR LITTLE ONE A
CHANCE! THAT IS ALL I ASK OF YOU!"

He had me by both lapels. I thought he
was going to kneel to me in pleading. I feared
he might kiss me. I raised him to his feet.
Then his manner changed—it became domi-
neering, hectoring, almost threatening.

I will pass briefly over the events of the suc-
ceeding hour, including our return to his lair
or office. Accounts of battles where all the

losses fall upon one side are rarely interesting to read about anyway. Suffice it to say that at the last minute I was saved. It was a desperate struggle though. I had offered the utmost resistance at first, but he would surely have had his way with me—only that a train pulled in bound for the city just as he was showing me, as party of the first part, where I was to sign my name on the dotted line A. Even then, weakened and worn as I was, I should probably not have succeeded in beating him off if he had not been hampered by having a fountain pen in one hand and the documents in the other. At the door he intercepted me; but I tackled him low about the body and broke through and fled like a hunted roebuck, catching the last car just as the relief train pulled out of the station. It was a close squeeze, but I made it. The thwarted Mr. Pickerel wrote me regularly for some months thereafter, making mention of My Little One in every letter; but after a while I took to sending the letters back to him unopened, and eventually he quit.

I reached home along toward evening. I was tired, but I was not discouraged. I reported progress on the part of the committee on a permanent site, but told my wife that in order to find exactly what we wanted it would be necessary for us to leave the main-travelled paths. It was now quite apparent to me that the abandoned farm-seeker who stuck too closely to the railroad lines was bound to be thrown constantly in contact with those false and feverish metropolitan influences which, radiating from the city, have spread over the country like the spokes of a wheel or an upas tree, or something of that nature. The thing to do was to get into an automobile and go away from the main routes of travel, into districts where the abandoned farms would naturally be more numerous.

This solved one phase of the situation—we now knew definitely where to go. The next problem was to decide upon some friend owning an automobile. We fixed upon the Winsells. They are charming people! We are devoted to the Winsells. They were very good friends of ours when they had their small four-passenger car; but since they sold the old one and bought a new forty-horse, seven-passenger car, they are so popular that it is hard to get hold of them for holidays and week-ends.

Every Saturday—nearly—some one of their list of acquaintances is calling them up to tell of a lovely spot he has just heard about, with good roads all the way, both coming and going; but after a couple of disappointments we caught them when they had an open date. Over the telephone Winsell objected that he did not know anything about the roads up in Conneccut, but I was able to reassure him promptly on that score. I told him he need not worry about that—that I would buy the road map myself. So on a fair Saturday morning we started.

The trip up through the extreme lower end of the state of New York was delightful, being marred by only one or two small mishaps. There was the trifling incident of a puncture, which delayed us slightly; but fortunately the accident occurred at a point where there was a wonderful view of the Croton Lakes, and while Winsell was taking off the old tire and adjusting a new one we sat very comfortably in the car, enjoying Nature's panorama.

It was a little later on when we hit a dog. It seemed to me that this dog merely sailed, yowling, up into the air in a sort of long curve, but Winsell insisted that the dog described a parabola. I am very glad that in accidents of this character it is always the victims that describe the parabola. I know I should be at a complete loss to describe one myself. Unless it is something like the boomerang of the Australian aborigines I do not even know what a parabola is. Nor did I dream until then that Winsell understood the dog language. However, those are but technical details.

After we crossed the state line we got lost several times; this was because the country seemed to have a number of roads the road map omitted, and the road map had many roads the country had left out. Eventually, though, we came to a district of gently rolling hills, dotted at intervals with those neat white-painted villages in which New England excels; and between the villages at frequent intervals were farmhouses. Abandoned ones, however, were rarer than we had been led to expect. Not only were these farms visibly populated by persons who appeared to be permanently attached to their respective locailities, but at many of them things were offered for sale— such as home-made pastry, souvenirs, fresh poultry, antique furniture, brass door-knockers, milk and eggs, hand-painted crockery, table board, garden truck, molasses taffy, laundry soap and livestock.

At length, though, when our necks were quite sore from craning this way and that on the watch for an abandoned farm that would suit us, we came to a very attractive-looking place facing a lawn and flanked by an orchard. There was a sign fastened to an elm tree alongside the fence. The sign read: For Information Concerning This Property Irquire Within.

To Winsell I said:

"Stop here—this is without doubt the place we have been looking for!"

Filled—my wife and I—with little thrills of anticipation, we all got out. I opened the gate and entered the yard, followed by Winsell, my wife and his wife. I was about halfway up the walk when a large dog sprang into view, at the same time showing his teeth in rather an intimidating way. To prevent an encounter with an animal that might be hostile, I stepped nim-

bly behind the nearest tree. As I came round
on the other side of the tree there, to my surprise, was this dog face to face with me. Still
desiring to avoid a collision with him, I stepped
back the other way. Again I met the dog,
which was now growling. The situation was
rapidly becoming embarrassing when a gentleman came out upon the porch and called
sharply to the dog. The dog, with apparent
reluctance, retired under the house and the
gentleman invited us inside and asked us to be
seated. Glancing about his living room I noted
that the furniture appeared to be a trifle modern for our purposes; but, as I whispered to
my wife, you cannot expect to have everything
to suit you at first. With the sweet you must
ever take the bitter—that I believe is true,
though not an original saying.

In opening the conversation with the strange
gentleman I went in a businesslike way direct
to the point.

"You are the owner of these premises?" I
asked. He bowed. "I take it," I then said,
"that you are about to abandon this farm?"

"I beg your pardon?" he said, as though
confused.

"I presume," I explained, "that this is
practically an abandoned farm."

"Not exactly," he said. "I'm here."

"Yes, yes; quite so," I said, speaking perhaps a trifle impatiently. "But you are thinking of going away from it, aren't you?"

"Yes," he admitted; "I am."

"Now," I said, "we are getting round to the real situation. What are you asking for this place?"

"Eighteen hundred," he stated. "There are ninety acres of land that go with the house and the house itself is in very good order."

I considered for a moment. None of the abandoned farms I had ever read about sold for as much as eighteen hundred dollars. Still, I reflected, there might have been a recent bull movement; there had certainly been much publicity upon the subject. Before committing myself, I glanced at my wife. Her expression betokened acquiescence.

"That figure," I said diplomatically, "was somewhat in excess of what I was originally prepared to pay; still, the house seems roomy and, as you were saying, there are ninety acres. The furniture and equipment go with the place, I presume?"

"Naturally," he answered. "That is the customary arrangement."

"And would you be prepared to give possession immediately?"

"Immediately," he responded.

I began to feel enthusiasm. By the look on my wife's face I could tell that she was enthused too.

"If we come to terms," I said, "and everything proves satisfactory, I suppose you could arrange to have the deed made out at once?"

"The deed?" he said blankly. "You mean the lease?"

"The lease?" I said blankly. "You mean the deed?"

"The deed?" he said blankly. "You mean the lease?"

"The lease, indeed," said my wife. "You mean——"

I broke in here. Apparently we were all getting the habit.

"Let us be perfectly frank in this matter," I said. "Let us dispense with these evasive and dilatory tactics. You want eighteen hundred dollars for this place, furnished?"

"Exactly," he responded. "Eighteen hundred dollars for it from June to October." Then, noting the expressions of our faces, he continued hurriedly: "A remarkably small figure considering what summer rentals are in this section. Besides, this house is new. It costs a lot to reproduce these old Colonial designs!"

I saw at once that we were but wasting our time in this person's company. He had not the faintest conception of what we wanted. We came away. Besides, as I remarked to the others after we were back in the car and on our way again, this house-farm would never have suited us; the view from it was nothing extra. I told Winsell to go deeper into the country until we really struck the abandoned farm belt.

So we went farther and farther. After a while it was late afternoon and we seemed to be lost again. My wife and Winsell's wife were tired; so we dropped them at the next teahouse we passed. I believe it was the eighteenth teahouse for the day. Winsell and I then continued on the quest alone. Women know so little about business anyway that it is better, I think, whenever possible, to conduct important matters without their presence. It takes a masculine intellect to wrestle with these intricate problems; and for some reason or other this problem was becoming more and more complicated and intricate all the time.

On a long, deserted stretch of road, as the shadows were lengthening, we overtook a native of a rural aspect plodding along alone. Just as we passed him I was taken with an idea and I told Winsell to stop. I was tired of trafficking with stupid villagers and avaricious landgrabbers. I would deal with the peasantry direct. I would sound the yeoman heart—which is honest and true and ever beats in accord with the best dictates of human nature.

"My friend," I said to him, "I am seeking an abandoned farm. Do you know of many such in this vicinity?"

"How?" he asked.

I never got so tired of repeating a question in my life; nevertheless, for this yokel's limited understanding, I repeated it again.

"Well," he said at length, "whut with all

these city fellers moving in here to do gentle-
man-farming—whatsoever that may mean—
farm property has gone up until now it's wuth
considerable more'n town property, as a rule.
I couldn't scursely say I know of any of the
kind of farms you mention as laying round
loose—no, wait a minute; I do recollect a place.
It's that shack up back of the county poor
farm that the supervisors used for a pest house
the time the smallpox broke out. That there
place is consider'bly abandoned. You might try
her."

In a stern tone of voice I bade Winsell to
drive on and turn in at the next farmhouse he
came to. The time for trifling had passed. My
mind was fixed. My jaw was also set. I know,
because I set it myself. And I have no doubt
there was a determined glint in my eye; in fact,
I could feel the glint reflected upon my cheek.

At the next farm Winsell turned in. We
passed through a stone gateway and rolled up
a well-kept road toward a house we could see
in glimpses through the intervening trees.
We skirted several rather neat flower beds,
curved round a greenhouse and came out on a
stretch of lawn. I at once decided that this
place would do undoubtedly. There might be
alterations to make, but in the main the establishment would be satisfactory even though
the house, on closer inspection, proved to be
larger than it had seemed when seen from a
distance.

On a signal from me Winsell halted at the front porch. Without a word I stepped out. He followed. I mounted the steps, treading with great firmness and decision, and rang the doorbell hard. A middle-aged person dressed in black, with a high collar, opened the door.

"Are you the proprietor of this place?" I demanded without any preamble. My patience was exhausted; I may have spoken sharply.

"Oh, no, sir," he said, and I could tell by his accent he was English; "the marster is out, sir."

"I wish to see him," I said, "on particular business—at once! At once, you understand—it is important!"

"Perhaps you'd better come in, sir," he said humbly. It was evident my manner, which was, I may say, almost haughty, had impressed him deeply. "If you will wait, sir, I'll have the marster called, sir. He's not far away, sir."

"Very good," I replied. "Do so!"

He showed us into a large library and fussed about, offering drinks and cigars and what-not. Winsell seemed somewhat perturbed by these attentions, but I bade him remain perfectly calm and collected, adding that I would do all the talking.

We took cigars—very good cigars they were. As they were not banded I assumed they were home grown. I had always heard that Connecticut tobacco was strong, but these specimens were very mild and pleasant. I had about decided I should put in tobacco for private consumption and grow my own cigars and cigarettes when the door opened, and a stout elderly man with side whiskers entered the room. He was in golfing costume and was breathing hard.

"As soon as I got your message I hurried over as fast as I could," he said.

"You need not apologise," I replied; "we have not been kept waiting very long."

"I presume you come in regard to the traction matter?" he ventured.

"No," I said, "not exactly. You own this place, I believe?"

"I do," he said, staring at me.

"So far, so good," I said. "Now, then, kindly tell me when you expect to abandon it?"

He backed away from me a few feet, gaping. He opened his mouth and for a few moments absent-mindedly left it in that condition.

"When do I expect to do what?" he inquired.

"When," I said, "do you expect to abandon it?"

He shook his head as though he had a marble loose inside of it and liked the rattling sound.

"I don't understand yet," he said, puzzled.

"I will explain," I said very patiently. "I wish to acquire by purchase or otherwise one of the abandoned farms of this state. Not having been able to find one that was already abandoned, though I believe them to be very numerous, I am looking for one that is about to be abandoned. I wish, you understand, to have the first call on it. Winsell"—I said in an aside —"quit pulling at my coattail! Therefore," I resumed, readdressing the man with the side whiskers, "I ask you a plain question, to wit: When do you expect to abandon this one? I expect a plain answer."

He edged a few feet nearer an electric push button which was set in the wall. He seemed flustered and distraught; in fact, almost apprehensive.

"May I inquire," he said nervously, "how you got in here?"

"Your butler admitted us," I said, with dignity.

"Yes," he said in a soothing tone; "but did you come afoot—or how?"

"I drove here in a car," I told him, though I couldn't see what difference that made.

"Merciful Heavens!" he muttered. "They do not trust you—I mean you do not drive the car yourself, do you?"

Here Winsell cut in.

"I drove the car," he said. "I—I did not want to come, but he"—pointing to me—"he insisted." Winsell is by nature a grovelling soul. His tone was almost cringing.

"I see," said the gentleman, wagging his head, "I see. Sad case—very sad case! Young too!" Then he faced me. "You will excuse

me now," he said. "I wish to speak to my butler. I have just thought of several things I
wish to say to him. Now in regard to abandon-
ing this place: I do not expect to abandon this
place just yet—probably not for some weeks
or possibly months. In case I should decide to
abandon it sooner, if you will leave your address with me I will communicate with you by
letter at the institution where you may chance
to be stopping at the time. I trust this will be
satisfactory."

He turned again to Winsell.

"Does your—ahem—friend care for flowers?" he asked.

"Yes," said Winsell. "I think so."

"Perhaps you might show him my flower
gardens as you go away," said the side-whisk-
ered man. "I have heard somewhere that flowers have a very soothing effect sometimes in
such cases—or it may have been music. I have
spent thirty thousand dollars beautifying these
grounds and I am really very proud of them.
Show him the flowers by all means—you might
even let him pick a few if it will humour him."

I started to speak, but he was gone. In the
distance somewhere I heard a door slam.

Under the circumstances there was nothing
for us to do except to come away. Originally
I did not intend to make public mention of this
incident, preferring to dismiss the entire thing
from my mind; but, inasmuch as Winsell has
seen fit to circulate a perverted and needlessly

exaggerated version of it among our circle of friends, I feel that the exact circumstances should be properly set forth.

It was a late hour when we rejoined our wives. This was due to Winsell's stupidity in forgetting the route we had traversed after parting from them; in fact, it was nearly midnight before he found his way back to the teahouse where we left them. The teahouse had been closed for some hours then and our wives were sitting in the dark on the teahouse porch waiting for us. Really, I could not blame them for scolding Winsell; but they displayed an unwarranted peevishness toward me. My wife's display of temper was really the last straw. It was that, taken in connection with certain other circumstances, which clinched my growing resolution to let the whole project slide into oblivion. I woke her up and in so many words told her so on the way home. We arrived there shortly after daylight of the following morning.

So, as I said at the outset, I have definitely given up my purpose of buying an abandoned farm and becoming an abandoned farmer. This spring we began looking about the Upper West Side for an abandoned flat.

Judging by the entrance halls and the interior decorations in the new buildings we have visited thus far, they are probably the most abandoned flats in the world.